"From the mountains a shadow reaches forth
. . . fell dark, bound by a spell grown old. You
shall journey, and you shall find, a home of
ancient wisdom, a place of ancient evil . . .
what are now two shall be three . . . and then
five, to face that not of earth . . . reach within,
then without for strength. . . ." Zwyle's voice
trailed away as she looked at me, her eyes once
more direct. "Beware, Lady Joisan. Your future
is indeed shadowed, and I can see no more
clearly. But this I know—you walk in step with
great danger."

"I shall guard," I told her, wishing almost
that she had not done the foreseeing for me,
though I knew she meant it well. Which is
better, to be warned of danger and live conscious
of its shadow, or walk blindly, content in the
sun's light while that lasts?

GRYPHON'S
EYRIE

Look for these other TOR books by André Norton

FORERUNNER
MOON CALLED
THE PRINCE COMMANDS
WHEEL OF STARS

ANDRÉ NORTON AND A.C. CRISPIN
GRYPHON'S EYRIE

TOR

A TOM DOHERTY ASSOCIATES BOOK

GRYPHON'S EYRIE

Copyright © 1984 by André Norton and A.C. Crispin
Illustrations copyright © 1984 by Judith Mitchell

First printing: December 1984
First mass market printing: March 1985

A TOR Book

Published by Tom Doherty Associates
8-10 West 36 Street
New York, N.Y. 10018

Cover art by Boris Vallejo

ISBN: 0-812-54736-5
CAN. ED.: 0-812-54737-3

Printed in the United States of America

This book is dedicated, with many thanks, to Hope Tickell, George Tickell and Randy Crispin, who provided invaluable assistance during its writing.

Prologue

What does a mastersmith do when he would forge a sword or axe to fit the hard palm of a fighter? He draws forth that raw material which gathers on the bones of the earth and works cunningly, with all his craft, over many days—even years—until there is that within him which shall say:

"Enough! The task is done as well as your art and all your striving can make it."

So it is also with the songsmith, who wrestles with self, skill, and words—for words are the rough ore which must be worked upon with all the patience of the fashioner. They must be heated by heart-fire, chilled with fear, pointed and edged with great care. Again, time has little meaning, for often the end of a song is a long time coming, because those whose fortunes it records do not win their place in legend between the setting of one day's sun and the light of dawn next morn.

Is this not so of that Tale of the Gryphon (which was at once a crystal-enclosed bauble of an amulet, again an Adept near forgot by even time, and lastly a man and a

woman true-forged into something greater than they had
even thought that humankind could yearn to become)?

There was Kerovan of Ulmsdale, whose cursed mother
dabbled in black lore, striking an evil bargain that she
might bear a child to be a tool of Power, serving her
purposes alone. That son did indeed carry on his body the
stigmata of the Dark, having amber eyes and cloven hooves
for feet. Yet all her bespelling failed in the end, for the
Great Ones, both Light and Dark, are not easily summoned,
nor lightly dismissed. So that the Lady Tephana, knowing
in her heart she had failed, assumed a pious horror of the
babe and urged that he be sent for fostering far from her
sight.

However, her lord Ulric, hot for an heir to follow him
in Ulmsdale, took note that the child be well trained,
befitting one of his rank, and Kerovan paid close heed to
the man-at-arms sent to lesson him. From Jago he learned
much of the skills of war, both in personal combat and in
the art of battle tactics and strategies. But in his isolation,
he turned also to the Wiseman Riwal, who hunted strange
knowledge in bits and pieces to be found in the Waste,
then seemingly deserted by the fabled Old Ones.

Lord Ulric also sought to protect the rights of his long-
desired son by bringing about a childhood axe-marriage
between the boy and the Lady Joisan, daughter of the
House of Ithkrypt, in those days before the invaders rent
the Dales from the sea's edge to the Waste. Wed they
were, still there was no meeting between the two of
them.

Little notice had Joisan from this lord whose gryphon
coat of arms she now wore 'broidered upon her feasting
tabard. Until one name-day there was delivered into
her hands an amulet which was plainly not of human
fashioning—a crystal globe in which was enclosed a tiny
gryphon. The whole, she came to realize, was a thing of
vast Power. Kerovan had found this talisman of the Old
Ones in the Waste (that desolate land shunned by

humankind, yet still roamed by strange creatures) and had been moved, against his will, to send it to her. Mistress of some small arts of healing, of herbal lore, and learned a little from what she had read in old abbey parchments, Joisan carefully prepared for her rulership as Lady of Ulmsdale. Nor was she then aware that the Lady Tephana still worked against her son, thinking to replace him with a true Dark heir in the person of his cousin Rogear.

To all schemes there is a season, and it was the invaders from Alizon-Over-Sea who broke this game so played in the north. For Kerovan marched with Ulmsdale's levies before he could bring his bride home, and as the war raged, Ithkrypt was overrun.

Saved through the strange Power of her unknown husband's chance gift, Joisan, and those left of her people, escaped, to wander the wilderness. There Kerovan, having answered a summons from his dying father, and so near walking into raw betrayal by his Dark kin, chanced upon them.

Though he recognized his lady, she knew not him but thought rather that this stranger was (because of his odd eyes and feet) one of the Old Ones. Thus she was laid open for the trickery of Rogear, who came, calling himself "Kerovan," to lay a bemusing spell upon her—drawing her into the Waste, that, through Joisan, Tephana might harness the Power of the gryphon.

Kerovan, tracking them to a bloody site of sacrifice where they strove to compel the Dark to their will, there stood firm with his true lady, calling upon Powers he feared mightily in her behalf. And because of his invoking of the Powers of Light, those who summoned the Shadow were, in turn, summoned, to death and Dark. Then Joisan, seeing her lord in the bright force of his spirit, knew that, in truth, they were indeed wedded, even as gold may be inlaid into steel for all time to make a weapon fit for arming a hero. But in Kerovan there remained the memory of his dual heritage, causing deep doubt, and he chose to set aside all custom's binding for her sake, riding from her.

Into the Waste he went once more on a mission for the Lords of the Dales—to perhaps enlist some remaining Old Ones against the invaders. Then Joisan put mail over her body, a helm on her head, and swung a sword at her belt, to follow. His trail she sought, knowing that no false pride was greater than the love in her, even as the weight of the gryphon—his gift—lay outwardly on her breast.

Divers strange and terrible ventures did these two have, apart and together. Kerovan rode ever with the belief that, in him, there was the smoldering fear of a divided heritage. However, Joisan was strong with the strength of one who fears more for another than herself.

Through captivity and darkness, and at last together, went these twain, until they fronted the beginning of their true destiny—which was a battle such as shook their part of the world. Five stood for the Light—Kerovan, Joisan, the gryphon, released at last from his long captivity in the crystal globe, his ancient master Landisl, and Neevor, a wanderer who had played a part several times in the tangle of Kerovan's life. While for the Dark was Galkur, the cloven-footed, who claimed Kerovan as "son." Which was a lie, yet such a lie as to weigh upon a young heart and spread much poison, even after the fall of the Dark Lord.

This dread weight Kerovan carried with him, even into the new land, and it remained ever a burden to plague him.

Wander they did, but together, and once more the land was troubled by the Shadow and they must stand to it, more knowledgeable perhaps this time. Again they were not alone, for; if no Adept arose from the past to front the Dark by their side, there were others bound to the Waste, a longing in their hearts ever pulling at them: Elys, who was of Witch blood and wise training, also he who rode ever as her shield mate and battle comrade, Jervon, and thirdly the boy Guret who had no arcane learning—only great courage.

The Tale of the Gryphon is not a new song to be word-built, but an old one to be added to—for out of a great endeavor there is spun in turn a longing for that which we ourselves may lack or never see. And what finally became of those who dared stand against the Shadow—

Ah, it takes a songsmith to summon full skill, looking into hearts, listening down the years to half-remembered tales, to use all which can be drawn or scraped from time itself to answer that. Thus comes into words the third part of the tale of Kerovan and Joisan, telling what they wrought—and were wrought—by the years in Arvon, during the fullness of time, and, with new cup-comrades, to endure and battle always the darkness.

Eydryth
Songsmith

1

Joisan

Our world . . .

I stood in the dimness of the lamplight, the newborn child in my arms, looking out across the lake to the east, and the coming dawn. A long night . . . my weary body cried out for rest, yet I felt no desire to brave the greying darkness and leave Utia's house. The effort of climbing down the house-ladder to our tiny boat, tethered securely to a ring in one of the huge stone pillars thrusting up from the lake's depth, was too much. I loosed one hand, still holding the child against my breast, as I pushed back a straying lock of hair.

A dawn wind arose, rippling across the lake, to send waves lapping about these age-old standing pillars which the quiet fisherfolk of Anakue had discovered untold years ago and put to use as supports for their water-protected homes.

My lord Kerovan and I had chanced upon many strange things both wondrous and terrible during our wanderings across this new world of ours—Arvon, the holder of secrets. The past troubled my mind as I watched the stars pale and dwindle in the east. From that east and north we had come, discovering a way down from those mountains now only a smudge of shadow against the sunrise-paling sky. I remembered that first morning after our struggle against the Dark Lord, Galkur, when we stood together on the slopes of those distant heights, looking out upon a land that seemed, after the frost-seared stretches of the Dales and the desolation of the Waste, to be a blurred tapestry of gold and scarlet, vivid against a backing of tall evergreen forests.

Then my lord and I had been near drunk with that beauty, feeling still the exultation of those who treasure life doubly because they have lately faced its ending. My mind filled with a heart-raising warmth, my cheeks flushed as I remembered well that first night together after our victory, when Kerovan became my lord in truth. Though the mountainside had been cold, our heat of body and spirit filled the world . . . our new world, this Arvon.

A fair land, truly, for the most part. Yet there were ancient pitfalls aplenty, to trap the unwary, that we had also learned during these past three years of wandering . . . of our wandering without end, for it seemed that nowhere was there a place we might claim for our own. Though we had found temporary dwellings among several peoples such as these simple, kindly fishers, always there was something within my lord which grew restless, pushing him on, so we would take to the road again.

The baby in my arms stirred, recalling me, with a start, to the here and now. He opened a tiny mouth in that reddened face, still molded by the stresses of birthing, to squeak, uttering a small mouse-sound.

Sun began to finger the lake, staining the water with crimson glory. I held the child up to the window so those rays might touch his thatch of dark hair. "Your first sunrise, small one. What do you think?" He blinked sleepily at me, unimpressed.

"Utia's waking, Lady Joisan." I turned, to see Zwyie,

Anakue's Wisewoman, spooning a strengthening cordial between the exhausted mother's pale lips.

"How does she now?" I returned to the woman's side, touched fingertips to her throat. The pulse I found was still fast, but stronger.

"Better, I think. She lost much blood, but I think she'll strengthen after a few days. 'Tis a good thing both of us were here, Lady, or we might have lost her."

I nodded tiredly. The baby had been a breech delivery, and nigh a month too early. I had been hurriedly summoned from one of the net-tenders who had run a hook into his hand, to discover Zwyie trying to calm Utia so she might determine how the child lay. It had taken every bit of healcraft I had learned from my aunt, Dame Math, as well as lore I had gained during our roving, to sing the labor-wracked woman into a relaxed state. We had worked together the rest of the night, mixing herbs and cordials, chanting, calling upon Blessed Gunnora's help to give her strength. And Gunnora had been with us, for both mother and child survived.

Utia's eyes opened. She was too weak to speak, but I guessed her desire. "The babe is well, Utia." I knelt on the woven rush floor covering, holding forth the child that she might see that tiny wrinkled face. "You and Raney have a fine son."

The woman's pale lips curved into a tender smile as, with an effort, she raised her hand to touch the fuzzy darkness of the baby's hair. I bit my lip as I laid the child beside her. There was a hidden emotion here which wakened in me a strange longing, akin to pain. My arms now felt empty of something far greater than just the light weight of a babe.

"Leave them now to peace, Lady." Zwyie was beside me, although I had not heard her come. "You, too, must rest, eat. . . ."

Numbly I went to the table, swallowed a few mouthfuls. The full weight of this night's work seemed to settle on me. It was all I could do not to slump and sleep, my head on the board.

The morning sun was now well up, light shimmering brilliantly across the water. Through the door I could see all of Anakue plainly. Those pillars with their wooden houses atop, the spidery bridges linking one to the next . . . all but the one that stood a little apart. That house was reserved by custom for the Wisewoman of the village. Until my lord and I had come to Anakue—nearly a year past—Zwyie had lived there alone. She had given us lodging in her loft. Our chamber was small, but after months on the trail, living on the open land in all weathers, trading what skills we had between us for a night's lodging here, a meal there, it had become the first real home I had known since the Hounds of Alizon had stormed Ithkrypt's now-shattered walls. I had wistfully dreamed of perhaps building a house of our own on the lake's shore, near the smokehouse where each day's catch was brought for preserving. If only my lord . . .

"How does he, Lady Joisan?" Zwyie might well have followed my thoughts, though between us was no true mindspeech, such as my lord and I sometimes shared. Still, all those who work within the Craft are conscious of much that cannot be seen, touched, smelt, or tasted by ordinary senses. And Zwyie and I had become close—I thought of her perhaps as an older sister, though I had never had one. . . .

I looked up to face her dark blue eyes, beautiful and long-lashed in an otherwise broad, plain countenance. "The . . . dreams come oftener these days. Then, when he wakes, he is . . . overcast . . . his features altered a fraction, as though another dwelt in him. . . ."

"Shadowed? You mean the Dark?"

"I do not think so. . . . No! He is not so cursed; but after these dreams, he will not speak aloud of what troubles him. His mind is closed to me also. Each time he awakes, he searches out his weapons to clean, oil, polish

. . . as though what has plagued him during sleep can be met and conquered by steel."

"Steel . . . cold iron *is* a defense against some forms of the Shadow. The land hereabouts harbors many who embrace the Dark. That is why Anakue stands surrounded by running water—which is also a defense, since evil cannot cross it."

"That I well know. What I cling to is the talisman he wears—that wristband of the Old Ones. So far it does not warn. And my ring remains unchanged." I looked down at the cat's-head ring I had found in a manor once occupied by Old Ones—those, I was sure, of the Light. Rainbow prisms flashed across its surface, as the rose-gold color of it mirrored the newly risen sun.

"Look ever to the ring, Lady. As long as it holds life, all will be well, though you may have cause to fear that it is not so."

The Wisewoman took from her belt a tiny pouch made of dried fish-skin, darkened with age. "I have not done this in long and long, but . . . reach within with your left forefinger; stir these."

Wondering, I cautiously dipped the finger into the pouch, felt therein many tiny sharp objects. I stirred them, felt one prick my flesh, so withdrew my hand hurriedly. A red drop stood out clearly on my skin.

"Good, blood always strengthens the bespelling. Now . . ." Zwyie upended the bag on the tabletop. The contents scattered across the sanded surface. Peering closer, I saw tiny fishbones. The Wisewoman studied the wide-flung pattern, then spoke with a lilt close to a chant. Her voice was so low I had to strain my ears to hear.

"From the mountains a shadow reaches forth . . . fell dark, bound by a spell grown old. You shall journey, and you shall find, a home of ancient wisdom, a place of ancient evil. . . . What are now two shall be three . . . and then six, to face that not of earth. . . . Reach within, then without for strength. . . ." Zwyie's voice trailed away as she looked at me, her eyes once more direct. "Beware, Lady Joisan. Your future is indeed Shadowed, and I can see no more clearly. But this I know—you walk in step with great danger."

"I shall guard," I told her, wishing almost that she had not done the foreseeing for me, though I knew she meant it well. Which is better, to be warned of danger and live conscious of its shadow, or walk blindly, content in the sun's light while that lasts?

Behind us, the baby began to cry.

"Quiet, small one." I went to pick up the child, cuddled him against my shoulder.

"Do you hold him, Lady Joisan. We shall bless him now." Zwyie reached into her bag of simples and herbs, bringing out two sprigs of dried leaves. Lighting a white candle, she chanted softly as she passed these several times through the smoke. Then she nodded to me, and I laid the child down on the table, steadying him so he would not roll.

The Wisewoman brushed each of the tiny feet with the brittle sprigs of angelica and vervain, as together we recited the ritual words: "Gunnora, Lady who protects women, and the innocents born of women, guard this child. Let not his feet carry him near the Shadow, rather let him walk in the Light in all ways and times."

I held up each of the little fists so she could touch them in turn with those protecting herbs. "Let also these hands work in the service of life and the Light."

Lastly she brushed the child's forehead. "Let his mind remain clean and untainted, grant him the strength of will to naysay any thought born of the Dark." She paused, then both of us repeated in turn, "So may it be always by *Thy* will."

I carried the child back to his mother. Utia roused, looking better for her short rest. "Utia"—I held the child before her after the custom of her people in which Zwyie had lessoned me—"this is your goodly son. Look upon him, name him, that he may have life well set before him."

As her eyes fastened eagerly on her child, again that ache I could not rightly put name to welled within me. "His name is Acar," she whispered.

I settled Acar safe beside his mother just as footsteps sounded on the dock ladder. Now came Utia's husband, Raney, and her sister, Thalma. Since what both Utia and the babe now needed most was rest and the comfort and praise of her kin, Zwyie and I took our leave, Raney's somewhat garbled thanks loudly following us.

The small boat bobbed as we clambered down and began to wield our paddles, sending the craft in the direction of the Wisewoman's house. We sat side by side, silent in our weariness. But I remembered, with a chill not born of the morning air, Zwyie's dire foretelling.

"I watched you hold the babe," Zwyie said suddenly. "There is an emptiness within you, my lady, and that is not surprising. Come with me to Gunnora's shrine tomorrow, ask her for a child."

"That I cannot." I kept my eyes steady on the approaching stone pillar supporting our temporary dwelling.

"Why?"

I discovered that I could not look directly at Zwyie. "It is . . . because of my lord."

"Why, Joisan?" Her question rang like a challenge. "He is a man, that is plain to any with eyes to look. Surely his . . . differences are not such as to prevent him from—" She broke off, plainly searching for suitable words, her own eyes suddenly downcast.

I smiled wryly at her. "No, that is not it at all, sister. My lord is indeed a man, and in spite of his . . . differences, as you term them, to me he is very good to look upon." I took a deep breath as I dipped paddle into the grey-green water. "No, I speak of this troubling which has descended upon him at intervals during our wandering time in Arvon.

Now it has come to plague him again—more strongly than ever before. I am afraid, of what I cannot say. . . ."

"This 'troubling' raises a barrier between you?"

"None of my building. Only Kerovan fears, that I know without his telling, and that fear drives him . . . apart."

Zwyie gave me a sharp, knowing look. I realized that she understood that which I could not have put into frank speech—that my lord had not turned to me as a husband for more than a month now.

The familiar catch of sadness burned at the back of my throat. Every night he either feigned sleep or contrived, with ever-thinner excuses, to be elsewhere. I wanted to ask why, but my few attempts to approach the subject had brought only a painful silence, inner knowledge that my questions hurt him in a way unknown to me.

If only . . . I remembered the last time we had been heart to heart together, and my hands tightened on the grip-smoothed wood of the paddle.

I had awakened suddenly in the early morning to find him tossing in his sleep, his face marked with that disturbing "otherness" I was sure betokened sendings from elsewhere . . . but from whom . . . or *what*?

My heart beating frantically lest he not return from wherever that Other had taken his mind and spirit, I had shaken him into wakefulness in turn. His eyes—those eyes which had made me call him "Lord Amber" when first we met—opened, to focus on me.

"Kerovan?" I made a question of his name, because it seemed to me that strangeness still shadowed his features.

"My lady?" He smiled at me, and there was something in his smile setting my blood to racing. Never had he looked at me so . . . always he had been shy, diffident. Before our true marriage he had regarded all women with the suspicion that his mother's cruel rejection and betrayal had forced on him. Try as I might to be close to him, in me always lay the hurting awareness that no matter what our physical nearness, some essential part of him remained aloof.

"Are you well?" I touched his arm, felt the warmth of his weather-browned skin, the soft down hair, was reassured by its solid reality.

In answer that arm encircled me, pulled me down to his waiting kiss, to acknowledge that this time no weight of past fear and anger welled between us—there was only love for each other, blazing and alive.

The boat bumped hard against the tiny dock built out from the house pillar, jarring me out of memories. Zwyie gathered up her bag of simples, and I made haste to do likewise. Weary beyond thought, I climbed the ladder-stairs behind her. Sitting down on the kitchen bench, we helped each other off with the high, tight-fitting, fish-scale boots. The women of Anakue, except for feast-days, went clothed the same as the men, since they shared the fishing.

Stocking-footed, I climbed to the loft my lord and I shared. He was abed, sleeping deeply. One glance told me the troubling was on him again. When I had first seen him I had thought him one of the Old Ones, those beings with a semblance of humankind—but who controlled Powers and forces we of the Dales could barely sense. Now, his dark hair further darkened by sweat, features thinned by daylight worry and night sendings, his resemblance to the faces pictured in some of the old shrines and temples was even more unmistakable. That long oval face, the pointed chin . . . even as I hesitated, half-afraid that, if I woke him, Kerovan as I knew him would be totally gone, he opened his eyes.

I braced myself to meet that yellow gaze; however, he spared not a glance for me. Swinging out of the bed with the fluid grace of a trained swordsman, he reached for his breeches, pulled them on, then his under-jerkin. All his movements were hasty, those of a guardsman summoned to a post. Moments later he threw back the lid of the chest where we kept our possessions and pulled on his padded shirt. Then, with a dull clink, his mail followed.

"Kerovan, what's to do?" I crossed the loft as he tested the edge of his dagger on his thumb, nodding in satisfaction when a hairline streak of red welled. He paid me no mind—as if I had not spoken.

With an echoing clatter, our swords and swordbelts dropped in turn to the wooden floor. Then my own mail shirt was shaken free. "My lord!" I put hand to his shoulder, shook him. "What do you? There is no battle—"

He turned to me, eyes brightening. "Ah, Joisan! I was afraid I would have to send Zwyie to seek you out, and time is short. Here—" He thrust my mail at me, then piled padded undershirt, boots, and sword on top willy-nilly.

"Put them on!" he snapped, seeing my hesitation, then turned to dig out his backpack. Mine followed. Without another glance at me, he began filling them with the swift precision of one who has spent much of his life on the road.

"But Kerovan, *why*?" In spite of myself, anger sharpened my voice. I let the things he had piled in my arms slip to the floor.

"We're leaving." He glanced at me as though I were lackwitted. "We must go—today. Hurry." He returned to his strapping of a pack.

"*Why?*"

He paid me no further heed. I watched him, realizing that if I did not prepare to accompany him, I might well be left behind. Once, before our struggle with Galkur, he *had* gone forth alone, not looking behind, driven by his fear of closeness with me. Now, again, something was goading him, and there was nothing in his mind but the urge to run from—or to—*it*.

Reluctantly I dressed in my trail clothing, leathern breeches and boots, padded undershirt, then my woolen shirt, and, finally, my mail. That last hung harsh and heavy on my shoulders, the feel of it recalling to me vividly fear, hunger, and cold, those ever-present companions during war. For the first time in long and long, I wondered briefly how fared that struggle between Hallack and the invaders from the eastern sea.

Long before I was finished, my lord had packed our few possessions, begun pacing impatiently. I heard the scrape and click of his hooves on the hard wooden rungs of the ladder as he descended. But I cast a last longing look at our "home," as I twitched the bedcoverings smooth. Then, with a heart heavier than my mail, I followed him.

I could hear Zwyie from the kitchen. "What's to do, Kerovan? Where is your lady?"

"Here," I made answer. "We are leaving Anakue, Zwyie. Give our farewell and good wishing to all your people, if you will. Our thanks for all your kindnesses."

Why? Her question echoed in my mind, but she did not voice it aloud. Behind Kerovan's back I shrugged.

"Well, at least I can send you on your way with something in your bellies! You can surely stay that long, my lord!" At Zwyie's sharp voice, my lord nodded. I felt shame for him a little, though I do not believe he truly realized his discourtesy, as she hustled briskly about, putting up a pack of smoked fish, journeybread, and dried fruit.

Moments later she pushed the provisions into my pack, helping me slip the straps onto my shoulders. "Go with Gunnora's Blessing and aid, my lady." She pressed something into my hand. Looking down, I saw an amulet of Gunnora's, the carven golden sheaf of grain entwined with a grapevine heavy with ripe fruit. Tears near blinded me as I fumbled the leathern thong that held it pendant over my head.

"Thank you, sister." Between us I traced the symbol of blessing. Her eyes widened as my fingers left a faint trail of greenish-blue light to linger for a moment on the early morning air.

"You have learned much, my lady. Remember, trust

that within you, rather than things as they outwardly seem."

"Joisan!"

Kerovan already stood within the boat, the breeze tugging impatiently at his hair as though it reflected the haste which drove him.

Silently I descended the house-ladder, took my seat. Our paddles slipped in unison into the water. The boat headed for the shore. Kerovan kept his face steadfastly set to the south and west, never looking back. It was as if to him the village—those who had welcomed us there—had ceased to exist.

But I watched over my shoulder Zwyie's stocky figure dwindle and shrink, and discovered myself hard-pressed to hold back tears.

Kerovan

The compelling pull from the mountains was constant now, an ever-present siren call, striving to force me north and east. I had been a prisoner to this compulsion ever since we had entered Arvon. This was a land where beings and creatures whispered about as shadowy night-tales in High Hallack, bore solid form and nightmare reality. At times the drawing was so strong it worked upon me both awake and sleeping. At other times I would gain a measure of peace when that pressure was quiescent for months at a time, so I was able to hide my secret fear from Joisan and hope—how I hoped!—that freedom might be mine at last.

Now I could only stride, fighting the need to turn back and run toward those darksome mountains where lay in waiting—what?

That Joisan knew I was troubled added to the weight of my burden. Many times the dreadful confession was ready on my tongue, and I must fight with all the strength of long-engaged will to hide what I feared might be a sending from the Dark. It filled my mind constantly that

Galkur, loathsome to me in every way, yet with whom I had felt a perverse tie, had regained his Powers and sought to draw me to him, to torment with dreams and possess me by the leash of his will.

I had believed the Dark One vanquished, devoured by the very evil rising from his own nature. But suppose that was not so? What if he still stalked in these mountains, waiting to entice me again with his claim? I had, perhaps in great folly, repudiated Landisl's aid, wanting none of other inheritance save what a man might rightly claim through natural birth. Without it, what defense had I against fell sorcery?

What were my true weapons now? Only that wristband of the Old Ones I had brought out of the Dales, and a small piece of the blue stone-metal Landisl had named quan-iron. Such would count as nothing against the power of an Adept well along the Left-Hand Path.

Beside me, Joisan stumbled as a rock turned under her foot. Startled out of my morass of dire foreseeing, I caught her arm, steadying her.

"Are you all right?" Even in my own ears my voice was harsh.

She glanced up at me, her face drawn with weariness, eyes two dimming sparks within shadowed circles, the generous curve of her mouth drawn tight. "I am well enough, though I could wish for a moment of rest. It seems we have been walking forever, Kerovan!"

I glanced up at the sun, was shocked how far west it had traveled. We had left Anakue in the morning, not long after dawn. How could time itself be so forgot? Pausing, I looked back along our trail.

Anakue lay in the midst of a large lake, one of many such lacings of water between green stretches of meadows. Straining my eyes, I could barely make out a distant blue shimmer surrounded by green. We had come far, indeed.

Joisan dropped to her knees, fumbling in her pack. Taking out her water flask, she drank, visibly counting her swallows. I squatted beside her. Silently we shared a cake of journeybread, a few handfuls of dried fruit. For the first time since we had begun our journey, I was truly aware enough to survey our path with a trained scout's eye.

We had been ascending a long, gradual slope, following no marked trail. So far this had been easy enough, for underfoot was tufted grass still brownish from winter. Spring in these heights was not as advanced as about Anakue. The clouds overhead were edged with darkness, half promising storm. Three birds winged by, hovering against the pale blue of the sky. Black for the most part, their wingtips showed a flash of brilliant iridescent purple. Though I had never seen their like before, I sensed these were about their own business of living—not dreaded servants of the Shadow come to spy on us.

Some of the strain eased out of me, the pull had lessened once more. The northeastern mountains I feared had nearly vanished beyond our horizon. Hope sprang in me again—had I finally outrun the calling? Or was this naught but another false respite?

When had been the last time I was only Kerovan, untormented by any urge outside those all men feel? One bit of memory returned, instantly vivid. I flushed, fumbling in my pack, keeping my face averted, lest Joisan see and mindshare.

For she had a part in that memory. I had bedded down that night a whole man (if one such as I might ever be termed "whole"). Then during the late hours, I had awakened, that exciting, demanding "otherness" within me—making me free, unfettered. Some essential part of myself heretofore always bound, constrained, had been loosed from all chains. Joisan had been there, shaking me, her hair unbound, her breasts—molded beneath her thin shift—rising and falling with her quick breathing, as though she feared for me. And then— Recalling that moment, my hands twisted savagely in the tough cloth of my pack. Memory beyond that was tattered, hazy, as though seen through thick smoke or fog. Still I could not deny that my hands and my lips had sought her flesh, as, freed by that Other I feared was a Dark One, I had fiercely taken her—my gentle lady, to be used so!

I swallowed harshly. Beast my hooves branded me, and beast I had been that night. I must hold that shameful memory ever, lest such could happen again.

Though truly I had not touched her since—had feared even to meet her eyes, lest I read revulsion, rightful and just, in them. If Joisan turned from me, then what had I left?

Many times I had thought I must speak, talk to her of all lying unsaid between us. Strive as I might, I could never bring myself to such openness, fearing the answer she now had every right to make. Always Joisan had accepted my physical differences, even pretending that she found me good to look upon, following me uncomplaining through hardships and rootless wandering, remaining my only solace and friend.

Yet our companionship could not have been easy for her, comely as she is. I glanced at her covertly. Despite her exhaustion, now plain to read, any eyes would find her fair, with her soft red-brown hair, blue-green eyes, that slender, yet rounded, body.

Many times I had watched men's eyes follow her appreciatively as we traveled, fancying I could mark their surprise that she journeyed with one such as I. After all the troubles she had faced and endured as my wife, who could say what act might prove too much for even her gallant nature to face?

"I wonder how Acar fares?" Her words startled me out of thoughts I could never entirely subdue.

"Acar?" The name meant nothing, and yet there was a soft smile about her lips, stirring in me a warmth of feeling new to me.

"Utia and Raney's son, born last night. Zwyie and I brought him into this world, with Gunnora's help, and a hard-won battle that was." Joisan rested her head on her raised knees, rubbing wearily at the nape of her neck.

A child—what would it mean to see blood of one's own blood, bone of one's bone, the sharing? Oh, by all the Powers of the Light, such a sharing! I flinched within and that spark of warmth died. What right had I to long for such? What did it matter that a fisherman had now a son, and I, once the heir of a powerful lord, had no prospect for even a home, much less a child?

I put aside that thought, realizing that this woman who had made, uncomplaining, a day's march long enough to tire a seasoned liegeman had done so with no sleep for nigh on two days!

"Then you did not sleep last night?" Hesitantly, awkwardly, lest I give offense by my touch, I put an arm around her shoulders. "Why did you not say so? It is time to camp anyway, and you must rest. Can you go on to the top of the slope? A better site may lie beyond."

·She raised her head a fraction, smiled a little wryly. "Assuredly, my lord. I told you three years ago that you could not leave me behind. Have I not proven that promise more times than I care to remember?"

I shouldered both packs in spite of her protest, and we climbed the remaining slope. At the crest we stood together looking out over the countryside beyond.

Ahead, perhaps a half day's journey tomorrow, lay foothills, though these did not rise into heights such as separated Arvon and High Hallack. Small stands of fir and pine studded the rolling hillsides, and I marked the silver flash of a stream not far below us. I pointed to a thicket near that rivulet. "There. Running water, wood for a small fire—a good spot."

The sun had set as we completed our camp for the night. Overhead the stars alternately disappeared then blazed as clouds streamed by. Here in this pocket of a valley we were sheltered from the wind driving those, our tiny fire making a brave show against all shadows. I had strung one of the fish-scale blankets from Anakue on a rope, anchoring it to two saplings for shelter should rain come.

We ate, then I settled back against my bedroll, feeling the tug and ache in my leg muscles—I had grown soft while we lodged in the fisher-village. Joisan reached for her bag of simples and began sifting through them. Holding a handful of dried sprigs, and what looked like an ordinary spool, she began chanting softly.

"What do you, my lady?" My voice in the quiet of the night was again harsher than I had intended. She did not look fully at me, but there was a determined set to her chin.

"I am going to set safeguards upon this place, that we may sleep sound."

"You know that I wish no tie with Powers, Joisan. It is best not to trouble so. Like draws to like. Even though what you summon may be of the Light, still even a spark of such may stand as beacon for the Dark."

"Using herbs and some red thread to call up a protective charm is hardly high sorcery, Kerovan." She did not look at me as she put away what she held, a frown line showing between her brows, though she offered me no argument.

Now I wondered just how much of such lore Joisan had learned during our years of roving. When I met her for the first time, she was already no ordinary maid, possessing courage and sense usually known only by one far beyond her years. Yet I also knew she was completely of humankind, bearing no taint of that other blood so evident in me. . . . Was it possible that one such as she might learn to wield true Power? Could encounters with forces beyond those known to humankind have altered her, so that now she was indeed one to command Power in her own right?

The thought made me shift restlessly, alarmed. I knew that Joisan had learned much about simples, herbs, and healing from her aunt, Dame Math, and from the ancient Past-Abbess of Norstead Abbey. I had watched her seek out Wisewomen in each of the villages and settlements of Arvon we passed through. But I had never before thought of my lady as one to hold Power within *her*. . . . I had always linked what Power I had seen evidenced with the crystal gryphon . . . and that was lost to us, now . . . lost in the struggle against Galkur. . . .

My thoughts had circled treacherously back to those that had plagued me for so long. I moved to feed the fire, then noticed that Joisan, whom I had believed asleep, was now sitting bolt upright on her bedroll. In the darkness her eyes were naught but dark smudges in the vague blur of her face. As the flames leaped brighter, I could make out her perfect stillness, as though she listened. When I made to stretch out beside her on my bedroll, her hand shot out unerringly, grasping my shoulder. I could feel the bite of her nails through my jerkin.

"Do not move." Her voice was a drifting breath against my cheek. Alarmed now, I reached for her hand, put my other to sword hilt.

"What is it?" My voice was as soft as hers had been. Through the contact of our hands, something was happening, flowing from her into me, awakening a sense I realized now had lain dormant since our fight with the Dark One. It was as though I could *see* a shadow drifting down the slope toward us, but that sight came not through my body's eyes, but from that other sense.

Cold, that darkness was, bitter cold, carrying with it a stench like carrion. In my ears arose a droning whine, and under my hooves a thudding vibration shook my body. Not even knowing why I did so, I drew naked blade across my knees so it lay between us and that horror.

And yet . . . it was strange, for that shadow did not truly seem to be *here* at all. My mind filled with a confused image of *something* moving along mountain paths, a yellowish something glowing sickly. It was shot through with malignant streaks of red, as though it fed on blood—and worse.

Suddenly, blown apart by a gust of clean wind from the west, that shadow vanished. I realized that it had never truly been there. What we had seen had been an image or sending of a reality lying far distant.

"You are right, my lord." I knew Joisan shared the thought in my mind. "I know not how, or why, but what we saw just now has no reality in this time and place. It is the ghost of . . . something." She shuddered once again and I set an arm around her, wishing that I might enfold her closer, protect her; but that I dared not do, I thought bitterly. I could not even protect myself from what called to me from those mountains. And what we had seen just now emanated from the same place, of that I was certain also.

"Why was this shown so to us?" I asked, more of fate itself than of her. It seemed too unfair that we should now be plagued with a new danger, when the old one appeared insurmountable to me.

"I know not. That . . . thing came from those mountains." Joisan turned her gaze northeast. "It is possible that there is some channel between those heights and us, and that along that channel can be drawn images of what runs there. Or this could be foreknowledge, or a warning. Arvon holds much we never knew in the Dales." She bit her lip, and I tightened my hold around her shoulders at the fear in her voice and her calm bravery in the face of it. "I *do* know, however, that what we saw is part of this land, no shadow without reality. That haunter of mountain ridges exists . . . somewhere."

We sat for a while longer, but naught else arose to disturb us in the night. Joisan's head slowly dropped onto my shoulder, and I knew she slept. Turning my head, I nuzzled my mouth against the softness of her hair, scenting the herbs of its recent washing. "Josian. . . ." There was so much I wanted to say to her, but could not . . . my lips could only form her name.

When I eased her back onto her bedroll she awoke, beginning to sit up. "Stay," I said, pulling the blanket across her. "I will take the first watch. Sleep, my lady."

"Very well."

Then came nothing but the quiet sound of her breathing.

Thus I sat, sword in hand, watching the stars. The clouds had thinned into occasional ragged wisps, and I was fleetingly grateful that at least we did not have to worry about rain.

I had intended to let Joisan sleep and not call her to watch, but, as the night went by, I needs must stand and pace the length of our small camp to keep from falling asleep. It had been long since I had had a restful night, and that, added to our day's journey, had taken their toll of my strength. When I found myself dozing as I stood, I realized I must wake her.

It required only a light touch on my lady's shoulder to bring her to full awareness. I hardly had time to stretch out and pull the blanket up before sleep claimed me.

Sleep . . . and dreams. The pull returned to me. In my dream I was light as thistledown, swift as thought, in my race back to the mountains I fled so determinedly by day. There, I knew, lay all that I ever had and ever could desire, the end of strife, my home. As iron to a lodestone was I drawn, knowing immediately my direction and destination. It was close—close—

There was a sound in my ears, a thunder as though great wings beat around my head and shoulders. I was being shaken violently—

"Kerovan! Wake!" I blinked stupidly, found I was standing upright, pack in one hand, sword in my other. Joisan barred my way, her hands still gripping my shoulders.

"What—" I dropped the pack, then sheathed my sword. The world swung, then steadied, as I realized I was on the other side of our campfire, headed up the slope down which we had come earlier. The pull was a screaming ache within me, and I felt sweat start out on my forehead, so great was the effort it took not to push my lady aside and run.

"*You walked through the fire, Kerovan.*" The small hands still holding my shoulders trembled, then tightened their grip. "I called to you, strove to halt you, but you walked through the fire before I could stop you. Are you burned?"

Feeling now the warmth as I saw the scattered coals, I sank to the ground. I examined one hoof, but its hard substance seemed to have taken no harm. For once perhaps I should feel thanks that my feet were not flesh as were other men's.

Joisan brought a brand from the fire, handing it to me. She knelt, reaching for my ankle. "Let me see."

"No!" Never had I allowed her to touch my feet, the source of so many of my troubles—I felt my face burn at the thought.

"I have no time for such folly now, my lord. Hold still."

There was a note of command in my lady's voice that I had never heard before—Lord Imgry, High Commander of the Dale Forces, might well have envied such a tone. I held the brand as she studied closely first one, then the other of my hooves.

"You took no hurt I can discover." She sat back, facing me. I cast the lighted branch back into the fire, glancing around. The brush of the wind promised that dawn was not far off, though the darkness was still complete.

Joisan's voice reached me again, still holding that force of command. "And now, my lord, I think we had best talk. I will hold with no more evasions or silences. It is time for the truth."

I moistened dry lips. "About what happened tonight to me?"

"What has happened this night, last night, and so many

nights since we entered this land. What torments you so, Kerovan?"

I swallowed, sought for my old control, found it shattered beyond repair. Then, in a voice I scarcely knew as my own, I told her of the pull from the mountains, how it had waxed and waned, and what I feared might be causing it. She listened intently, then, when I had finished, sat in thought for several minutes.

It seemed very long to me before she spoke. "I cannot pretend to understand all that is happening, my lord. There is Power here, but I feel none of the cold of the Shadow about it. Though that may mean nothing, for mayhap it has disguised itself beyond my limited sensing." Far off in the night something screeched, probably an owl. Joisan continued, "But this I do know. We two cannot continue as we have heretofore done."

My heart froze within me; suddenly breathing itself was pain. I strove to steady my voice. "Then you will go back to Anakue—alone? I cannot blame you, Joisan, I only ask you to let me escort you. . . . These lands are wild, and I—"

Her words cut across my stumbling ones like a sword. "Always you doubt me, Kerovan! What must I do to make you believe that I could never company with another— that I want only you? No, what I am saying is that I think you must fight your fear of Power and the using of it, and allow me to protect us as best I can. This will be a task greater than any I have ever attempted, and I cannot be sure of success. But it seems I needs must try, and to this you must aid me."

So great was my relief that Joisan held no thought of leaving me that my inner distrust of any magic seemed at that moment very small compared to the other fear. "Very well. My thanks for your help, my lady. And"—I drew a deep breath—"what I can do . . ." Though I added no more words she must have known what I found so hard to voice.

As she sorted through her bag of simples for the herbs she would need, Joisan sent me, with a torch, into the neighboring grove of trees. "Search out an ash, Kerovan. I believe I sighted one as we came downslope. Failing that, look for a hazel bush. I must have a proper wand, blessed under the moon." She glanced at the sky, then frowned. "So hurry, my lord, for the moon is far spent."

The grove was dew-wet, overgrown with brush, a thicket which I cursed as I tripped and blundered my way, torch held high. Finally I sighted the slender leaves and grayish trunk of what I sought and called to my lady.

She came, carrying something in her hand. I stepped forward. "Shall I break a limb for you?"

"No! This only *I* must do." Approaching, she laid hand to the bark, spoke softly. "Good tree, hear my plea."

Slowly, with difficulty because of the underbrush, she walked around the ash, turning always to her left. Thrice she circled so, chanting softly:

"Ash tree, strong tree, I beg of you a bough to aid me in protecting one I love. Well shall I use your gift, in the service of the Light. My thanks shall stay with you always, O great tree!"

Pausing, she knelt, scraping at the earth above its roots. "May my offering nourish your soil, may you grow ever stronger and taller." Leaning over, I saw what she buried—a piece of journeybread. "It is forbidden to take without giving freely in return," she whispered before I could question.

Standing tall now, Joisan raised her hands to one of the short, lower branches of the ash. With a quick snap, she broke the limb. The break was clean, no dangling bark remaining—almost as if the tree had willingly relinquished part of itself in response to her plea.

As we returned to the fire, her fingers stripped loose all bark. I watched as she carefully rubbed pinches of herbs from her bag against a sharp stone, before using it to scrape free any remaining shreds.

Then gathering the discarded bark, Joisan crumbled it into a mound on a flat stone, adding more herbs to the small heap. "Angelica, valerian, trefoil, and vervain," she identified each sprig she selected. "All protection herbs." Mixing the handful together, she cupped it, before throwing it into what remained of our fire.

Taking up the ash limb, she knelt and passed it seven times through the resulting smoke, chanting softly in a language I did not recognize.

Drawing herself up to her full height, she touched the tip of the peeled branch to the ground, then, taking her water flask, poured several drops along its length. Holding the branch full into the moonlight, she chanted, "O wand of ash, I consecrate thee to my use. By the virtues of earth, air, fire, and water, be truly filled with Power, and let that Power be of the Light." Looking up, she held both hands above her head, the wand between them. "Gunnora, Lady of the Moon, aid and succor me in what I do now. So may it be always by *Thy* will."

A moment only she remained so, then, turning back, instructed me matter-of-factly, "We must wash before beginning."

I followed her to the stream by torchlight, nearly stepping in it in the darkness. Joisan knelt, laving her hands and face. At her gesture, I did likewise.

The water, mountain-fed, was cold enough to make me sputter, and my lady's voice sounded amused. "By rights we should both bathe, Kerovan. Be thankful I do not order you all the way in, and then make you stand bare for the ritual!"

When I had finished, she held a small vial unstoppered and, after anointing herself with its contents, touched my forehead and wrists with a scented oil. "Rosemary, for protection."

We returned to our packs, and Joisan surveyed me critically by the light of the torch. "Lay aside sword and knife, Kerovan." With quick movements she unbound her hair, shaking it loose to lie across her shoulders.

I unbuckled my swordbelt, pulled my knife from its sheath, feeling nearly as naked as if she *had* made me strip. "Have you aught else of iron or steel about you?"

My hands went to the buckle of the belt to my leather breeches. "That, too," she ordered.

"Let us hope," I said ruefully, doing as she commanded, "that in this we are not set upon by outlaws or wild beasts, my lady. I shall look a fine sight trying to find my sword with one hand while holding up my breeches with the other!"

Joisan was already laying out her wand and paid me no attention.

"Come you over here, my lord, where the ground is clearer."

I stood where she bade me, watching her gather more herbs, her spool of thread, and several candles from the bag. Placing them in the center of the tiny clearing, she proceeded to draw a circle around both of us with the wand. "Do not step outside the circle until this rite is complete, Kerovan. To do so may cause great harm."

By the faint light of the fire I saw that the candles were red, and that there were three of them. My lady placed them at equal points within the bounds of the circle, pushing each into the soft earth until it was firmly wedged. Then she unreeled the red thread, until it followed the path of the circle, scattering more herbs as she did so. Lastly, she lit each candle with a twig from the fire. Her movements were quick and deft, naysaying the doubt she had expressed earlier in her own abilities.

At last she approached me, holding out her hand. "I will need your strength in this, my lord, and what you hold of Power."

The old protest was instantly on my lips. She shook her head. "We both know that within you Power resides, though you keep it buried. We have need of it now."

Taking a deep breath, I grasped her hand. Joisan closed her eyes, then stooped to touch wand to the ground before her. Almost immediately the ash length began to move, drawing lines in the soft dirt—but not as though my lady's hand guided it, rather as if that branch followed its own path. In a few quick lines, a globe took shape, then, spreading out from it on either side, what I recognized as wings.

Joisan opened her eyes, taking a soft, urgent breath as she gazed upon the symbol on the ground.

"That is not what you meant to draw?" I asked.

"No. I had in mind a pentagram . . . that being the most common sign for invoking Power. But this . . ." She studied the marked symbol. In the firelight I could see her frown.

"Do you know aught of this symbol?" I fought to keep the fear I felt out of my voice. Was this something out of the Dark taking over, as I had feared from the beginning?

"I have seen it. It is of the Light, that I know. But the symbol I saw before had outstretched wings, while these are half-furled."

"Why did this take shape?"

"I do not know . . . unless it is because, without your knowing, the Power within you took a hand, Kerovan."

I began to protest, but she shook her head. "Such an act is not something you would be conscious of, my lord." She glanced again at the symbol, then nodded. "Each element in a spell shapes as it will. This is of the Light, and will serve, perhaps better."

Holding the wand before her, she began to chant again, her syllables rising with the lilting intonation of a song. I listened intently but could make out no distinct words.

I felt a tingle in my palm against hers, a prickling that ran up my hand, along my arm, then continued to my shoulder. Where it went, my flesh numbed, as might a limb that has lain too long in one position. The prickling tingle continued. Looking down at my arm, I could almost *see* the strength draining out of my body to my lady's. Her singing grew louder, now, more commanding.

With an effort I raised my eyes to gaze about us. The candle flames no longer flickered in the faint breeze. They burned brighter, stood straight. While around us—

I blinked, and only Joisan's warning squeeze upon my fingers kept me motionless. Around us the air had taken on a faint glow. Blue-green, it curled upward from the circle my lady had sketched, climbing higher with each breath I drew. I could see through that wall of light, as it climbed to eye level—then it was well above my head, walling us in with a faint haze of radiance.

Joisan's voice rang out, startling me out of my bemusement. "May this which I have fashioned tonight serve to guard and protect my lord, day or night, for as long as is needed."

Gradually the light faded. She watched it go, then turned to me. "How is it with you now, my lord?"

I had become so engrossed with the rite that I had forgotten the reason for it. Now I turned, faced toward where I knew those beckoning heights lay, waiting.

Nothing . . . nothing in me but the knowledge of *where* the pull came from. But there was no drawing as a part of that now.

"It's gone!" I turned to Joisan, grasped her shoulders in my relief. "Gone, Joisan!" I pulled her to me, hugging her exultantly. "Powerful magic have you worked tonight, my lady wife! I had not thought you could summon such."

She raised her head, her eyes bright in the moonlight. "If you had not aided with your strength, I could not have, Kerovan. I am so glad you are free at last."

Her lips were soft, alive under mine as I kissed her. Then, as I drew back, thinking how long it had been since we had been one, realizing that now there was nothing to keep us apart, she sighed deeply and sagged in my arms, limp.

Alarmed, I swung her up, carried her over to the bedroll.

As I laid her on it her eyes fluttered open again, and she spoke, her voice as faint as though she were far distant instead of inches away. "Summoning and controlling the Power . . . 'tis heavy work."

"Are you . . . all right?"

Her eyes closed. "Must . . . rest. Sleep. . . ."

I studied her anxiously but soon realized that she was indeed asleep. Pulling the blanket up, I sat beside her, watching the moon set and the faint flush that precedes true dawn lighten the eastern sky.

It was midmorning before Joisan awoke, and we set off again after a hasty breakfast. I felt so light, so free, not having to fight the summoning from the mountains, that the slope before us seemed the most inconsequential of barriers.

Still keeping to the south and west, we crossed the foothills and by midafternoon had descended onto a huge flat plain of rolling grassland which extended as far as I could see.

There were no tracks, no road, no traces at all that people abode in this plainsland—just scattered signs of wildlife.

We had stopped for a rest, sharing some of the Wise-woman's dried fruit, when we heard a faint sound. Joisan glanced around. "What was that?"

I was already standing, peering westward. "I don't know. It came from that direction." I pointed.

"It sounded like something in pain, Kerovan."

We shouldered our packs, moved toward a ridge of trees and denser brush that must mark a stream or river. Halfway there, we heard the sound again, more distinct now. Joisan began to run.

Shouting to her to take care, I pounded after her, but she had the lead and had gone some distance before I could catch up. I nearly ran into her, for she had stopped to look intently at a dark form on the ground before her.

A horse. It lay on its side, stomach distended, so still

that for a moment I thought it dead. Then the flanks heaved, shiny and rippled with sweat, and the legs thrashed again.

"A mare," Joisan said, moving toward her. "And trying to foal, by the look of her."

We moved closer. Joisan was right, I saw; the mare was in labor, and in trouble. Horses foal very quickly, if all goes well, but from the torn-up sod surrounding this one, it was evident she had been struggling for some time. Her coat was very dark, true black (which is rare among horses), and the mare's small, fine head showed clearly that this was a valuable, blooded animal.

My lady knelt by that head. "Poor girl, will you let me help you?" The mare's large, dark eyes, white-rimmed with pain, opened as Joisan stroked her muzzle and neck. "Easy, easy. Kerovan"—she looked up—"stay by her head while I feel how the foal lies. We must lose no time, or she will die."

Soothing the horse, I watched as Joisan rolled up her sleeves and made a quick inspection of the birth canal. "One of the foal's forelegs is caught, Kerovan, and I cannot loose it." The mare thrashed, and I held her head pressed against the ground. Then Joisan was beside me, one hand pulling loose an amulet she wore beneath her mail.

"I will sing her into a painless state, if I can. You must try and free the foal, yours is the longer reach and greater strength. Have you done such before?"

"When I was a boy I used to follow Riwal, the Wiseman, when he tended the farm animals. I have seen him do so once or twice."

"Even small knowledge will have to do. Reach downward toward the mare's belly, and find the foreleg. Pull it up so it rests beside the other."

I pulled off my mail, stripping also quickly to the waist, as Joisan began to sing. When the mare's eyes closed again, she nodded, and I began.

It was an awkward business because I had to lie nearly prone. Each labor contraction squeezed my arm, but I persisted between them, until finally I located the snagged foreleg. Bringing it up toward the birth canal, I pulled, feeling the foal's nose resting on top of my hand.

The mare groaned and shuddered, and suddenly the foal slid out, still clad in its protective sac. Joisan smiled at me. "Well done, my lord. I shall call upon you as a midwife more often!"

I ripped loose the whitish, translucent covering and began massaging the foal's ribs. It took a deep, gasping breath. The mare climbed to her feet, then delivered the afterbirth. Busy with the foal, I heard Joisan exclaim as the mare lay down once more. "Kerovan, she—"

Suddenly the mare heaved again, and a second foal was born! I hastily pulled the first to one side, and together Joisan and I tended the second.

The second foal was much the smaller, though both were fillies, greyish in color, with darker manes, tails, and legs. Soon the mare stood again to deliver the second afterbirth. Joisan cared for her, giving her water from the stream into which she poured a strengthening cordial.

Some time later, nickering softly, the mare nosed the larger of the two foals, licking, then prodding at it gently until it climbed to its unsteady legs and finally began to nurse. But when the other foal also gained its feet, the mare laid back her ears and nipped viciously at it, warning it away.

"I was afraid this would happen." I frowned, studying the rejected filly. "When twins are born, most times the mare casts off one—usually the smaller and weaker of the two."

"But . . ." Joisan stroked the tiny castoff. "If she doesn't feed soon, she will die. . . ."

"We can try milking the mare," I said, knowing that sometimes—only sometimes—one could save rejected young in this way.

"Every *half hour?*" Joisan bit her lip, putting a protective arm around the foal's neck. "And for how many days . . . *weeks?* We have little in the way of supplies, Kerovan."

"I know. . . . Perhaps the mare's owners will seek her out. They may be better equipped than we to raise the foal. If not . . ." I took out my knife, watching the lowering sun flash red on the blade. "Perhaps it would be kinder to take the foal's life cleanly rather than be forced to leave it to suffer when we must move on."

Joisan shook her head, her eyes very solemn. "You do not understand, my lord. I am a healer, sworn to practice my Craft on any and all creatures needing my aid. I must do whatever I can to save this foal, even if it means staying here to tend it."

I stared at her, then at the mountains I could no longer see, but which I knew still lay in wait for me. Joisan's protection—how long could it be expected to last? "But, my lady, what if your spell-guarding does not hold? My deliverance lies in distancing myself from those mountains. . . ."

"I know." She looked back up at me. "But I cannot let her die, Kerovan! I am oath-bound to healcraft!" Joisan's cry was so vehement that the filly started.

"But . . ." I gestured, feeling helpless, then ruffled the little castoff's fuzzy mane. "This is a hard thing, I know, but I can think of no answer save for me to leave and you to stay."

Joisan

"But there must be!" I cast a desperate glance at the black mare, contentedly licking her first foal, while my fingers absently stroked the other baby's muzzle. It lipped at them with toothless gums, trying to suck. Kerovan's amber eyes caught and held mine. The chilling distance that had lain in their depths when he fought the pull from the mountains was gone. Replacing it was such sadness that I quickly laid a comforting hand on his arm.

I knew my lord had always felt closer to animals than to his own kind, for it is their nature not to judge by appearance, rather to respond to that which lies within a person. The little castoff's plight stirred him deeply.

Those amber eyes . . . they tugged at me, their golden color awakening the ghost of an idea . . . amber. . . .

My hand flew to cup Zwyie's amulet, clutching tightly that ripe amber sheaf of wheat entwined with grapes. Gunnora!

I turned back to the mare. "Kerovan, we must get some of the mare's own milk onto the hide of this little one. Squeeze some onto your hands, then rub it over the foal."

He hesitated, as though he questioned what I intended, but instead obeyed without further comment. I walked a little apart so I could see the mare, the two foals, both lying down now, and my lord all together. The afternoon sun had darkened slightly as it edged toward its western bed, changing the sky's hue to near the amber of the pendant. Overhead I could see the faint white day-ghost of the moon's disc. I closed my eyes, raising my face to that shadow of moon, picturing in my mind Gunnora as she is always described (though none can claim to have seen her with eyes of the body), for, time out of mind, she has been truly spirit.

A woman . . . ripe of body, yet slender of waist, with dark hair and eyes, wearing a mantle of rich amber, a precious amulet twin to mine. . . . I filled my mind with that image, holding to it with all the will toward life I could summon. Also silently I thought-spoke, words that held no proper shaping, yet welled up from my heart.

Gunnora . . . you who are mindful of womankind, our support and aid in times of pain and fear . . . you who nourish the seed when it is sown, who raise up the ripe fields . . . I ask your aid to waken and strengthen the will to motherhood here, so that one in great need will not die. . . . So may it be always by Thy will. . . .

For moments counted only by the beats of my heart I held her image before me, striving to reach . . . *touch*—

A warmth spread from between my breasts, outward-flowing along my body. Those dark eyes—they were no longer those of the woman in my mind-constructed image—they were *real*. For a long moment they looked directly into mine.

Then that contact was gone, and the warmth that had been nigh unto heat gentled. Blinking, I looked around, feeling the tough grass blowing about my ankles once more, then a caressing puff of breeze against my cheek.

Kerovan stared at me, his wide eyes fixed on the amulet.

I looked down, to see that symbol still glowing, pulsing in time to my lifeblood's flow.

He wet his lips. "Joisan?"

"Here," I made answer. What had he seen in those few moments that he should look at me so?

"For a space it seemed . . ." He shook his head, long fingers absently pushing back unruly locks of dark hair, for his helm lay upon the coils of his doffed mail. "It was as though someone else stood there. A second only—too fast for my eyes to make sure."

The black mare nickered low in her throat. She bent her head, took a step forward, standing nose to nose with our little outcast. I caught my breath, then the horse began to lick her second newborn. With spidery legs outthrust, the filly made her unsteady way to her mother's side, began nursing greedily, her little whiskbroom tail switching from side to side.

"Thank you," I whispered, watching, that absurd tightness I had felt watching Utia and Acar clutching once more at my throat. "So may it be always by *Thy* will. . . ."

Kerovan's arm circled my waist, and we stood so for a moment—then his grasp tightened until I drew breath sharply in near pain.

"What? Kerovan—" Now I could hear it, too. The rolling thrum of hoofbeats.

My lord swung around, stooping to grasp sword-hilt, setting himself still mailless between me and those oncoming riders. My heart pulsing not now in joy, but fear, I tightened fingers on my own blade, half drawing it. Fingers as steely as my weapon reached back, grasped my arm, staying its motion. "No, Joisan. There are too many."

Every impulse in my body urged me to draw. Swallowing, I sheathed blade. My lord had the right of it, and with one part of my mind I admired his wisdom and restraint as he slowly, deliberately, hooked his thumbs in his belt, waiting with an outward show of ease.

As the riders swept toward us, I counted twenty in the

band. All bestrode mounts clearly of the same fine breed as the mare behind us, though colors ranged from grey to a brown mottled with small white spots. Their riders were equally colorful.

As they reined in to face us silently, I was surprised to see that both men and women made up the band, dressed alike in loose-sleeved linen blouses bright with embroidery. Their trousers were also linen, of coarse wild flax, tucked into high soft boots laced with dyed leather. Some wore beautifully patterned blankets, a simple hole in the center to form a loose surcoat.

All were clearly of the same race, dark of skin, hair, and eyes, with high-bridged noses and cheekbones. Most wore their hair braided, some of the women making colorful cords part of that twining. Copper necklets set with rough stones caught the late sun's rays with flashes of crimson, indigo, and jade-green.

Each rider carried a short spear, wickedly barbed.

After a long moment's hesitation, the lead rider, a brawny man of middle years with a thick fringe of lip hair, touched heels to his mount's flanks, moving to front my lord. The common speech of Arvon sounded harsh and strangely accented as he demanded:

"How do you come here? And why? Could there be dreams of horse-stealing?" His short fingers twirled easily, and suddenly the spear was leveled at us. "Let me tell you, the Kioga take not kindly to such."

Kerovan shook his head in denial. "No horse-stealing, only the saving of a horse . . . and a valued one, by the look of her."

The leader's teeth showed in a grin that held no humor. "So say you, outlander, and so would say anyone caught as you are. But Briata would never have wandered so far from the herd, even for foaling, unless—"

"Obred, look!" That cry cut across his words. Startled, I looked to its source. A young woman, red-and-gold cords threading her long braids stared wide-eyed, pointing. *At me*.

Confused, I glanced behind me, wondering what strangeness had caused her to look so. Gasps and mutterings were audible from the band of riders.

The leader, Obred, suddenly touched hand to forehead, bowing so low his scrag of mustache nearly grazed his mount's mane. "Your pardon, Cera. I did not see what you are. Please forgive, Wise One."

My lord was also staring at me, his gaze fixed on my mail shirt. Hastily I looked down.

Gunnora's amulet was less bright now, but the sun was also nearly gone, and the amber glow still waxed and waned from it in time to my heart's beating. I took a breath that was more than a little shaky. Kerovan nodded slightly, mindsharing, and I knew he was in full agreement with my measurement of our now-averted peril.

I wet dry lips, found a voice that only will kept steady. "Through Gunnora's Will I was able to help Briata, but she and her foals still need tending. My lord and I will leave that to you, now, and be once more on our way."

"Foals? *Two?*" Obred's eyes made a quick search of the tall grass, fastened on the bigger filly stretched out asleep. "Truly, Cera, a miracle! Twins, and both alive! Has Briata accepted both?"

"Yes, thanks to my lady." There was pride in Kerovan's voice as he spoke, such pride as to bring the blood up in my cheeks.

I turned to gather up my pack even as Kerovan now resumed his clothing and mail shirt, then straightened as Obred dismounted, shaking his head. "Of course you will not go, Cera, not until we have had a chance to thank you. Briata is Lead Mare, and without her our herds would lose their way. The Kioga take not such debts lightly, and ours is truly beyond repayment. But we will make what amends we may."

Kerovan hesitated, looking at the shorter man, clearly

in doubt whether to accept his offer of aid. The Kioga leader drew his dagger from his belt-sheath, offering it to my lord. "My knife-oath on it, Lord. You and your lady have earned aught we can do to ease your way and give you comfort. We can only hope you will bide long enough to let us erase some part of our debt."

A swift mindtouch came then from Kerovan, although his eyes never wavered from the older man's face. *Say you yes, Joisan? I believe he speaks truth. . . .*

I believe so, too, I returned.

My lord nodded, then clapped his bare hands together, afterward raising his right hand in the salute of one warrior to another. "To the House, greeting. For the welcome of the gate, gratitude. We thank you, Obred."

A short time later, mounted on two of the Kioga horses, we reined away from Briata and her foals. The two Kioga whose mounts we now rode were to stay behind with the Lead Mare, caring for her until tomorrow, when she and the foals would be fit for travel.

The setting sun dissolved in a crimson-and-gold splash over the western horizon, shading to purple the undersides of the clouds as we rode. Obred set a quick pace across this level plain, and I was glad that the gelding I bestrode was smooth of gait, for I had not ridden since we left High Hallack. Soon muscles used only to walking began to pull and tug, and I found myself hoping that the Kioga hold would not be far.

"Yesterday, walking, I felt myself grown soft." I turned to see Kerovan grimace ruefully. "Today, riding, I am certain of it!"

I laughed. "You echo my thoughts, my lord. Still, compared to the mounts of High Hallack, we should be thankful to be astride horses such as these."

"They are beautiful," Kerovan agreed, running a hand over his mount's shining neck. "Spirited, quick to the rein or leg, yet gentle and calm."

"Our horses are our lives, and we theirs," Obred said,

turning back in his saddle, his face a blur in the fading light. "The Kioga would not exist, save for the speed and wisdom of our mounts. Long ago, they brought us out of death and ruin to a new life, each man and woman riding his or her Chosen, carrying naught save what his or her mount could bear. Our sign is the Mare." He gestured at the southern sky, where a few stars were beginning to show. "She is followed during the springtime by her Twins."

He reined his horse back, lowered his voice so it should reach our ears only. " 'Tis also said that when the Mare and her Twins come to walk this world's earth, the Kioga will find an end to roving—our true home."

I thought of the strange Gate we had passed through three years ago, only to find ourselves in Arvon, wondering if Obred's "new life" referred to such. Their dissimilarity to any other peoples we had yet encountered argued they were not native to this land. His recounting also told much of their immediate acceptance of my lord and myself upon seeing the twin foals. Uneasily, I hoped that this "true home" they spoke of was not something they would now expect to spring up from naught to confront them . . . though I could well sympathize with their longing for a place that was theirs alone, and an end to roving.

As the darkness deepened, our pace slowed. I rode loose-reined, allowing my mount to pick his way, depending on his night-sight, so much more acute than my own. Several times I saw Obred urge his mount to the fore, conferring low-voiced with the lead rider, the young woman who had pointed at me. I guessed that the Kioga had ranged far from their grazing lands in search of their Lead Mare, and a prick of disquiet touched me again. Obred had the right of it when he'd said Briata should not have wandered so far, even for foaling privacy. It was almost as though she had been led . . . and we to find her.

I shivered. Once before my lord and I had been so directed, chivied by (seemingly) accidental circumstances to a confrontation between the Dark and the Light. I glanced over at Kerovan, wondering. Could his fears be truth? Was it Galkur, seeking to reclaim what he had proclaimed his?

We approached a grove of trees, silver-limbed in the moon's glow. As we drew near, I noticed something cleaving the forest like a giant's sword-slash—halving it perfectly. A road, running straight and bare, its length catching the light until it seemed a shining river. Dimly, muted, I could hear the cries of night birds as Obred swung his horse toward that road, and I, conscious of a sudden lightening of heart, made to follow.

A shout split the night—"Obred, hold!" My gelding shied and skittered as Kerovan, putting heels to his mare, sent her crashing to the fore of our small group, swinging his mount to bar our path. A blue-green glare of light illuminated his features, emanating from that wristband of the Old Ones he always wore. "Hold! Let no one who values his or her spirit set foot on that road." He swung about in his saddle, turning to face us. "Look at it! Through the light of my wristlet, look at it! Look well!"

Narrowing my eyes, I gazed at that arrow-straight way again.

Looking through the honest glow of my lord's talisman, I saw with eyes freed of bedazzlement or glamourie. That road appeared now a phosphorescent glaze laid over rank darkness, like the shine of decay overlaying ancient rot.

I heard a retching noise, saw Obred leaning far off his mount. I could smell it now, too—the stench that betrays a Shadowed place. Fighting nausea, I turned away from that hideous trap.

After regrouping, we rode on once more, but with a difference this time. Kerovan and I rode to the fore, with the Kioga leader, in case any more such places lay in wait. Obred turned to my lord as we rode. "My thanks for saving my people, Lord Kerovan. Would you consider accompanying us on the morrow on our ride in search of new spring breeding-grounds? Such a warning talisman as you bear could prove a great boon in this haunted land."

What think you, Joisan? I am minded to go, if only to gain more knowledge that may aid us in our journeying. . . . Kerovan's mindsharing reached me clearly.

I hesitated, thinking what it would be like to be alone among strangers . . . but the realization that my lord seemed to have found in these Kioga a people he could be at ease with decided me. In all our journeying there had been no companionship for him save my own, and if he had found such now . . .

I am minded to stay with these folk for a while . . . and it would be good to have a scout's knowledge of what lies ahead. . . . I made him answer.

"I will ride with you, Obred," my lord agreed.

"For all my people, I thank you. Where did you find that wristlet?" the Kioga leader asked.

"In a stream, not far from a place of the Old Ones. Uncounted years it must have lain there, for our people do not venture far into those lands, long abandoned as they are. But this came to me as if made for me alone, though doubtless many ages separated its fashioning and my birth. . . ." He laughed reminiscently after a moment's pause. "Doubtless this will please you, Obred. My *horse* had the true finding of it. Hiku led me to its resting place."

Obred chuckled in turn, then sobered again. "It has saved you before?"

"A number of times." Kerovan's voice sounded wistful as he continued. "Usually it has only served to warn, although I have evidence it has greater Powers—Powers I have no knowledge of . . . such learning has never been mine. I was trained as a warrior, and those skills were given ample testing, for there is war overmountain in High Hallack."

"So we have heard, through traders. Mostly the Kioga keep to themselves, but no one shrugs away or forgets tales of war in neighboring lands. You and your lady fled when your home was destroyed?"

"Yes, into the Wastes, along with our people. But the paths into Arvon are few, and so far we two have encountered no others of Dalesblood in our wanderings."

" 'Tis said this winter past some of the blood of Arvon returned to this land, and that riding with them they brought brides from out of the Dales. The trader swore that this joining came about as a result of some bargain struck between the Wereriders and the Dale Lords."

The smooth pace of my lord's mount beside my own faltered a bit, as though his legs had clamped hard on the mare's sides.

"The Wereriders? Struck a bargain with the Dales?"

"Such was their price for their swords. They fought for the right of the Dalesblood, though under their own command and in their own way—and many are the rumors and stories whispered about the strangeness of that way— still, it seems they battled to some purpose. The trader Klareth told us that the war in High Hallack is over."

The war over! I glanced over at Kerovan, saw the vague shape of his face turned also to face me. The knowledge gave me joy, but such joy as I could feel only for others—in me there was not the slightest urge to return to the Dales, seek out my blasted Keep of Ithkrypt, and rebuild— although I felt relieved that those of my people who might wish to do so now could.

And you, Kerovan? Silently I asked that question. *Do you think now of returning to Ulmsdale?*

His returning thought came swiftly. *You know that I do not. The part of me that struggled against those demons from Alizon is glad of their defeat—but I have no home there anymore.*

I agreed with his assessment, but his final words reminded me once more that, in truth, there was no place we could look to as our own. I sighed, reminding myself to be grateful for the temporary hospitality of the Kioga.

A few minutes later, we rode into that hospitality. Lights, people—after the silent darkness of our ride, the Kioga camp (for hide tents betokened what I had already suspected, that these people were nomadic, following their herds) seemed aswirl with those eager to welcome us. One short, stocky woman seemed to be their leader, for Obred, upon dismounting, went directly to her, conversing with her quietly. Kerovan aided me from my horse, and we stood together in the torchlight as they approached.

"Our Chief, Jonka." The woman inclined her head graciously at Obred's words, smiling.

"Obred has told me of our debt to you, a debt I acknowledge freely, for Briata is my Chosen. I offer you aught that the Kioga can give for comfort. Abide with us in peace and honor as our guests." She gestured, and a young girl approached, in her hands a guesting-cup.

I wet my lips with dark liquid, then swallowed gratefully. Wine, sweetened with herbs and honey, its fragrance heady and rich. I passed the silver vessel to Kerovan, who also drank. Jonka completed the guesting ritual, sipping from the cup, then tossing a few of the remaining drops in the air, toward the moon's near fullness, splashing the last on the ground.

"Valona." She gestured and the young girl who had borne the guesting-cup came forward. "Show our guests where they may rest and refresh themselves. I must see to the guesting-feast."

It was near bliss to shed the weight of my mail, wash in herb-scented water. Valona brought our packs to the tent, aided by another little girl who pressed her palm to her forehead in a respectful salute but was too shy to speak. I pulled my clean jerkin from the depths of the pack, grimacing at its wrinkles.

"I could wish for my best tabard and gown, if we are to be honored with a feast," I said to Kerovan, who was busy rummaging through his pack.

"And, I, also—wish for the tabard, that is. Still, they

cannot expect much in the way of scented fripperies from two who have crossed the plains and delivered foals today, can they?"

"Let us hope not," I murmured, wincing at the knots in my hair as I combed.

A few minutes later, washed, combed, and arrayed in our best (poor though that might be), we followed our little guide between the rows of tents to the sounds of laughter and the smells of food.

We ate sitting cross-legged on the brown-tufted grass, but the variety of the meal—as well the excellence of its cooking—belied the lack of ceremony in our seating. Fish and waterfowl, rice mixed with nuts and spring onions, fruit and bread—after two days of journey rations, the Kioga feasting seemed to eclipse even the grandest in my Uncle Cyart's Great Hall before the war had come.

Nobody spoke much until the end of the meal, when our cups were again filled with the honeyed wine. Jonka sat on my right, dressed now in a plain linen gown brightened by an embroidered bodice and sleeves, with the skirt divided for riding. The woman's only outward sign of authority was the silver crescent marked with a horse's head that hung on her breast, but the dark eyes looking into mine were wise, accustomed to command.

"Tell us, Cera, how you came to find and save Briata."

Hesitantly I related the events of the afternoon, giving mention of my lord's assistance in the delivery but stressing that it was only by the Will of Gunnora that both foals had been safely born and accepted.

"Gunnora?" Jonka brushed back a strand of long dark hair, raised her brows questioningly. "Is Gunnora the one whose symbol you bear?" I nodded assent. "Many are her Names, and all true. To the Kioga she is the Great Mother, the Mother of Mares. . . ."

"In my travels I have seen her sign linked with several Names," I agreed. "I am only grateful that today, when I called, she heard."

As the feasting drew to a close, Jonka and Obred withdrew to discuss tomorrow's scouting journey to search for a new breeding-ground. I relaxed, sipping at the last of my wine, my eyes studying our new companions. The torches glittered on gemmed necklets and bracelets, sparking bright colors everywhere. The Kioga dressed to suit their cheerful, talkative natures, so different from the rather taciturn fisherfolk of Anakue. Everywhere smiles and frankly curious glances met mine as I looked—

No. Not everywhere.

In the shadow of one of the tents, a woman crouched, studying us with eyes so dark they seemed to reflect none of the firelight—rather, resembled pits in her stony countenance. I could *feel* her stare laid across my face, like a cold hand in the night.

It was an effort to wrench my eyes from that contact. I turned, found Valona sitting beside me, smiling shyly. "Valona, who is that?"

She turned, scanned the crowd obediently. "Which one, Cera?"

"That one—" I moved to point, but the tent's shadow was empty. "She was there a moment ago . . . a woman, wearing a dark cloak."

"With eyes that keep everything inside?"

"Yes. Who is she?"

"Nidu, the Shaman." The child moved a little closer to me. "She has great Power. . . ."

I thought of that dark, gaunt face and could well believe the child's words.

There came a soft tread behind me, then the Chief's voice. "You and your lord must be weary, Cera. I will show you to the guesting-tent."

We followed her to the large tent where we had washed earlier. The Kioga tents were woven of horsehair, with differing designs stitched upon them using thin strands of braided, dyed horsehair. A patterned blanket divided the sleeping area from the rest of the tent. Jonka gestured to an ewer of water and a towel sitting on a heavily carved chest. Beside it was a wicker-seated stool and, resting on the stool, a clean nightshift.

"Traveling is wearying, Cera, and it is hard to pack all one could wish for upon one's back. I hope this will do well enough. We are almost of a height, but I am somewhat the broader!"

"It's beautiful," I said, my hands caressing the thin, finely woven linen embroidered with delicate, pale stitches. "I thank you, Jonka."

She motioned upward toward the top of the tent. "It is our custom to open the top of our homes in good weather so we may see the Mare as she rises. But if you prefer, I can pull the flap to—"

"I am used to seeing the stars as I lie abed, Jonka. Open will be fine."

"I bid you a good night and fair rising, then, Cera."

"And to you, Jonka. Thank you again."

Kerovan echoed my good night, lifting the blanket, then disappeared into the sleeping area. I washed again, then slipped the nightshift over my head. Jonka had the right of it, it was too loose, but my hands lingered over the thin fabric and the beauty of the stitchery as I tied the bodice-lacings. It had been long since I had worn women's dress, and the feel of the skirt was pleasant as I shook my hair loose, began to brush it.

Overhead the moon shone only a day away from fullness, its light silvering the tent into sharp contrasts of dark and light after I snuffed the candle on the low table.

The moon . . . the light . . .

My eyes were drawn upward, fixing on the sign of Gunnora hanging in the sky—uncounted distance away, but seeming to me now, at this moment, almost within fingertip range.

The moon . . . the light . . .

I found that I was standing, arms and legs apart, my head thrown back, my whole being seeking, reaching for that light and what it betokened. On my breast was again a warmth, and loosing the laces of the nightshift, I found my amulet once more glowing.

It was as though that symbol drew to it all the light of the moon, changing and reflecting back that glow in amber radiance. In me there came a stirring, a touch of something I could understand only dimly with my mind, but which my body responded to as ancient and ageless fate. . . .

I was moving, my steps taking me toward the sleeping area. The dividing blanket rasped my nails as I pulled it aside. Kerovan lay curled on the pallet, dark head resting on one outstretched arm. At my tread his eyes opened, widened.

"Joisan—the light—"

My fingers touched his lips, quieting him. His hand came up to circle my wrist, as his mouth pressed a kiss 'gainst my palm. "Joisan . . ." My name was a spoken caress, while a whispered echo filled my mind. His touch was as light as the whisper of wings upon my body, but this time he was truly himself, and there was nothing held back—no hesitation or fear to separate us. I found myself freed, also, by his warmth—free to give and take as never before . . . free to share. . . .

Filled, consumed by that uniting, that sharing, we fell at length into exhausted slumber.

Kerovan

Bright sunlight woke me from sleep so deep it was naught but a dark, dreamless void. For long moments I lay blinking at strange surroundings, unable to recall where I was or how I had come there. My eyes fastened on the bright blue of the blanket curtaining the sleeping area from the rest of the tent, its curving lines of white reminding me suddenly of swirling waves upon the sea. . . . As though that pattern suddenly anchored me to the past, memory surged back.

The Kioga . . . Obred, Jonka, and that strange dark woman Nidu . . . was it only yesterday we had come here, been welcomed with such joyful celebration? And then, last night . . . I turned cautiously onto my side, careful not to wake her, and regarded Joisan.

She slept deeply still, russet hair thick-locked about her face and over her shoulders and breast, the sunlight awakening gold among the reddish-brown strands. Around her neck she still wore the amulet that had glowed amber to the beat of her heart—it seemed for a moment that I could again feel that talisman's warmth against my own chest.

I reached for her, longing to feel her skin beneath my fingers, then stopped, chary of waking her. Yesterday had been a day to tire the strongest, and she doubtless needed her sleep. Yet a selfish portion of me continued to wish she would wake. I wanted to experience again her arms about me . . . her kisses, warm and yielding, then by turns demanding. . . . I wanted—

Joisan's eyes opened, then she smiled sleepily, moving to brush hair out of her eyes. "As Jonka would say, fair rising, my lord."

"Looking upon my lady is the fairest part of my waking," I said hesitantly, almost afraid to meet her eyes and see laughter in them. I knew so little of courtly ways that pretty speeches—even when meant wholeheartedly—came awkwardly to me.

Her hand moved to brush my hair, touch my cheek. Mindsharing, I knew she understood my words, felt her appreciation of them. I turned to touch her, gathered her close, eager for—

"Lord Kerovan!" Someone scratched at the tent flap outside. "I would not disturb you, save that our morning meal is ready, and the mounts saddled. We must break our fast and ride." Obred's voice sounded embarrassed as he finished, "I know it is but poor manners to call a guest, but it is nigh unto noon, and we have far to go."

I sighed deeply, rolling onto my back, away from Joisan. Trying to mask the irritation I felt, I made quick answer. "A fine scout I am, sleeping the day away! I will be with you directly, Obred. Thank you for calling me."

Joisan managed to look both amused and disappointed. "Who are you to think you have no courtly ways, my husband? I have seldom heard rank falsehood voiced in such a semblance of truth."

"I would stay instead with you, Joisan . . . today, and tomorrow, and the next. . . ." Again I reached for her. But she was already rising, shaking her head.

" 'Promises made lightly are still promises to be held

to,' " she quoted, her smile holding more than a little of devilment about it.

Grumbling, I made ready for the day.

When we had broken our fast, Obred turned to me. "Now we must see you mounted, Kerovan. Come with me to the Unchosen herd."

We walked quickly over the level plain, threading our way between the tents of the Kioga. In the daylight I could see that they were mostly dark brown, or black, with one or two (including the one that had been ours) dyed indigo. Each had a different design upon its flap. Small children ran by us in a group, playing some game. Older ones passed, carrying baskets filled with linen to be washed, wild grain to be ground, or younger brothers and sisters they tended. All smiled in greeting.

"I like well your people, Obred," I said frankly, reflecting inwardly that never had I felt so at ease in the presence of so many of my own kind before.

"And I, too," echoed Joisan. "In all our long travels, seldom have we been so welcomed."

"A small return, surely, for the saving of Briata. Lero and Vala brought mare and foals in some hours ago, having started with the dawn. Already the fillies are running, trying to play with each other. A fine pair they'll be to train!"

"And Briata?" I asked.

"Standing by with great forebearance, especially when both decide they are hungry at the same moment. You should see her expression."

We laughed.

After crossing the camp, Obred gestured at the horses grazing to our right. "The herd of the Chosen." Two young boys rode, acting as herd-guards.

Several minutes farther on was another, smaller, herd. "The Unchosen. I had the youngsters cull out the yearlings and two-year-olds, as well as the breeding mares close to foaling. Now you must see which of our trained mounts shall Choose you, to be yours for the journey."

I looked at the score or so animals, all of different colors, but bearing clearly the Kioga stamp of breeding—small heads; strong, short backs; sloping croups; and deep chests. "How do I Choose?"

"You do not. The horse will Choose you. Can you whistle?"

"Yes."

"Then do so. The first animal to come toward you will mean you have been Chosen by that one."

Thinking back to my scouting days with the army, I put my fingers to my lips, trilling the early morning call of a hedge-grouse—our signal for re-forming after a dawn reconnaissance.

Several animals looked up, but only one took several steps in my direction. Nor did she turn away as I approached to lay hand upon her shoulder, but stood quiet, flicking her ears far forward, regarding me with calm interest.

A good-sized mare, fifteen and a half hands, I judged, her coat a dark bay dotted about the flanks and haunches with white spots near the size of my palm. A wide strip of the same color traced her forehead, and her two forelegs bore stockings to the knee.

"Easy, easy," I said, gentling her as Obred and Joisan joined us. "I gather I have been Chosen?"

"Aye. She is one of Jonka's breeding and training, is Nekia. Her name means 'night-eyes' in our tongue. She is keen-eyed at all times, but unusually so in the dark."

I stroked the mare's strong, arched neck. "Well, Nekia, shall we company together?"

She bobbed her head down, seemingly in acquiescence, then nudged me so strongly that I staggered, chuckling. "I have seldom seen such impatience!"

Obred smiled broadly beneath his mustache. "A good beginning, Lord. Will you mount?"

"But I have no saddle, no bridle for control—"

"Our horses are trained to the knee and weight, Kerovan. Many times I've ridden the whole day with my reins lying loose on my mount's neck, and never had to pick them up."

Cautiously I placed my hands testingly on Nekia's neck and back, then, when she remained quiet, vaulted up. It felt exceedingly strange to ride with no visible control, and when the mare moved out at the squeeze of my calf muscles, I needs must steady myself for a moment. But she slowed obediently when I tightened my knees, shifting my weight backward. By the time we reached the camp again I was marveling anew at the Kioga skill in training horses.

Still, it was with some relief that I found a light saddle and braided hackamore in Jonka's arms as she came forward to bid us farewell. While I made fast girths and adjusted stirrups, the remainder of the scouting party gathered. Looking around, I counted five other men, including Obred, four youths, and seven girls of varying ages. (Used to the keep-sheltered women of High Hallack, who were generally allowed only the gentlest of palfreys for mounts, I eyed these last with some surprise, only to realize before many minutes were past that they numbered among the boldest and best riders.)

Some of the party led extra mounts carrying light packs. "For hunting," Obred explained at my question. "On our return, we will stop to hunt if the sign is good, and we can be certain of reaching camp with fresh game."

His remark and the amount of supplies allotted each member made me realize this was no one- or two-day reconnoiter. This party was setting out for a journey of many days.

I glanced at Joisan as I guessed this, wishing mightily that I was not going. Last night had gone far toward healing the rift between us caused by my recent uneasiness, now I wanted to be with her . . . her only—

Still, as she had reminded me, I was bound by my word—and that I could break for no cause as small as merely my own wish. As the party exchanged final greetings, I leaned from my seat on Nekia to look straightly at my lady.

I would I could stay with you, Joisan . . . you know how much. . . .

I know, she assured me, her mindsharing a quick, warm touch. *I will miss you . . . but there is much for me to learn here, and Jonka has been so kind. . . .*

Taking her hand in both of mine, I touched my lips to it briefly, then turned Nekia quickly away, not looking back—for I feared greatly that otherwise my resolve would weaken.

Our riding was south, angling slightly to the east. The plains continued to roll, unbroken, save for brief clumps of trees clustering along stream or riverbanks.

When I questioned him as to our possible goal, Obred told me they searched for higher grazing lands. He explained that their animals were mountain-bred from generations back and fared best in pastures with greater elevation. "Putting a mountain under a horse's hooves breeds better muscle and wind," he commented, rising in his stirrups to scan the flat horizon ahead. "To the west lies a great desert, with naught but sand, scrub, and death to fill it. We hope that farther to the east we may find hills."

We camped that night near a stream. Tired from the day's riding, I lay down in my blankets, pillowing my head on Nekia's mane, as she also stretched out, as did the rest of the Kioga and their mounts. The mare's body was warm, her presence comforting under the star spread and the harsh glare of the full moon—but my thoughts sped to Joisan. I missed her with an intensity that surprised me. Never since our true marriage had we been separated, save when the demands of her healcraft had intervened . . . which was not the same, I discovered, as being leagues apart. I wondered if she thought of me . . . and so wondering, finally slept.

Twenty days' riding brought our small band to the bank of a great river, so wide we could not hope to ford it without boats or rafts. Obred turned again to the east, hoping to find a narrower stretch where we might swim our mounts across.

I found myself riding that morning beside a youth hardly more than a boy, sprouting as yet only a downy growth on his dark face. (In this company of bearded countenances, my habit of shaving each morning brought me some strange glances—several times I had been mistaken at a distance for one of the boys.)

"Fair rising, Lord Kerovan." He glanced at me diffidently.

"Fair rising to you," I made answer, unable to remember his name—if indeed I had ever known it.

"I am Guret, sir."

I gave him a warrior's salute, bringing a flush of pleasure beneath that faint shadow of beard. "Thank you, m'lord—but I am no warrior yet. I am still practicing for the Festival of Change."

"Festival?"

"Aye, more than a month from now. All those who have been Chosen"—he affectionately slapped the neck of the fine chestnut stallion he rode—"must show their skill as hunters and herd-protectors. Then we will be accorded a voice in the Council."

I thought of my own rite of manhood—when my father, Ulric of Ulmsdale, had ceremoniously given me the sword I still wore. I knew well how it felt to pass in the space of one day from untried youth to man—remembered how the heavy weight of new responsibility had seemed to press upon me, leaving me feeling even more of a boy, far less than a man. . . .

It was almost as though Guret read my thoughts, for his voice grew subdued till I must strain to hear him.

"At times, it seems to me that the Festival cannot come

too soon, and I wish it were tomorrow. And at others, it seems that it is rushing toward me like a wasp-stung horse, and that I stand frozen in its path. . . ."

For long moments I was silent, debating whether I should attempt to answer the half plea I heard in the youngster's voice. Always, except with Joisan, I had kept my own counsel, standing apart from others . . . but can one live forever so? Even as I told myself to hold to silence, I heard my own words:

"It seems to me that only those who have no understanding of what makes a true man rush headlong. Those like yourself, who doubt and consider, are those who prove to be the wisest, the most mature. . . ."

"Perhaps you are right, Lord," he replied thoughtfully.

We rode on in silence, hearing only the rushing of that great river. I found myself wondering if the stream flowed into some distant sea far to the south. This land was wide . . . in all our wanderings, Joisan and I had seen only a small portion of it.

"From whence did you and the Cera Joisan come, m'lord?" the boy asked.

"From overmountain." I turned in my saddle, pointing at those heights which I could no longer see but always felt—although, thanks to my lady, that once-compelling pull remained at bay.

"*We* came from those mountains, too." Guret frowned. "Last winter the Council decreed we should move on, though the harvest was rich, our horses fat. One of our scouts was slain—by something in the mountains. Then we made haste, even riding through snows belly-deep in the passes."

Something about his words raised a prickle of unease. For the first time in days I thought of Galkur—whose touch meant death and defilement such as no human spirit should bear. . . .

I shivered suddenly, convulsively, and the sudden tightening of my legs made Nekia dance beneath me.

"What are those lands like, overmountain? What manner of people live there?" Guret had not noticed my reaction. "I have asked the traders when they came, but even they had not traveled so far. I would like to roam this land, see what lies beyond our small territory."

I thought of the Dalesmen whom I had companied with in war, sat beside at feastings—those same men who had drawn away from me with sidelong looks barely hiding their distrust, their fear, once I had thrown aside the special boots my father had given me, made to conceal his heir's "difference." But such memories were not fit for sharing with this eager-eyed youth. . . . Instead, I let my thoughts run back farther in time, back to the two Dalesmen who had accepted me, even as now the Kioga appeared to. . . .

"The land of High Hallack is wide, and gently rolling eastward, which is why it is called the Dales by its people. Each lord has his Dale, with his menie of armsmen to defend it. One of my father's armsmen was Jago, my tutor in the skills of war and arms. Yet he taught me more than swordplay. . . .

"The Dales were not always tenanted by humankind, but bear traces, even as Arvon does, of others, those we call the Old Ones. They lived in Hallack long long ago, and our legends say that when first our people came into the Dales, they were already empty of their presence. But traces of them remain, and some men and women who thirst for knowledge and wisdom try to seek out such ruins. Such a one was Riwal, the Wiseman, who roamed the Waste in search of things he had little hope of understanding, yet was driven to try. I accompanied him on many such searches, and once we found a wondrous talisman from ages past. . . ."

I continued, telling more than perhaps I had intended, for Guret listened so intently. When I finally stopped, he protested that he must hear more.

"Yes, more, Lord Kerovan!" A voice echoed shrilly

from behind us. I turned to see a smaller child, a girl, heels beating a steady rhythm on her fat gelding's sides in her effort to keep up with us.

"Nita!" Guret's chagrin was plain. "How long have you been there? You know it is ill-mannered of you to listen to speech not intended for your ears!"

She raised a small, defiant chin, and in doing so, her likeness to the boy became even more pronounced. "It was Lord Kerovan's story, it is for *him* to scold me if he is angered." She turned dark eyes to me, suddenly sobering. "*Are* you angered, m'lord?"

I found myself chuckling, and sobered, making an effort to keep my voice stern. "No, I am not, but your brother has the right of it. It is *not* well-mannered to listen to others, unless they know you are doing so."

"Well"—she smiled serenely—"you must let me ride beside you from now on so I can listen freely, for truly, Lord, your story was among the finest I have ever heard."

I glanced sideways at the scowling Guret, then noted with relief Obred's upraised hand, our signal to halt. "No more stories now. Perhaps another time."

The Kioga leader beckoned me toward him, and I touched heels to Nekia's sides, drawing up beside him. "What think you, Kerovan? Do we try it? This is the narrowest it has been."

I looked to the river, judging those brown depths, noting the swirls and eddies betokening a strong current. "Single file, perhaps, with each rider leading his or her mount, until forced to swim."

"Aye." Turning to the others, he shouted instructions, and we began the passage.

I was the first, leading Nekia, until suddenly the bottom disappeared from under our hooves, and I found myself swimming, catching hold of the plunging mare's tail, speaking to her as calmly as I could, "Easy, girl. Just a few more . . . easy. . . ."

The silty water lapped my chin, and sputtering, I kicked

harder. Before me Nekia surged up, water streaming from her saddle and flanks, then my own questing hooves found purchase—

A shrill scream rent the air, coming from behind me, fading even before I could turn, ending in a bubbling gasp. Slapping Nekia's rump as hard as I could, I turned back, knowing the mare won free onto the bank.

Striking out back toward the other bank, I held my head high, striving to see what had chanced. Something large thrashed in the shallower water, grunting in panic, and I could hear shouting. My searching eyes fastened on a smaller form bobbing helplessly in the grip of the current, swiftly disappearing downstream. I flung myself after that figure, swimming as rapidly as I might, until I, too, found myself gripped by the main thrust of that current.

Stroking hard to keep my head up, my eyes fixed on the now feebly struggling victim, I knew a brief gratitude that my mail and weapons were securely fastened to Nekia's saddle—and that I wore no boots to drag me down. Years had passed since I had swum with Riwal in calm ponds, following Jago's stern lessonings in keeping myself afloat— never had I fought a current. It was all I could do to keep myself from being overborne by the rushing waters—what hope had I of aiding that other?—even assuming I could reach him or her. . . .

Summoning all my strength, I quelled such hopeless thoughts and swam on, only to see the other slip beneath the water when I was less than arm's length away. Before I could think, my body arced into a dive, both hands outflung, groping in the muddy flow.

My lungs rebelled, blood pounded in my ears—air! I *must* have *air*! Agonized, I kicked myself forward, still flailing my arms—

And touched! My fingers brushed cloth, grabbed, then I was swimming upward, toward life and air, that handful of linen clenched tight in my fist.

The finest of wines served at a High Lord's feasting

could never have tasted as wondrous as did that first mouthful of blessed air when my head broke water. Snatching quickly at what I held, now seeming naught but a lifeless bundle of rags, I heaved, bringing a face into view. Stroking awkwardly, one-handed, I began the long pull for shore.

After only a few feet, the air that I had gulped so greedily razed my chest like fire. The muscles in my arms and legs seemed at once weighted and weak. I could no longer see the bank, as my sight dulled.

Closing my eyes, I kicked frantically, feeling the limp weight along my side bearing heavy on me. Tightening my grasp stubbornly, I kept fighting . . . fighting . . . the water grasped me, pulling me down. . . .

So dulled were my senses, for long seconds I did not realize that the hold I felt upon my shoulder was that of a real hand—a hand that became many hands, dragging me from the river's deadly embrace.

Looking up, I could see Obred's face . . . hear dimly his shouts for help. More faces appeared. I was lifted, carried . . . carried into darkness. . . .

A huge pressure squeezed my ribs, though I moaned in feeble protest, trying to lever myself up.

"Easy, Kerovan. Lie still. You tried to drink half that accursed river." A voice spoke from above me—Obred's, I realized fuzzily.

I was lying facedown, the harsh brush of the plains grass beneath my cheek. That gripping pressure came once more, and this time I did squirm my way to my hands and knees—only to be racked again—this time by nausea. I could well believe that I *had* swallowed half the river from the quantity of water of which I painfully rid myself, Obred's big, hard-palmed hands gently supporting my head.

Finally I was able to look about me with a measure of intelligence, though my head still whirled, and I wanted nothing more than to collapse in sleep.

A knot of people clustered around another figure stretched on the ground. For a moment I thought sickly that all my effort had been for naught, and that that other was dead—then I saw one foot twitch. Staggering, I made a shaky progress toward the little group.

Guret crouched over that small form—my breath caught painfully. It was Nita I had pulled from beneath the water. One of the women massaged her ribs fiercely, then stooped to blow her own breath between the child's blue lips. There was no sound save for those rhythmically breathed puffs of air—once, twice, thrice. I lost count, and still the woman worked. . . .

A gasp from that soaked bundle, then another. An excited mutter from the grouped Kioga strengthened into a muted cheer as the girl on the ground began to breathe normally again.

Long moments later I turned away, realizing suddenly that if I did not sit, I would fall. Obred's arm encircled my shoulders.

"Once more we owe you a debt we cannot possibly repay. You went after Nita, with full knowledge that your own life might be forefeit in the doing. I have never seen such courage."

I sat, shaking my head in negation of his words. "Give me no such credit, Obred. I reacted before I could think—if I had thought, then I might well not have been able to summon the will. One cannot name that courage."

"You will never hear otherwise from my lips, Lord."

"What happened?" Now that I sat in the full light of the sun, with no sound but the rush of the river and the murmur of the others, the whole incident seemed unreal. Were it not for my soaked clothing, I could well imagine it had never happened.

"Nita's horse slipped on a stone and fell, throwing her into the river. None of us were close enough to catch her."

I heard a tread behind me but was too exhausted to look

up until I heard Guret's voice addressing Obred. "She is still sick from the water she swallowed, but she will be fine."

The boy dropped to his knees beside me and, before I could naysay his action, took my hand between both of his and pressed it to his forehead. "Lord, I am in your debt. Accept me as your liegeman, as is right."

"I will accept you as friend, Guret, and be honored in the doing." I found my voice, still rough from the rawness of my throat. "More than that, no. I am only thankful that Nita will recover."

We talked a bit more, then I slept, while Obred oversaw the river crossing. When I awoke it was time for me to cross again, thankful that there had been no more mishaps. We camped that night on the opposite bank. I sat leaning against my bedroll, listening to one of the women recount a long story-song, about the spirit of the river, in the shape of an otter, playing tricks upon two would-be Kioga trappers. It was a funny telling, and I found myself laughing with the others.

Something touched my shoulder. Turning, I saw Guret, his arm around Nita's waist. The girl looked weak and shaken still, but there was something of the old glint in her eyes. "*You* should be story-telling, Lord Kerovan. Everyone has heard of Otter and his trick, but only Guret and I have heard of the gryphon 'prisoned within a crystal globe, worn about a lady's neck, and she all unknowing it was a live creature."

"Nita!" I made haste to seat her beside me. "Where have you been?"

"I was the last to cross. Obred strung a rope, and I came through the river like a basket of rocks, with a loop tied around me. I told him I would cross with my horse, like any other, but he would not hear of it. He told me that you were already gone across, and I should not tempt the river to recapture what it once had within its fist."

She paused, then looked once more straightly at me,

her voice trembling. "I owe you my life, m'lord. I—" She swiped impatiently at her nose and eyes, tried once more. "I thank you. . . ." Then she began to sob, and I touched her shoulder, dismayed to see brash Nita so undone. Her body quivered with convulsive shudders.

"It is the reaction to near death," I told her brother, feeling helpless. "I have seen men taken so, after battles." Clumsily I put an arm around her, drew her to me, wondering a bit if she would protest. But she did not, and we sat so for a long time, the only sound Nita's quiet sobbing.

Finally Guret spoke, his voice pitched for my ears alone. "Lord? Are you truly a man? Or are you one of the Dream Spirits Nidu speaks of when she drums herself into a trance and walks other worlds?"

I looked over his sister's head at him. "Truly a man, Guret, naught else. Though at times"—the youth's dark eyes seemed to compel honesty from me—"I have been filled with the presence of another, from the past. One who is not of . . . this world. Although that was a long time ago."

"Yet you have these." The lad gestured at my hooves, curled beneath me as I sat.

I felt the old chill sweep through me but fought to keep my voice steady. "I was . . . born so. There was . . . other blood in my family, so say the tales. We are linked to the Old Ones."

"And that is why you have the Power."

"Who told you that?"

"Everyone can see that you are different, and the night you came, Obred spoke of the warning you gave that helped ward the rescue party from one of the deadly Shadowed places. You wear that." He nodded at my wristband. "One not having the Power could not do so."

"Perhaps you are right," I admitted reluctantly, "but I have no lessoning in such. Nor want any, if truth be known. I have no desire to be different inwardly, as I already am outwardly."

The dark eyes glinted in the firelight. "Perhaps it is as you told me this morning. One who does not worry about holding responsibility—or Power—is not one who should have it."

I smiled, albeit a little grimly. "My own words return to haunt me—but perhaps we should *both* consider them. . . ."

That night, with the silent camp sleeping around me, I found myself wakeful as I lay in my bedroll. Memories of Nita's rescue played themselves over in my mind, in a slowed-down manner, against my will. I saw, as if from outside myself, the spinning current, Nita's small form, my own movements—seeming incredibly clumsy and ineffectual. Sweat sprang dank and clammy on my body at the realization of just how close death had come to claiming me—and Nita—beyond all rescuing. *And against death,* I thought, shivering though the night was balmy, *man has no defense at all. . . .*

Not so, responded another part of my mind. *Most men have those of their blood to follow them, and so, in a fashion, live on.* I thought of Guret's clear-eyed gaze, of Nita's pert friendliness, and felt a pang of envy for their parents. What would it be like to have a son or daughter of my own to counsel, to comfort, as I had done today with Guret and Nita?

Joisan and I had been truly wed for three years, now. To my knowledge she had never used her Wisewoman's learning to prevent conception, yet we had no children. This must mean that she could not conceive by me—once again I was too different from pure humankind.

I thought of my own boyhood when my father, though offering me all any son and heir was entitled to in the way of food, clothing, and training, had nevertheless held me at arm's length insofar as any closeness, any sharing, was concerned. That his distance was partly due to my mother's ensorcellment in her effort to turn him against the "monster" he had fathered, I had discovered only after his death— when it was too late. I remembered my childish vows, when, hurt by Ulric's rejection, I had sworn that if *I* ever had a son I would never behave so . . . and then I recalled the soft, longing note in Joisan's voice when she spoke of Utia's child. . . .

I took a deep breath, realizing that my hands were balled into fists, nails gouging my palms. Opening my eyes, I willed myself to relax, looking upward at the moon, once again waxing, and at the bright, bright stars. Here on the plains, with no trees to interrupt their sweep, they arced overhead in such brilliant profusion that it made one dizzy to look upon them. I seemed to shrink within myself, my sorrow to become a silly, maundering indulgence in the face of such eternal indifference.

Yet something within me fought that sentence of insignificance—that negation of spirit. *I am a man*, I told those faraway uncaring watchers, *a man, and today I saved a life*. The thought brought with it a measure of comfort. Closing my eyes, I willed sleep.

For the next ten days we rode, moving ever southward and to the east, our eyes searching the horizon for Obred's looked-for mountains. On the morning of the eleventh day, when he chanced to ride beside me, I asked him why he and the Kioga had abandoned the mountains from whence Joisan and I had traveled—and if he and his people had originated in those heights.

"To answer your second question first, no. When I was still such a small one that I could barely ride alone, we came to this land. Nidu opened the way—" Catching my look of surprise, he nodded affirmation. "Yes, the same Wise One you have seen. My race is long-lived, true, but Nidu's Powers have given her a lifespan known to few. She is old, yet seems not to age. . . . It is best not to question one with Power. She drummed and sang, and we rode into a greyness . . . and when it faded, we were here, in this land."

"Why did you leave your old land?" I asked, thinking that Joisan's suspicion about these people having traversed some Gate from another world or time now had more substance in the face of Obred's explanation.

"I was too young to understand much, and the Elders never liked to speak of it . . . but I remember hiding in one of the wagons and peering out, only to see some of our young men and women marched away in fetters, linked by neck-collars and chains. My mother was among them. Tall, thin men with light hair and eyes rode beside them with whips. Thus we were a strange band when we came into Arvon—numbering only the very old and the very young, with few riders who could be reckoned in their prime. . . ."

"That is a heavy memory to bear," I said slowly, thinking that, in its way, his fate had been even harsher than my own. "You must have missed your mother."

"Perhaps in the beginning. I do not remember much. Only that one sight stayed with me. But here, things were different. We were free, roaming our mountain home with none to fear—until this past winter, that is, when that . . ." He paused, seeking for words. "That *thing* . . . that runner of mountain ridges claimed Jerwin's life. Guret and I were among those who saw *it*, and one view was enough. We packed and marched with the breath of the Ice Dragon burning at our backs, lucky enough to traverse the passes without causing an avalanche, but none who had seen *it* ever thought of turning back."

His words seemed to bypass my mind and sink directly into my body, causing a stirring at the back of my neck, as of little icy slivers pricking the flesh. My breath caught, then I managed, "*It?*"

"Everyone who saw it had a different perception of it, Lord, but all agreed it was uncanny—a thing against true nature. Yellowish, swirling, it seemed to me, and cold,

colder than death, ranker than decay. It hurled itself up
the ancient mountain road with the speed of a hunter, and
young Jerwin happened to be caught in its path. He . . .
froze . . . stood looking at it . . . while we shrieked for him
to run. His face—" Obred's voice caught, and it was a
moment before he continued. "Jerwin was my sister's
boy, you see. It was his first scout. And I am haunted by
the thought that he met a death that is not yet finished
. . . an unclean death . . . a never-ending death."

"I understand," I whispered, stirred by the horror of
his remembering and my own. "I, too, have seen *it*."

"You? When?" Obred was plainly startled.

"Just before Joisan and I came into your land. I did not
see its reality, only a shadow . . . a vision, if you will. It
was horrible."

"Aye." Obred tugged absently at the heavy droop of his
moustache, evidently thinking. "Did it appear to you much
as I described it?"

"Yes. Streaks of red running through a yellowish mist
. . . a droning sound like angry bees, or perhaps some
insane music. . . ."

"I heard nothing. So it was with each of us; some things
seem the same, some perceptions differing with each
watcher. Nidu was the only one who saw it clearly—or
thought she did."

"What did she see?"

"A hunt. Men and monsters pursuing a creature from
legend. An unholy mixture of woman and bird-thing . . .
grotesque and ugly. Like a harpy in Arvon's old legends."

Harpy? My mind skittered through memory, finally
seizing on one of the tiny figures my friend Riwal had
collected on one of our many forays into the Waste, hearing again his words as he labored to fit together a broken
body and leg. "True, this is a woman's body, Kerovan,
and what looks to be the leg of a bird. But they join
perfectly, so. See? It is a pity the other leg is lost." And I
had stood in wonder at the one-legged creature with a

woman's trunk bearing the head and extremities of a bird of prey. Something about the rapacious expression on the tiny face had made me shiver and draw back, as though the creature might snap its fanged beak suddenly, then launch itself at me.

"A fearful thing, a harpy," I said, the memory of the tiny carving vivid before me.

Obred nodded. "Following Jerwin's grim death—after the creature rolled over him, there was naught left we could even bury or burn—we decided that we must leave. We did, and now we search for mountains again, safe ones, clean of the Shadow."

Automatically we both scanned the horizon, still featureless. There were only the plains—

Narrowing my eyes, I put out a hand toward Obred. "Look! To the west, there. What is that?" It seemed to me that a small mound broke the wave of the grass in the distance.

"I don't—yes, I see it!" Signaling to our followers, we rode toward that hump.

Perception is distorted on such a featureless expanse. I realized in a few moments that the mound I had glimpsed was much closer than I had originally thought, and consequently much smaller. Nekia's trot lengthened into a smooth canter, ground-covering and gently rocking. Moments later we drew rein before that solitary object.

"A well!" Obred exclaimed. "But how did it come here, so far from any dwelling?"

I studied the high sides, made of ordinary stone, mortared roughly together. From deep inside I could hear the entrancing gurgle of water. Small bushes clustered about the well's base, bright with large orange blossoms.

Obred reached down and jerked his waterskin free of its fastening on his saddle. "At least we can replenish our supplies and drink our fill. It seems as though we've been short of water forever." He began to dismount.

It was then that I felt the tingle on my wrist. Looking

down, I saw the wristband of the Old Ones glow even in the brilliant sunlight, shining blue-green. Along its surface runes twisted, red-gold in color. I stared at the talisman in near disbelief, for the well was such an ordinary, homely structure, it was difficult to believe—

Heat erupted from the band, near searing me in its intensity. I found my voice. "Obred! No!"

The Kioga leader continued his slow pace forward, not even turning his head. I glanced back at the rest of our group. Most sat their horses with fixed gaze, eyes blank. A few looked uneasy. I seized upon a familiar countenance, putting all my will into my shout. "Guret! We have to stop him! To me!"

The boy pulled his eyes from their fixed stare at the well, his dark gaze centering on mine. Then, slamming heels into his stallion's flanks, he crowded through the others, reaching me in moments.

Turning Nekia, I signaled to him, and together we followed Obred's broad back. Even as we raced toward him, he had almost reached the bushes—

Bending down, I grasped the Kioga leader's shirt with both hands, controlling Nekia with my knees and weight. Guret, on the man's other side, did the same. "To the right!" I shouted, and as one, both mounts wheeled on their haunches, turning away from the well.

I urged Nekia away, digging my heels into her sides as much for balance as to urge speed, for the man's body was a heavy weight. Sudden pain lanced into my hand. Turning, I saw Obred's teeth locked tight over my left thumb and forefinger, their whiteness swiftly eclipsed in red as blood flowed. Agonized, I tightened my grip, praying to any Powers that might listen to let me sustain my hold until we won free of the well's influence.

A few strides further on, Obred's jaws parted, and he slumped in both our holds, limp.

Tightening both knees, I signaled Nekia to halt. Obred slid from my numbed grasp onto the plain, facedown.

"Take care of him," I told Guret, turning the mare back toward the rest of the Kioga, only to see one—two—three—then a fourth rider slip from their saddles, heading for the deadly trap. I raced past them.

"Stop!" I turned Nekia to face them, drawing steel, resolving that any who would not heed would die cleanly by my sword, rather than be trapped by the Shadow.

One or two hesitated as the blade swept from my scabbard, then stopped, blinking. Acting on a half-remembered tale, I drew the steel through the air between the group and the well, and the cold iron did indeed break their fixed gaze. "Back—get back!" I crowded Nekia closer to them, still swinging my sword, keeping the blade ever between their eyes and the well. Several mounts took a hesitant step back, in response to their riders' signals. One by one, gradually, all the Kioga retreated, until when we were perhaps twoscore feet from the structure, the compulsion abruptly ceased. The Kioga milled in confusion, one rider falling from his saddle in a faint, several others clutching their heads and crying out.

Guret came forward, half supporting a shaken Obred. I dismounted, warning, "Do not look toward it. It may be that once nearly caught, one is more susceptible the next time."

Obred shuddered. "I do not believe most would have a second time, Lord. That—that foulness—" He spat, looking for a second as though nausea would overcome him at the very mention of the well.

I turned to look at the rock-and-mortar trap, surrounded by those huge, unnaturally brilliant blossoms. Cautioning Obred and Guret to remain where they were, I moved closer, sword held between me and the well, my wristband flaring. With great care I circled it, studying the rocks, the blossoms. Wherein lay its threat? Would its victims cast themselves in? As I stepped, something crunched underfoot, and looking down, I saw the skull of a deer, bits of hide still clinging to the bone-whiteness. A little farther on, a pronghorn's bones lay bleaching—then something that looked like a small wildcat's. On impulse, I lowered the sword from between me and the well—

At once I felt its lure, though that call was muted, no doubt by the wristband I wore. The trickle of water was in my ears, water of life, water of eternity. To drink of that water would make me immortal . . . invulnerable . . . give me the wisdom of the ages . . .

It was not until I staggered a half step forward that I realized how close I had come to being ensnared. I jumped back, bringing my sword up once more, only to see movement around the base of those rocks. *The flowers*—

I blinked. Had it only been my imagination, or had those blossoms actually moved away from the steel? I lowered the sword again, watched the blossoms strain toward me, writhing, rippling—their petals moving, opening like hungry mouths, entrancingly lovely . . .

Hastily I raised the sword again, and they were only flowers once more. Guardedly I completed my circuit, noticing many more bones nearly hidden among the tall grass, as though cast aside after a feasting.

As I approached Obred and Guret from the other side of the well, the Kioga leader led Nekia to me. "Mount, Kerovan. Let us get hence from that thing, before it lures us again. I thought for a moment it had you."

I shook my head, refusing the proffered reins. "I cannot go, yet." I cast a look back at that Shadowed trap, and fear tightened my voice. "I must do what I can to seal that thing. It shall not be left to draw others—animal or human."

Guret's hand closed on my arm. "But Kerovan, you said yourself you had no lessoning in use of Power! How can you do such a thing?"

"I don't know." My words were forced from me, honesty compelling that admission. "But I do know I cannot ride away free, leaving that thing also free, to kill again."

Turning, I pulled away from his grasp, walking back toward the well.

5

Joisan

Barely a fortnight after my lord's departure with the Kioga scouting party, I began to wonder if I might be with child. My woman's cycles had always been extremely predictable, but this time the moon had waned into darkness and still—nothing. Also, my midwife's training made me alert to other small signs that could mean my body was preparing to shelter another life than my own.

Not truly knowing myself whether I hoped for or feared confirmation of my suspicions, I reminded myself that the strain of the past few weeks—leaving Anakue, Kerovan's erratic behavior in the face of that drawing from the mountains—could well have disordered my body's rhythms. Each morning I told myself that this day could well lay to rest all my doubts . . . while those days slipped by, each like unto the other, leaving me to question—with only time to provide firm answer.

My days in the Kioga camp left me with too much time for such solitary speculation. As an honored guest I had no assigned duties, and those I could assist with, such as weaving the coarse linen thread spun from the wild flax growing along the riverbanks, were tasks that give one much time for thought. I spent long hours in conversation with Jonka, learning about the Kioga, how they had come to the plains, and was chilled to discover what had driven them from their mountain home—the same creature (or one like unto it if one were to imagine the doubled horror of *two* such) that Kerovan and I had seen that night on the hillside.

For some reason (perhaps to turn my speculations in any other direction—even an unpleasant one), thoughts of that mountain terror returned again and again to haunt me. I found myself wondering if it had always existed, a wrongness blighting the land since time itself was new, or if it had been created by some perverse follower of the Dark. . . .

Sometimes at night I dreamed of it while lying alone in the guesting-tent, waking shaken and chilled, missing Kerovan's warmth and strength more each time. We had always looked to each other for all companionship and happiness, as though we moved within a circle drawn by love—as a wand draws a pentagram for protection in a spelling. As the days passed, I wondered if, supposing that the drawing from the mountains was finally broken, we could extend that encircling warmth to include another, welcome a child. . . .

With such hopeful speculation I barricaded myself against doubt and fear, for as the days passed, my certainty grew. At times I lay wakeful, hands pressed to my belly (though it would be long before any movement fluttered there), striving to ward off misgivings with reason.

Every woman fears a little when she first discovers she is bearing—I perhaps more than some, for I had presided at many birthings in past years. Fear of pain . . . fear of that ultimate aloneness that is labor . . . fear of change . . . fear of the possibility—however remote—of death. Rationally, I knew that I was well suited physically for childbearing, healthy, with a strong yet supple frame.

Women of my mother's family for generations had been given to easy labors and birthings. Still I feared—a little.

But growing even more quickly, nigh eclipsing fear as the moon began to wax full again, was my eagerness to hold, touch, see my son or daughter. As I moved about the Kioga camp, my eyes were drawn naturally to the babies and young children, and I grew to know several of the young mothers—though my secret remained mine alone.

One of the young women, Terlys, was also alone while her husband was off with the scouting party, so I began to take my evening meal in her tent, helping her with her two lively youngsters, Janos, a boy of five, and Ennia, her daughter. Ennia was barely out of her cradle, but at times it seemed to me that she could crawl faster than her mother and I could walk, so busy did she keep us . . . untangling her from the spinning basket, snatching her from imminent immolation in 'the cooking fire; once I turned my back for what seemed a bare moment, only to find her playing with her mother's copper necklet, sitting serenely between the front hooves of the herd-gelding tethered outside the tent!

Gunnora be thanked, the horse, as though he knew he must not move, stood like a rooted oak as I retrieved the baby. I carried her back into the tent, walking with knees that only will kept steady beneath me, as all the dreadful possibilities of the situation rose before my eyes. After I handed Ennia over to her mother, explaining how I had found her, I cut a thick chunk of bread, salted it, then fed to the gelding, scratching his ears and thanking him for his forebearance.

Returning to Terlys's tent, I helped her change the baby into a clean dhoti, folding the thickness of the cloth carefully, so it would not chafe her little legs and bottom. Worn out by her exertion, Ennia was asleep before we slipped the clean tunic over her small head. Holding her carefully against my shoulder, I moved to put her in the wicker cradle. As I tucked the blankets around the sleeping child, Terlys's voice reached me. "You need one of your own to care for, Lady Joisan."

I looked up, startled, to see the shadow of a smile about her lips, wondering if she had guessed. Perhaps I might have told her, then, if the tent flap had not rattled with Janos's return from the practice field where he was learning to ride.

"How did it go today, Janos?" I asked, a little worried. Yesterday he'd returned dirty and scratched from a fall taken over the pony's head when (acting with the waywardness most ponies possess) it had decided to buck rather than trot in a circle.

"Much better, Cera Joisan." He grinned, showing the gap between his front teeth. "This time Pika went where *I* said, not where she wanted."

His mother hugged him. "Good, good. No more falls, then."

"Well . . ." He turned ruefully to show us the seat of his linen trousers. "I didn't say *that*. But"—he brightened—"today I got back on all by myself!"

That night when I left Terlys's tent, picking my way carefully between the rows of tents and wagons, I saw that the moon was at her fullest and determined to ask Gunnora (for she is especially mindful of women who are bearing) if I indeed carried a child and, if so, for portents of its birthing. With this in mind, I made my preparations with special care, for I had never had need to try divination of this kind before.

Under the moon's glow, I walked slowly to a nearby field, seeing there the distant shapes of the horses, hearing their muffled snufflings, the tearing of the grass as they grazed. Near the western side, protected from the animals by a makeshift hedge of cut thorn, was a stand of wild grain. Carefully I harvested a handful of the green heads, murmuring the proper thanks as I did so.

Returning to my tent, I poured these into an earthen

bowl, adding wine until the grains bobbed in the dark
liquid. Inhaling the fragrance of the grape deeply, I recited a silent invocation, asking Gunnora to bless and aid
me, lastly holding the bowl so the rays of the moon shone
full upon it. Then I settled down, cross-legged, closing my
eyes to all about me, clearing my mind. Scrying is not a
talent that all Wise Folk possess—as in all things, some
are better at one thing than another. I had never tried
such by myself before . . . but something seemed to be
urging me to do so . . . whispering throughout my being
that I must *know* . . . must *know* . . . must . . .

When my mind seemed clear and steady, I leaned
forward, loosing the lacings of my shirt so that Gunnora's
amulet dangled free, still warm from its touch upon my
breast. Without touching the amulet with my fingers, I
lifted it by its thong over my head, then dropped it into
the earthen bowl with the wine and the grain. When the
red liquid was again still, I looked therein.

In the wavering glimmer and shadow cast by my single
yellow candle, I could see the bowl and its contents
clearly. I gazed at the surface of the liquid, trying to open
my mind to any sight, any message forthcoming. The
candle flame reflection . . . my own wide eyes . . . there
seemed to be nothing but those shifting flickers of red . . .
then gold . . . red . . . red-gold . . .

I was floating above myself, looking down upon a young
woman with slender shoulders, red-gold hair lying loose
over them. Her/my face was hidden, of course, but my
vision seemed expanded, intensified, so I could see the
thing beyond the thing plain to normal sight . . . a wavering glow surrounded her very faintly, blue-green, brightening about her head, then shimmering into violet just
below the faint outline of the shoulder blades beneath the
linen shirt . . . violet, the color of the purest Power, that
magic of the spirit . . . few of this world can harness it.
The violet light brightened, pulsed, its throbbing quick
and regular, as of a heartbeat. I seemed to see a white

glow within the violet, at its heart, a quicksilver glimmer of something . . . *something* . . . something which seemed to be enlarging infinitely, expanding to fill the universe, and at the same moment to be dwindling to the tiniest of specks, smaller than the human eye can discern.

One cannot look upon something which *is*, and yet which *cannot be*, for long—mercifully the mind blanks itself, shuts out a sight so terrible, so awesome, so wondrous.

I came to myself lying on the floor of the tent, the bowl of wine overturned, the sticky dregs draining into the earthen floor. Fortunately it had missed staining Jonka's woven floor mat.

Slowly, hardly daring to think on what I had seen, I picked myself up, feeling very tired but strangely peaceful. After cleaning and drying the amulet and putting away my materials, I snuffed the candle and went to bed.

Lying in the white light of the moon, I closed my eyes, breathing deeply, feeling myself drift toward sleep. Only then, relaxed and serene, did I think about my scrying and the child it had revealed I indeed held within me. That violet glow . . . *Little one,* I thought, as though my son or daughter could mindshare already, *what/who were you before? An Old One, it must be . . . one whose Power eclipsed any bare scratching for knowledge and wisdom I may have gleaned. . . .*

It has been speculated by some of my race that none of us comes into this world with no previous existence. Instead each of us lives many lives, with our actions in previous incarnations determining our pattern of existence in this present one. I had had direct knowledge of such a truth when Landisl revealed himself to Kerovan as one who bore ancient identity with my lord. Perhaps, in some previous time, they had been one being.

Was it through this heritage of long-ago Power that this child held such identification? Was it only Kerovan's seed that betokened a lineage of time-forgotten might? I thought of my aunt, Dame Math, and how she had brought the very stones of vanished Ithkrypt down, crashing upon the hated invaders of Alizon. That usage of the Power had resulted in her death, but such a death as would make any warrior proud. One aged woman had leveled a fortress built to stand centuries . . . no small feat of sorcery. And I . . . with little lessoning beyond that which I had gathered in working with Dame Math and other Wisewomen, I had strengthened my will . . . my Power, until I could rightfully claim some small knowledge of the ancient Craft for myself.

No, our child did not owe its entire heritage of Power to my husband . . . I had a part in that making, also.

Then another thought struck me, and I found myself smiling in the moonglow. It was also entirely possible that the Power I had sensed in the child developing within me was strictly its own, owing naught to any lineage. Let it be enough that Gunnora had answered my question, given me positive knowledge. I thought of Kerovan, tried to picture him with a small bundle in his arms, looking as discomfited as most new fathers when first they gaze upon the squeaking reddish creature they must claim as their offspring.

Would he be pleased? With all my being I hoped so, longing for his return. Perhaps this would provide incentive for him to settle in one place, build a home. Though he had proven a capable midwife when Briata foaled, I did not fancy the thought of delivering our son or daughter in the middle of the wilderness somewhere, without a Wisewoman standing by—one trained in midwifery, possessing capable, experienced hands.

Counting in my mind, I realized that this child would be due about Midwinter Feast, when the breath of the Ice Dragon was at its fiercest. I closed my eyes, feeling sleep steal over me again, resolving drowsily—but firmly—that my lord and I would be settled in a holding of our own (be it cottage, Keep, or tent) before then. . . .

During my time in the Kioga camp, I had had no reason to practice my Craft as a Wisewoman, except as I had needed for myself. I could not forget the dark, closed face of Nidu, and it seemed to me that prudence might be the best course—to walk mum-faced, doing nothing that might seem to challenge the Shaman's position.

Two days after my efforts at scrying, however, I was given no choice in the matter. Terlys's voice reached me while I was still within my tent early one afternoon. "Joisan! Joisan! You must come!"

I arose hurriedly, as the hanging shielding the opening of my tent burst inward at the force of her entrance. "Joisan!" Terlys, usually so calm, clutched at me frantically. "Your Wisewoman's knowledge—Janos is sick—you *must* come!"

"I will come." I made haste to gather my bag of simples, overlooking its contents for my healing materials. "What ails him, Terlys? Calm yourself, tell me aught you remember."

"I—he woke this morning with a headache, but seemed otherwise fine. Then this afternoon he lay down, saying he was tired. Just now, when I went to wake him, I could feel his fever before I even touched him. He will not wake, only tosses, moaning!"

"Fever . . . high fever . . ." I looked into the bag, satisfied myself that I was as well prepared as might be. "When we reach your tent, put water to boil. I must make a tisane of black willow and saffron."

In the dimness of Terlys's tent, I examined Janos. His fever was so high that his skin felt tight, stretched, and his eyes were sunken far into his head. I feared that if his body were not cooled immediately, he would have convulsions.

"Hurry, Terlys," I said, pulling the child's clothing off. "We'll take him outside, to the stream. Bring clean cloths and your ladle. We must lave him with cool water."

We attracted some attention from the Kioga as we

hastened toward the nearby stream, Terlys with Janos in her arms. I following with my bag of simples and a steaming pot. Jonka hurried over. "What chances, Cera?"

"Janos is very ill." I hastened my steps as Jonka fell in beside me. "He has a high fever."

"Where is Nidu?" Jonka asked.

Terlys did not turn as she answered, "I asked, but no one knew where she went, only that she has not been seen since morning."

Reaching the bank of the stream, I hastily helped Terlys place Janos on a woven mat, instructing her to wet the cloths, then place them on his body. "When his skin has adjusted slightly to the coolness of the water, then use the ladle to pour it directly over him."

While she began dipping and wringing the cloths, I hastily anointed myself with a healing oil, afterward lighting the three blue candles I had brought. Keeping one eye on Terlys as she labored over Janos, assisted by Jonka, I made a hurried but fervent invocation: "Gunnora, Lady who guards the innocent, bless and heal Janos of his fever. Help me in what I would do to aid him, in the Name of all Spirits of the Light. So may it be always by *Thy* will."

Taking the still-seething pot, I measured pinches of the black willow powder from my simples bag, followed by several of the saffron, then a minute portion of sandalwood for good measure. Swirling these three together, I waited for the water to cool, schooling myself to calmness, relaxing my tense muscles. I must put aside all impatience—use the proper disciplines.

Closing my eyes, I breathed deeply, willing patience, a positive spirit. Little is gained in healing magic until the would-be healer can attain a calm, relaxed state and frame a convincing mind-image of the subject as completely healed. . . . Concentrating on an image of Janos happy, riding his pony, I swirled the tisane until it was cool enough to pour some into the blue crystalline cup I kept for medicinal doses.

Moving to Janos, I touched his forehead. Terlys's efforts with the cool stream water were helping—praise Gunnora, the tisane would make the fever vanish completely. Supporting the now half-conscious child, I urged the contents of the cup on him. He grimaced at the taste, but under his mother's and my urging, swallowed, then swallowed again. Covering him then with a light sheet, we sat quietly for a little while. I held Terlys's hand in mine, instructing her to think of Janos as well, as healthy. Keeping that image in my mind, willing his recovery with all my strength, I did not hear footsteps approaching from the other side of the stream.

"What chances here?" The harshness of that query made me jump. Opening my eyes, I saw Nidu standing on the other bank, her hooded eyes, usually so blank, blazing angrily.

Terlys answered, when I held silence. "The Cera Joisan helped when Janos was taken with a sudden fever."

"Helped!" Nidu's disbelief was patent. "Dousing the poor child in a stream? Gagging him with potions? He needs drum magic, Terlys . . . not this—this—"

What further slight she was about to voice was never uttered. Jonka's cry of surprise made all of us turn back to Janos. "Look, there is sweat on his forehead! I think the fever is breaking!"

Hastening back to the little boy, I felt his forehead and chest with relief; Jonka was right. Terlys carefully wiped the moisture from his brow, crooning softly to him, then was rewarded when he opened his eyes for a moment. "Mama . . . I'm thirsty. . . ."

"May he have water?" Terlys turned to me

"Of course. Such high fevers deplete the body. Give him water that is cool, but not cold."

As we prepared to carry Janos back to the tent, I looked about for Nidu, but she was gone. After seeing Janos safely asleep, I gave the remainder of the tisane I had brewed to Terlys, explaining that he was to have another dose at sunset, then the last in the middle of the night.

"If he needs more, I will brew it in the morn," I told her, "but I doubt it will prove necessary. Make sure he is protected from chills, and keep him quiet for all of tomorrow, at least. I will—" I stopped as the sudden thought struck me that perhaps I should step aside, let Nidu have the final words in the boy's case. . . .

"I will stop by tomorrow afternoon, if I do not see you in the morn," I said firmly. Janos was for the moment my charge, and I could do no other than to see him safely well again. If Nidu could not understand the obligations binding one pledged to healcraft, then she was but a poor healer herself.

"Thank you, Cera Joisan." Terlys took both my hands in hers. "You have given me back my firstborn, and someday I feel sure you will know what a gift that is. I am beholden, and Rigon and I freely accept our debt to you. I will watch for any way I can repay your kindness."

"There is no way I can thank *you* for the warmth of your fire and the companionship you have shown me, Terlys." I took both her hands in mine, more moved than I could express easily. "Gunnora's Blessing upon you, upon yours."

There was a tightness at the back of my throat as I left the tent, and I wondered for a moment at the depth of emotion Janos's healing and Terlys's words had aroused in me. . . . It was as though all my inner feelings had been thrust outward and were now lying just beneath my skin. Why? I had always been one trained to strong control, the masking of my thoughts and feelings—part of the lessoning I had received in preparation for running a Keep, before the war had ended that future for me.

Suddenly the answer to my new sensitivity came to me, and I smiled to think how purblind I had been. Many of my patients had described this feeling of being "thin-skinned" to all and sundry while they were carrying—did I think that I, because I was a healer, would be immune?

"You smile, Lady." The cold words came from behind me. Whirling, I saw Nidu step out from the side of the nearest tent. As usual, the Shaman went robed in her hooded gown of coarse linen dyed dark brown, almost black. A small drum swung from her belt, and her fingers caressed the head of it, producing a faint thrumming. "Why do you smile? Do you have some secret happiness? Or could it be you were thinking of how you made me look foolish just now?"

I found that the drum's barely discernible rhythm made it hard to concentrate, but I managed to summon words. "Of course not, Cera Nidu. I am just glad Janos is better."

"Thanks to you, of course. . . ." She moved closer, her fingers moving more quickly. "It seems you have a certain magic of your own, which, though it is no match for mine, still must be reckoned with. That is . . ." The thrumming of her nails on the hide top of her drum grew louder, and she swayed to its beat. "If you have any wish to stay here. Do you, Lady?"

"I . . . do not know." To my horror I found my pulse beginning to quicken, even as these drumbeats did. "I must stay here until my lord returns from the scout. Then, I know not what we will do. I wish no trouble. I came when Terlys called, because she has been my friend here."

Her eyes were jet, black and stony in her thin face. "You speak truth, I see. Still, there are times when those who wish no trouble nevertheless find it. Your summonings have disturbed the Dream Spirits who answer the drumming for me. My pipe visions are clouded. You must leave, and now."

"I cannot. My lord—"

"Your lord, Joisan, has troubles enough of his own. He meddles, Lady, even as you do, and he has not your feeble lessoning. Look." Raising her hand palm outward, she brought it before my eyes, so I could see clearly the lines thereon. The muttered beat of the drumming increased still further. I attempted to step back, away from that threatening hand, but could not move. I looked at her palm, unable to look away, and even as I did so, I could see a swirling there . . . a clouding . . . a picture, growing . . .

Kerovan stood in the middle of an endless plain, sword out, the wristband he wore glowing, flaming, the runes along it pulsing brilliant red and gold. Beyond him was what appeared to be a well—but it was hard to see the exact shape, the miasma of the Shadow rose so dark about it. My breath caught as I realized the Dark was drawing, calling to my lord, and that he was answering that challenge. Legs braced apart, head up, he faced the thing, so real in the farseeing I felt that I must reach out, grab his arm, drag him backward from that noisome menace striving to entrap him.

"Kerovan!" I strove to force words, then a mindsharing, but his attention did not waver from what he faced. Was this an illusion Nidu created? But he was so *real*—he stood close enough that I could see the faint shadow of beard on his cheek, see the wind whip his unhelmed hair, longer now than when he'd ridden away. Why could he not *hear* me? *Kerovan!*

Slowly he moved toward the thing, one step . . . another—

"Kerovan!" My cry startled me as well as several of the passing Kioga. I blinked, shivering, my heart thrumming, although the drum was now silent. Nidu still fronted me, smiling, but that twist of lip held nothing about it of friendship or human goodwill. Slowly she lowered her hand. "See, Lady? Your lord may well not return from the scout. You had best ride on without him, and be grateful to leave safely."

Anger swelled in me, hot and bursting, like a wound poisoned within. I longed to draw the dagger at my belt or, better still, seek out my sword, lying paces away in my tent. But anger leashed and controlled in the face of another's heat is ofttimes a more potent weapon. I willed my voice to calmness.

"You know I will not do so, Nidu. I await my lord's safe return. He has faced the Shadow before, and triumphed."

"Think you so? Would you like to see what is even now happening to him?"

I dared not accept her offer to call up another farseeing for me—I could well imagine that to do so would open the door to whatever illusion this woman wished me to view. Kerovan's death—or worse. Also, to accept a gift of magic knowingly from one who means you ill can tie the receiver to the giver—with dire price.

"No." I made my answer firm and without further speech stepped aside, walking without haste to my tent.

Once safely inside, out of sight of both friendly and unfriendly gaze, I collapsed on my sleeping pallet. Shudders shook my body, sobs wrenched my throat. That evil thing—and my lord walking toward it! Did he still live? I had voiced brave words for Nidu's ears, but my mind kept returning to Kerovan's steadfast determination to avoid all knowledge of powers beyond those of humankind. Yet in facing such a foe, ordinary steel, even if swung in the most expert swordsman's grasp, would avail little. If Kerovan tried to fight such a menace so . . . I closed my eyes, willing any trace of mindsharing, so that I might *know* . . . but nothing awoke in response to my efforts. For the next several days I tried many times to contact him, although with little hope. Our mindsharing had always been a tenuous thing at best, occurring mostly when we were within speaking distance, or in physical contact. To hope for such at what must be many days' journey away . . . Yet still, at intervals, I found myself questing, calling—only to touch nothing.

Each night I fell on my pallet, exhausted, for the forming of a child during the first three moons is taxing for a woman's body. This I had heard many times and found it true, though thankfully I was never plagued by any sickness.

Except for my unaccustomed fatigue, I felt well—barring the constant worry about Kerovan's well-being.

Another concern pricked at me during those days, something I tried unsuccessfully to attribute to my pregnancy— the dreams began.

Each night, as I dreamed, I became another person, a young woman, but one not altogether of humankind. I never saw myself mirrored in any surface, but my hands bore elongated curving fingers, with a faint pearly look about them, as though they might be covered with the tiniest of scales. On my arms (for the short tunic I wore left them bare) fluffed a noticeable white down, also bearing an opalescent sheen.

At first I would wake at once when the dream-awareness that I was this Other came to me, but as each night followed, I found myself enclosed within that Other's body for longer and longer periods, seeing through her eyes. As this Other I lived within a Keep, stone-walled and old, old beyond measuring, aged far beyond even the most tumbled ruin we knew in High Hallack. Gazing out my window across the heights (for this Keep surmounted a mountaintop), I knew this place had stood for aeons.

Yet *I* was not old—rather, I was young, perhaps even younger than my dreaming self. Those rocky heights held no fear for me; I knew each path, each cliff, each crag. Nearly every day I climbed down the mountainside to the valley with its river, its grassland, and the forests it sheltered.

I loved the bare crags of the mountaintop, but even more I felt myself truly at home in the valley. The birds, animals—even the trees and grasses held a special affinity for me, and my world contained no greater joy than that I found sitting beside a woodland stream or running free across the meadow.

These scenes—of wandering through the forests or climbing the mountain—dominated the dreams for many nights. Strangely, I felt no threat, no fear of that Other during my waking hours. Each night I went to bed knowing I would so dream, and each new morn found me rousing from deep, satisfying sleep that was normal in all respects—save one. Unlike the dreams I had experienced all my life, the details of these dreams were not lost upon waking, nor did they fade as the day's hours passed. I began to feel more and more strongly that I was seeing through another's eyes each night in order that I might be told a story—a story whose meaning would eventually become clear. For some reason I never doubted that there *was* a significance to the dreaming . . . and as the nights passed, there grew a certainty that I was, in some manner, linked to that Other.

Perhaps it was because my days were so filled with worry for my lord's well-being, but I began to actually look forward to my dreaming, to learning more of that Other. One day, as Terlys and I sat outside her tent combing the flax to make it ready for spinning, the hot sun of late spring struck heavily upon my eyelids, so I closed them. Feeling drowsy, yet still awake enough to feel the warm breeze, hear the shouts of the children, I rested for a moment. The sun's rays turned my shut-eyed vision into red . . . then, even as I nodded, the redness changed . . . darkened, became the deep green of the inner forests. I could hear the rippling of a stream . . . a stream that lapped cold about my ankles as I waded—

I jerked up, and the vision was gone. Still, my breath came short for a moment as I considered that I had entered the world of my dream Other while still waking. Could I now do so at will? And was that a good thing? Never had I felt any taint of the Shadow about these sendings . . . but, as I had told Kerovan, the Dark has many forms and faces, some appearing very pleasant, very fair.

Terlys was staring at me. "What is it, Joisan? For a moment you looked frightened. There was a strangeness upon you . . . just for a second, then it was gone. Are you well?"

"Completely," I answered. "I found myself dozing here in the warm sun, that's all."

"I can finish the combing. You go back to your tent and nap. I will send Janos to fetch you in time for the baking. Remember, today is the Festival of Change."

Trying to hold back a yawn, I climbed to my feet. "I *do* feel sleepy still. Thank you, Terlys."

As I made my way back to my tent, I mentally calculated how many days my lord and the scouting party had been gone. The moon would shine tonight near-full, so it had been more than twice a score of days. The party had only carried supplies for one month.

Jonka had reassured me only last evening that all was well—that they had undoubtedly found game and were hunting, as planned, and that she still held hopes they would return in time for the Festival. I also hoped, with all the fear and loneliness I had felt since Nidu showed me that vision of Kerovan facing the Shadow, that she was right. My lord and the others *would* return safely—I could not let myself think otherwise!

Kerovan . . . my thoughts were full of him as I lay down in my tent. I thought of the night we had lain here together, the night our child had begun. . . . For a moment it was as though I could feel again the warmth of his body. My eyes grew heavy, so I shut them, seeing the vision of my husband, even as sleep took me. Kerovan . . .

I was farseeing again, seeing him, seeing the rest of the scouting party, with my lord riding at its head. He wore mail, and his helm was pulled down to shade his eyes, but still I knew him.

I watched from some indefinite height as they rode toward the camp, though I could not hear them. The plains rippled strangely, seeming now grey, then again their normal spring green. . . . They were nearing the camp. I marked the swiftness of their passage, for but a moment ago, nearly a league had separated us—

A sound of feet approached the tent, then the rattle of the tent flap! Kerovan! I sprang to my feet, raced to meet him, feeling such relief that he had returned safely that I moved light as a feather borne by a strong wind. Kerovan! He was silhouetted in the opening as I ran toward him—

Suddenly my sight sharpened as the sunlight behind him picked out the flash of steel in his hand. His sword, unsheathed? But why?

I tried to halt, but was still borne forward, only to see his hand raise, the blade's brightness flash toward me with all his experienced grace. That brightness became a stab of pain so great it was molten.

I looked up from the sword transfixing my middle, only to see the ultimate horror—Kerovan's face bore a smile. . . .

A shriek of anguish and hideous pain ripped itself from my throat, awakening me. I was lying on the pallet, safe, though the echoes of that stabbing awoke within my belly when I moved, convincing me that the pain, at least, had been real. A sword-thrust had been aimed at me, rightly enough, but no physical one. A *spell*. . . .

Unsteadily I stood, feeling the prickling hairs at the back of my neck with a trembling hand, the other shielding my middle. But no further twinges resulted. I drew a deep, sobbing breath, half of anger, half of relief. Someone had tried to hurt me, had tried to kill my baby, but apparently had not succeeded—thanks be to Blessed Gunnora. Cupping my amulet, I sent up a brief and doubtless incoherent thanksgiving to the Amber Lady.

"Joisan!" Jonka's voice came from outside the tent. "Are you safe? I heard you scream. . . ."

"I'm fine," I called to her, trying to steady my voice as best I could. "I was moving the sleeping pallet and a mouse ran across my foot." I gave a laugh I did not have to feign to sound shaken. "I feel foolish."

"Nonsense. Anyone would have been startled." Jonka's

tone was reassuring. "Fair day to you, then. I will see you later, at the Festival."

"Thank you, Jonka."

Disgusted at having had to sound like a fool before the Chieftain, I made haste to give at least some of my explanation veracity, tugging at the heavy pallet, moving it a few feet away. As I did so, I saw something light that had been stuffed underneath the mats. Snatching it up, I realized it was one of my linen chemises. Carrying it over to the light filtering past the door flap, I examined it closely. As I turned the garment over, something fell from it, onto the floor—and at the same moment I saw someone had cut a large jagged square from the front, on the left, heart-high.

Going to hands and knees, I opened the bottom of the tent flap wider, studying what lay on the packed earth floor, careful not to touch it. Small, oval, black—a stone lay there, upon its dull surface faint, lighter scratchings that could have been runes. . . .

A spell, right enough, and this stone its focusing point. Wrapped in my own garment, placed beneath where my body would rest, I stood for a moment trembling, consumed with rage and hate, wanting nothing so much as to show Jonka these things, tell her of my pregnancy, and demand Nidu's death. Any who could summon such magic bore more than a small taint of the Shadow, making the Shaman one unfit to serve the Kioga. Evidently her jealousy had caused her to tread paths verging far from the Light.

But what proof had I, really? A ripped garment and what could have been a stream-washed pebble with naturally light veining—save I knew it was not. No, I must find that stolen piece of cloth, see what it enfolded. Then I could accuse Nidu, if that seemed the best course. Or, her magic having failed in its purpose this time, perhaps she would try nothing more. It is a far different thing to aim a spell at someone unprepared and unwarned than to duel with a knowing opponent. I could not match Nidu's Power, of that I was certain, but in my bag lay simples that could set up formidable protections against evil. And as soon as Kerovan returned, we could leave the Kioga camp. I had never been one to shrink from a battle, but now I had to think of more than my own safety.

Having made my decision, I held Gunnora's charm toward the cloth, careful not to touch it, for the fabric was now tainted.

"Blessed Lady of the Harvests, aid me. Where lies the other piece of this my clothing, that I may protect myself?" Slowly I passed the amulet over the linen three times widdershins, for the force that had touched it had definitely been against—not for—nature.

A small glow brightened the talisman, and I felt a definite tug in my hand, to the right. Hastily I gathered my bag of simples, tidied my hair, ordered my clothing, then, keeping the amulet enclosed in my hand, went out into the camp. I also carried the black pebble, wrapped once more within the linen.

Following always that slight tug from the amulet, I left the camp, heading for a small stand of woods bordering on the stream to the north. As I went I tried to keep my mind calm, seeking, not allow the anger within free rein. But the question of whether I should tell Jonka of Nidu's actions continued to plague me—as did the question of why the Shaman's spell had failed.

Finally, after a sweaty tussle with thorns and underbrush (for the amulet's tugging led me straight and I dared not turn aside to search out a path), I found what I sought.

An elder bush—of course. Elder by its nature lends itself to the darker spellings—exorcisms, banes, and the like. A miniature figure bobbed in the faint breeze, roughly carved, made from some woody substance. Eyeing it more closely (though still keeping a careful distance), I thought perhaps that it had once been a root. There are several such that can be used—ash, bryony—but somehow I was sure that Nidu had used no half measures in this spelling, that what I was looking at was true mandrake, extremely rare and potent . . . especially in spells involving fertility. The small form had been wrapped in my linen square, then pinned to the trunk of the elder by a bone needle thrust through its tiny midsection.

Sickened anew by the hate that must have motivated such wrongness, I used my belt knife to shake the bush until the poppet fell free. Then I looked about me for a rowan tree—for rowan is the most powerful source of protection against any and all magics. There was one only a few paces away.

Worrying the doll onto the remains of the chemise, careful still not to touch it, I carried the entire evil package over to the slender tree that I sought, addressing it:

"Good rowan, I beg you to use your power to rid this bespelling of its threat. I ask it in Blessed Gunnora's Name, and by the Power of Light."

Digging quickly with my knife, I hollowed out a hole in the soil within the shelter of the rowan's branches, but still a goodly distance from its root, for I did not wish to endanger the tree. Then I used knifepoint to topple the bundle into the earth, afterward carefully filling in the hole, patting it down firmly.

Taking a garlic bulb from my bag of simples, I stripped away its papery outer covering, then, after separating it into its individual cloves, I pressed each small section into the packed earth firmly. With the point of my knife I drew a protective rune, whispering, "Bind evil, rest here always. Harm none," three times.

Lastly I sprinkled a pinch of salt over the spot, then rose, shaking dirt from my skirt. As I straightened I suddenly felt that brushing at the back of my neck that betokens a watcher. I tried to reassure myself that it was only that my nerves were still strung tight as threads on a loom, and had almost succeeded when I heard a footstep. Knife in hand, I turned to face that watcher.

6

Kerovan

With each step I took toward the well, my pace slowed a bit. More and more fervently I wished instead to be astride Nekia and riding away. Guret had the right of it—I was no sorcerer. I held no claim to such Powers as would arm a man in this kind of battle. To engage any manifestation of the Shadow without such protection was but rankest folly. I feared, and that fear grew in me as I walked stiff-legged closer to that foulness. Yet I could not turn back . . . partly pride held me, I suppose, but also a basic stubbornness that has always kept me opposing the enemy, even in what seemed to be the face of certain defeat. Such obstinacy cannot be termed real courage, however much it may sustain a man.

At last there were no more steps to take. I stood at the well experiencing again the seduction of its lure, feeling thirst parch my mouth and throat as I heard the gurgle of cool water. My hand went to my belt pouch, where I carried that sliver of stone-metal like unto the material fashioning my wristband. Quan-iron, Landisl had called it. In the sunlight it flashed as blue as my arm talisman.

Looking upon it broke through the ensorcellment that play of water had so easily wrought.

If only I knew more! Could I invoke any Power from this chip of blessed metal . . . *invoke?* I cleared my throat, my hand moved almost of its own will to raise the piece of quan-iron before me like a shield. My words were halting, my voice hoarse, but my plea was as sincere as any I have ever voiced:

"If there be Those Who Are of the Light who can hear me, then upon them I call: Aid me in what I would do. Help me break the force of this Shadowed One. I ask this humbly, for without the blessing of the Light, I am nothing."

Holding the chip of quan-iron in my right hand, I continued to stand, waiting, feeling the pain where Obred's teeth had pierced the skin of my left thumb. Blood continued to drip from that wound slowly into the dust. Suddenly it came to me! Blood! Used to strengthen any spell, it was the one element most often present in *both* good- and ill-intended magic. Slowly I clenched my left hand, holding it over the right. Three red drops struck full upon that blue shard. Color like flame blazed, as though I had poured oil or wine upon a fire.

Then, as though this fragment were a pen, with it I signed in the air . . . the winged globe I had witnessed Joisan's wand trace upon the ground more than a month ago.

Once, twice . . . thrice did I sketch that symbol before the well—and the last time, my effort glowed to life, hanging red outlined with bright blue, as though born of pure light. I was so startled that I nearly dropped that sliver (for my belief was less than half and I had not truly expected any answer). The symbol did not fade, instead held steadily before me, still like a shield. My hooves touched the edge of the growth that nurtured those blossoms. Drawing a deep breath, I hurled my talisman through the globed symbol so it dropped into the well's open mouth.

Earth heaved beneath my hooves, which I dug into the soil lest I be thrown down. From the mouth of the well puffed a cloud of murky, purple-black darkness. The ears of my mind alone heard a deep groaning, then a keening wail. My eyes blurred as that puff of vapor passed above my head, gagging me with its stomach-wrenching foulness.

Now the very shape of the well *changed,* moving like a sudden flow of turgid water into a stagnant pool. This thing . . . or creature . . . whichever it could be termed . . . was no more a well than I was High Dale Commander. By illusion, it assumed whatever shape would prove most enticing to prey. We thirsted, thus we had seen a well. Other bewitched travelers might have eyed fruit hanging heavy from a tree, or perhaps the entrancing shape of a beckoning woman, if the traveler was a man who had traveled leagues in loneliness.

The stone curb vanished, and in its place was *something*— something so alien, so inimical, that my eyes could not truly ascertain its real shape. For a second I thought I glimpsed a muzzle, or snout, teeth flashing scarlet within writhing wetness, then I was forced to shield my eyes. A brilliant blue light (the same color as the globed symbol I had sketched) poured from the spot, and that half-heard plaint shrilled. Hands over my ears, eyes squeezed tight, I crouched in the face of that final destruction—setting myself to endure for seemingly endless moments.

A hand touched my shoulder, and I glanced up to see Guret, Obred beside him. Nita held the horses a few paces away, her brown eyes huge. I arose, shaking, to look.

The ground was unbroken, marked only by a tumble of rocks, as though something had been torn up by the roots. Even as I watched, a thread of clear water bubbled among the stones, making a shining rivulet as it flowed amid the hollows. I held out my wristband, but this time there was no warning glow.

Guret clapped me on the back so hard I nearly fell and needs must brace shaking legs. "You did it! Powerful magic, my lord! And you said you had no lessoning in such!"

"I haven't." I stared incredulously at the newborn spring.

"But . . ." He turned to look over at the water. "How did you know what to do?"

"I didn't. I just guessed."

"Guessed?" Guret blinked.

"*Guessed?*" Obred's deep rumble sounded horrified, and I found myself grinning sheepishly, light-headed with relief. I shrugged.

"As you said, it worked."

A giggle from Nita made all of us turn. She glared, half-amused, half-angered, at my companions. "I don't believe you two! Isn't it enough that Lord Kerovan destroyed the evil? Must you make him explain *how* he did it?" She began to laugh, and after a moment we joined in—though I found myself weak, drained of energy and spirit.

After cautiously sampling the water, Obred deemed it pure, and we rinsed and refilled our limp waterskins. The horses drank, one at a time, then we humans, for to the Kioga the welfare of their mounts came always first.

That night, camped near the new-sprung rill, we held a Council, each giving his or her thoughts on whether to proceed in our scout or turn back. Guret's pointing out that a number of our younger riders might miss the Festival of Change, thus delaying their rightfully earned recognition as adults, weighed the balance in favor of return. I felt some regret that we had not found the mountains the Kioga craved so poignantly, but this was overlaid immediately by the thought that soon—soon!—I would see my lady. Joisan's image rode beside me by day, shared my bedplace by night. Now that we traveled toward the camp, not from it, I could scarcely contain my impatience. Our returning trip was made at a much swifter and more direct pace than the wandering one we had used heretofore. Our mounts sensed that home lay ahead, as a result we must needs curb their pace. Each morning Obred sent scouts ahead to locate game, and hunting was good.

Late one afternoon, I spied several trails of smoke marking the horizon ahead, and called Obred's attention to them. Shading his eyes with his hand, he gave a quick nod. "Aye. We're almost home."

Nekia had been moving at a steady trot beneath me. Now, perhaps in answer to an unconscious squeeze from my legs, she lengthened her pace to a canter, flicking her ears back, then forward as if to say, "Let's run, shall we?" Leaning over her mane, I shook the reins loose to give her her head. Her strides lengthened even more—the wind stung my eyes. There was no sound save for the quick thud of her hooves on the dry earth, the swish of the grasses parting beneath her flying legs—until, behind me, rose a chorus of wild whoops and shouts. The very air was filled with the rolling drum of hoofbeats as we swept down toward the camp like an invading army.

As I drew rein within the shadow of the foremost tents, my eyes were already scanning the running figures of the Kioga for my lady. Dismounting, I began leading the puffing mare around the middle ground, cooling her off, lest she founder or colic. Still Joisan did not come! Nekia's breathing slowed, steadied, and the sweaty patches on her flanks cooled, then began to dry. Seeing Jonka in the crowd of welcomers, I beckoned.

"Where is Joisan?"

"Several people saw her go toward the stream, that way." Jonka waved her arm toward the small woods lying to the north. "When the scouts marked the dust of your approach, I sent Valona to seek her out, tell her of your return."

As one we scanned the darker green of the trees, looking—

A flash of white! Two such! Even as I watched, Joisan, hand-clasped with Jonka's daughter Valona, emerged from the wood, coming swiftly. I waited, barely curbing my impatience, held back by Nekia's reins still in my hand. It went against Kioga custom to ask another to care for one's mount after a hard ride. A touch on my shoulder made me turn.

"Let me take her, m'lord." Guret reached for Nekia's reins. "By the debt I owe you, I will care for her as for my own."

"My thanks, Guret." I passed over the reins, gave the mare a swift pat, then turned and ran.

Dust puffed from beneath my hooves as I raced, yet time stretched much too long until I held my lady in my arms again. She did not speak, only laughed, then sobbed, and the clutch of her hands upon my shoulders told me clearer than any words that she had been greatly concerned for me. As for me, I could only hold her—now and again murmuring her name, feeling the warm softness of her body, smelling the herbs that scented her hair—hold her and thank all the Powers of the Light that we were both safe and together once more.

Finally we loosed our tight grip, stepping back to study each other. "Why were you—" I began.

"I saw you—" she said in the same instant. We laughed, then I insisted she speak first. Her smile faded, and I saw the echoes of fear shadow her eyes. "I saw you, Kerovan. You were facing what seemed to be a well, yet was not. It was of the Shadow—"

"Yes." Memory of that evil still had the Power to shake me a little. "It was something from the Dark right enough. I know not exactly what. Yet it was destroyed utterly by that chip of quan-iron I carried—you remember?"

"Yes. But how did you know what would vanquish it?"

I hesitated. "I asked for aid from any of the Light, and

the words and action just came into my mind. Perhaps the Old Ones answered . . . perhaps it was something *I* remembered from . . . long ago." I was thinking of that other heritage that had been mine, that had, on one or two occasions, filled me with the essence of Landisl himself. Seeing her nod, I knew she had caught my thought and agreed.

"But now *my* question." I gestured at the woods as we turned to walk toward the camp, my arm about her shoulders, little Valona trailing behind. "Why were you here . . . in the woods? Jonka said she had to send her little girl to seek you."

Her glance touched mine, then dropped as she watched her footing on the overgrown path. "I was searching . . . for an elder bush."

"Did you find one?" I saw the pouch she used for collecting simples hanging from her belt, concluding that elder must be one of the growing things that Joisan used in her healing potions.

"Yes." She made no further reply, only smiled at me, and I felt that warm touch in my mind, the equal of any kiss we had shared. When we reached the cluster of tents again, Valona ran off on some errand of her own, leaving us to stare at the bustle of activity. Men and women shook out their best garments, hanging them in the late afternoon breeze to air. The smell of roasting meat and baking bread made me—after nearly two months of travel rations— sniff avidly, while juices awakened in my mouth.

"What's to do, Joisan?"

"I don't— Oh!" She clapped a hand to her cheek, flushing. "It's the Festival of Change! I've had so many . . . other concerns . . . that I forgot all about it! I must help Terlys with the baking—I promised, Kerovan." She swung to face me, her eyes pleading. "It will only be a short while, then we will be together again."

I made a good show of concealing my disappointment. "Of course. But who is Terlys?"

She explained that she and Terlys had become friends while Rigon (Terlys's husband) and I were away. Within minutes we scratched at the flap of a brown tent colorfully appliquéd with scarlet strands of braided horsehair.

Terlys was a large, ample-fleshed woman with hair flowing so long it nearly reached her knees. Her lord, Rigon, I knew slightly from standing watch with him one night. He was a wiry, short man, spare of words as he was of flesh. But there was in his dark eyes a look that I had trusted from our first meeting.

Janos, their young son, circled me warily as any weanling colt, eyeing me measuringly, then, suddenly, he ducked his head and grinned. After Joisan had made me known to all of her friend's family, she bent over a small cradle, picked up a baby. "This, Kerovan, is Ennia." The small one blinked at me sleepily, thumb in mouth, then laid her head trustingly on my lady's shoulder. Seeing her do so, then catching the soft light in Joisan's eyes, pain twisted within me with knife force. I had not been mistaken— Joisan wanted children of her own—and those I could not give her.

I looked away, biting hard at my inner lip to control my reaction, then felt her soft touch on my arm. "Would you like to hold her, my lord?"

Shaking my head, I backed away, fighting to keep my voice unchanged—but it rang harsh in the stillness of the tent. "No. She'll only cry if I touch her." I cleared my throat, turning to the tent flap. "I am weary, my lady, and dusty from riding. I will see you shortly."

Ducking, I left the tent, hearing behind me Joisan's voice calling my name, then silence. I stood in the gentle wash of sunlight, blinking, while the old bitterness welled anew—why could I not accept that I would never be as other men? And now I must have hurt Joisan. I stood there, cursing myself, then turned suddenly at the sound of Guret's voice:

"M'lord Kerovan!" He hastened toward me, dodging the path of an old woman carrying a huge platter of bread. I waited until he reached me, then voiced the question every soldier learns early on—be he Kioga or Dalesman.

"The horses? Nekia?"

"Rubbed down, watered, then turned loose for grazing, m'lord. She is fine. I checked her legs and hooves."

"My thanks." My eyes traveled around the camp, noting the excited bustle. "Are you ready for your part in the Festival this evening?"

Guret's mouth stretched in a wry grin. "My 'part' so far seems to consist mostly of staying out of the way. My mother is baking and roasting, grumbling about how narrowly we timed our return, and my father is assembling the Council, on Jonka's order. That has made my mother grumble even more, since she must lay aside her cooking to attend."

"Why has Jonka called the Council together? Is that usual before the Festival of Change?"

"No." He looked troubled for a moment, then shook himself, shuddering like a horse in fly season. Plainly he was uneasy about this new turn of events.

Striving to turn the conversation in a new direction, I motioned toward the camp. "This is a shameful thing for a warrior to admit, but I know not where I am quartered. It was dark the evening we arrived here and I spent but one night in your guesting-tent. Can you show me where it lies?"

"Of course."

I followed him as he threaded the narrow spaces between the tent rows, until we came to the one I remembered. Joisan's touch, I saw immediately, was evident, lending a sense of permanence to even this temporary dwelling-place. Spring flowers, carefully transplanted, bloomed along the horsehair "walls," their perfumes warring with the sharp, spicy scents of the herbs hung up to dry, both within and without. Entering, I stripped off my mail, then my sweat-streaked shirt and under-jerkin. Guret reappeared in moments with a bucket of water, soap, and a coarsely woven towel. By the time I was washed, shaved, and had managed to tame the most unruly cowlicks of my hair, he had already laid out clean clothing from my pack.

Freshly garbed once more, I placed my pack within the sleeping area, glancing once at the pallet as I did so, feeling my blood stir. Tonight I would not rest alone. . . .

As we walked back through the camp toward Terlys and Rigon's dwelling, I noticed a large crowd of men and women ahead of us, dispersing rapidly, as though just dismissed from a meeting.

Guret looked up, surprise in his eyes. "The Council session is over. I wonder what is happening?"

I studied the faces of those closest to us, thinking that most did not appear pleased with the outcome—whatever it might be. Common sense told me that this meeting could have but little to do with Joisan and me, but even as I so reassured myself, Jonka appeared in the doorway of the tent marking our destination, with Joisan, a moment later, following her. My lady's eyes were troubled, while the Chieftain's normally round, good-natured features seemed pinched and fleshless. As we approached, she brushed past us with only a muttered word.

Hastening my strides, I reached Joisan. "What's to do, my lady? Jonka is upset about something."

"Was it the Council meeting? What happened?" Guret echoed, his voice strained.

Joisan twisted her hands in her flour-marked apron, half turning from us. As she did so, Terlys brushed aside the tent opening, the baby squirming in her hold, and answered. "It is Nidu, the Shaman. She has demanded—as is her right—the selection of a Drummer of Shadows tonight at the Festival."

Hearing Guret's soft, indrawn breath, I asked, "What does that mean?" I looked from one solemn face to the other, feeling a nameless fear stir coldly within me. "What is a Drummer of Shadows?"

Terlys's voice was flat—too flat. "By right, the Shaman is entitled to a youth or a maid to serve as assistant. If the Drummer shows aptitude for the Shaman's work, she may accept her assistant as an apprentice to learn her Craft. If not, the Drummer is released after a year, and another chosen by lot to serve her."

"What does the Drummer do in this 'service' to the Shaman?"

"Whatever Nidu wishes." Guret's voice was dull. "Drums to call up the Dream Spirits, those Shadows who give her Power . . . collects and prepares herbs, sweeps out her tent, walks at her heels, brings her meals . . . offers blood, spirit, and life for her spellings—"

"We have no proof of that," snapped Terlys, her obvious unease belying her words. "Tremon was never strong."

"Which is why he never should have been forced to serve when his lot was picked." Guret's mouth thinned to an angry slash. "He was my best friend. Even though I was so much younger, we cared deeply for each other. Then, after the selection, I had to watch him grow even thinner, paler. Many times I asked him what was wrong. Shame was in his eyes—but he was too frightened to answer. Then . . . he was gone. I know not what happened, what caused his death, but I know that it was *wrong*. She should not be allowed another selection!"

"Why has she called for one now? How long has it been since Tremon served her?" I asked, putting a hand on Guret's shoulder, feeling the tenseness of the lad's body.

"Nigh unto eight years, now." Terlys answered my second question. "As to why—" She broke off, shrugged. "I know not."

But I had not missed the quick start Joisan gave, and within my mind I sensed guilt, quickly smothered. "What do *you* know of her reasons, my lady?"

"Your lady is *not* responsible, Lord Kerovan!" Terlys's

anger was well leashed, but her words held a quiet warning. "She could do naught else but save Janos when he sickened."

I nodded slowly. "I begin to see. So in saving your little boy, Joisan unwittingly usurped one of Nidu's duties, thus angering the Shaman—who now feels she must assert her authority by calling for a Drummer to be selected." I looked over at my lady. "This is an unfortunate turn for us, Joisan, but, as Terlys says, I suppose it could not be helped. Did you try to explain to Nidu that you meant no harm?"

My lady's eyes held a spark in their depths that I had seen but once or twice before. "In following the tenets of my Craft, I owe apology or explanation to no one, Kerovan. Not even to you, most certainly not to Nidu."

Lifting the flap of the tent, she disappeared therein.

I sighed. "I can see that was not well said. I did not mean to imply that Joisan had done aught wrong. . . ."

Terlys gave a quick nod. "She knows that, Lord, as do I." She cast a swift glance at the tent. "She will be all right."

"Has she been well, Terlys?" I asked, and at her swift, inquiring look, I continued. "Her eyes . . . they look dark-shadowed, as if she is tired. And she seems . . . different. . . ." I trailed off, uncertain myself of what I wanted to say.

"Joisan is fine, Kerovan," Terlys said, then smiled suddenly, as though at some private joke. "I had best see to my baking."

As though Terlys's words had been a signal, the clash of a gong rang through the afternoon air. I turned, saw each of the young candidates emerging from his or her tent, dressed in their finest riding clothes, carrying weapons. I turned to Guret. "Are you ready?"

"No . . . I . . ." He glanced around at the others and several of them called and waved to him. Guret's expression foretold panic. "What will I—"

I took his arm, began hurrying him back in the direction of his parents' tent. "Then we have no time to lose!"

After speeding the young man through dressing and donning his weapons, I escorted him to the field that lay to the south of the camp.

The Kioga had set up areas for the young people who were the Festival candidates to demonstrate their expertise with the bow, lance, short spear, and throwing of the knife, both mounted and afoot.

"Stay here, hold your place in the line," I hissed to Guret, pushing him into the waiting group. "I will bring your horse."

The lad's stallion, Vengi, grazed unconcernedly in the western field. Fortunately I had ridden enough with his master that, when I called to him, he came willingly. Hastily I bridled him, then vaulted onto his back. Guret would do well enough without a saddle—many of his people never troubled to use them unless they had packs to transport.

Vengi, in spite of his hard run earlier in the afternoon, was well rested, snorting eagerly as he scented the other mounts, heard the shouts of encouragement from the crowd.

After seeing Guret safely mounted and ready for his trial, I looked up at him, giving him a warrior's salute. He grinned at me, brushing his dark hair back out of his eyes, before he returned it. "My thanks, m'lord. And when the time comes for me to offer blood and be accepted, will you stand with me? Tremon would have done it, but he . . ."

I nodded. "I understand. I would be honored."

As he rode away, I stepped back into the crowd, watching the young men and women. After a few minutes, I felt a hand brush my arm, turned to find Joisan beside me.

Hesitantly I touched her hand, then took it in mine. As we watched the candidates perform, our minds touched. I summoned thoughts:

I am sorry my words hurt you. Her fingers felt small and calloused within my own, and her mindsharing was a tiny, warm spark inside me. *They were ill considered. . . .*

Her answer came swiftly. *Think not on it, my lord. You were tired, and have not witnessed* . . . Her mental "voice" faded as her thoughts turned elsewhere, into pathways I could not follow with my so-limited abilities.

Witnessed what? Has aught happened since I left? I strained my eyes against the lowering sun to watch Guret cast his short spear at a target of horsehide stuffed with hay, then cheered when the barbed head sank true, nearly transfixing the dummy.

. . . will speak of it later, my husband. I gave a guilty start, realizing my attention had wandered from my lady's words. But her mindsharing was warm and rich with understanding. *The boy . . . Guret . . . you have become friends. I am glad. . . .*

He is a fine young man. . . . You should meet his little sister, Nita. She would make you laugh. . . . In swift mental flashes I told her of the girl's rescue from the river.

Her mindsharing in return was touched with such admiration and approval that I felt as if I had been praised as a Hero-of-Battles. I raised her hand to my lips, still keeping my eyes fixed on Guret's marksmanship trial. She did not turn either, but for a butterfly moment, her fingers touched my cheek.

As the sun fired the western plains before dipping beneath them, we gathered for the Ceremony of Acceptance. I stood beside Guret, with his father, Cleon, and his mother, Anga. Jonka and Nidu presided, taking position on either side of an ancient, many-stained horsehide. In her right hand the Shaman held a crescent-shaped blade. Group by group we advanced. Finally it was Guret's turn. Leaving the rest of us behind, he stepped forward, stood alone.

Jonka's voice was solemn. "Guret, son of Cleon, son of

Anga, do you offer your blood that the Kioga may flourish? Will your life from this day onward be lived as a barrier between any ill and the good of your people?"

"It will."

Stretching forth his hand, the boy held steady as Nidu moved the knife across his right wrist, the blade flashing quicksilver. Crimson flowed, dripping with a faint spattering upon the ancient horsehide, mixing with the red trails left by the previous candidates.

Nidu began to chant, her fingernails tapping upon the small drum swinging from her belt. Her sable sleeves flapped in the evening breeze, seeming suddenly to resemble huge wings. I remembered Obred's description of the harpy, then shivered as the Shaman's eyes met mine, almost as though she could mindshare.

Just then Jonka stepped forward, pressed a clean pad of linen to Guret's wrist, then embraced the young man. "Be welcomed, then! May the Mother of Mares favor you with wisdom in our Council!"

Cheers rose from the crowd surrounding us, and hastily I broke that eye-bond with Nidu to join the well-wishers. Minutes later we were seated on the ground, Kioga-fashion, enjoying a meal that completely erased from my mind the boring sameness of trail rations.

Joisan, freshly garbed in a linen dress that laced across the bodice and was brightened with many-colored embroidery, sat beside me. Her hair hung loose down her back, after the fashion of a maid. Watching her over the rim of my wine goblet, I thought that I had never seen her look more desirable. Even as I gazed so at her, she raised her eyes to meet mine, unsettling me further as I realized she was again mindsharing . . . that she knew my thoughts were of her, knew also the nature of those thoughts. . . .

It was hard to tell which warmed me more, her answering smile or the wine. Even as I thought of pleading tiredness after the long scout as excuse to retire, Jonka

rose to her feet. The Chieftain's face bore a cold, imper-
sonal mask in place of her usual good-natured expression,
and watching her, I remembered suddenly Nidu's demand for a Drummer. She raised a hand for quiet, and
the noisy, chattering crowd immediately stilled.

"Tonight is a night of celebration for us, but even in the
midst of our festivities we must not forget our duty.
Tonight Nidu has requested that we select for her a Drummer of Shadows to serve her in her service to us. Will all
of the Chosen between the ages of fifteen and nineteen,
who are unwed, stand, please."

The torches cast flickers of yellow-red across the som-
ber faces of the young men and women. Aided by Obred,
Jonka moved about the crowd, handing each a strip of
dressed skin. After every candidate had marked his or her
name, she said, they were to fold their strip and drop it
into the basket in the center of the clearing.

Nidu herself stepped forward when this was accomplished, her bony wrist and thin fingers doubly light
against the dark of her garment. Closing her eyes, the
Shaman thrust her arm into the basket, fingers searching,
searching . . .

My heart seemed to labor within me as my ears listened
to the faint scrabbling sounds those stirring fingers made
within the wicker hollow. A pressure began within my
head, as though a thundering sound awoke, just outside
the range of my ears—there, distinct, and yet not there at
all. I felt that I must stop what was happening, must cry
out, must—

Nidu withdrew her hand, her lips stretching into a
triumphant smile. Deliberately the Shaman unfolded the
strip she had drawn, but her eyes remained fixed on the
assembled Kioga.

"Guret is the Drummer of Shadows, under the law of
the Council. Guret, son of Anga, son of Cleon."

"No!" My lips moved soundlessly. It was as if a wind of
the Shadow had lightly scored my cheek. There was a

babble surrounding me, some of it relieved, some excited, some upset.

Numb, I felt Joisan's hand on my arm, her fingers trembling. "Come, Kerovan. There is nothing we can do about this tonight. Tomorrow we will talk with Jonka, see what can be done."

Shaken, I let her lead me away from the firelight, back into the shadows. "I must see Guret—talk with him. There is a way to change what has happened . . . there must be!"

"There is." At my quick glance, she nodded. I could barely see her face, pale against the darkness of the tents surrounding us, but her voice held conviction. "Terlys told me this afternoon that if a candidate chooses not to accept the selection, another is made by lot."

"But?" I asked, for her tone also made me sure such a decision carried its own penalty.

"It is considered a shameful thing to refuse. If he does so, Guret could well be shunned by his people for a long time."

"Better *that*, than Nidu's service—I mislike that woman. She witched the drawing!" I was positive I spoke truth.

"I agree. Tomorrow we can talk with Jonka and the boy."

"Yes." An idea was beginning to shape itself in my mind, curling tantalizingly just out of reach. . . . I yawned suddenly, feeling fatigue settle upon my shoulders like the weight of mail after battle. Tomorrow . . . tomorrow I would be able to think clearly once more.

Once inside our tent, I made haste to seek the sleeping pallet. I must have dozed, but awoke when Joisan also lay down. My hand went out in the moonlight to brush her cheek, just as hers had done mine earlier. "I am glad to be home, Joisan. I missed you . . . very much." As always, my words came awkwardly. Why could I never use with my lady the endearments other husbands voiced? Few indeed had been the times I had been able to even

think—much lest say—"I love you," for always it had
seemed to me that every time I acknowledged any feeling
for another—Riwal, Jago, my father—that person vanished from my life as irrevocably as though my words
doomed them. . . .

"I thought of you every day, every hour." Her whisper
came softly in the night. "I asked Gunnora to let you
come back to me, and the Amber Lady has answered my
plea, for which I give all the thanks that are in me."

The moon, waxing three-quarters-full, shone through
the open tent flap above us, revealing her face, the dark
tumble of her hair, the lacings of the nightshift she wore.
Shadows touched her, as revealing in their way as the
silver moonglow, bringing to life the slight hollowing of
her cheek, the fullness of her breasts beneath the shift
. . . a fullness that seemed new to me, arousing. . . .

My hand trembled slightly as I touched her cheek
again, and I cast about for words to answer her. "Perhaps
it was the Harvest Lady, then, who helped me in the
river, or with the well. But Joisan, you said that things
had also happened to you while I was gone. What passed?"

She hesitated for a long moment, then, as I gently
moved my hand upon her shoulder, she spoke, her voice
a little breathless. "We agreed, my lord. No problems
from the outside world tonight. Tonight shall be ours
alone."

"But—"

"Just we two, this night. Not Guret, nor Nidu, nor . . .
any other. . . ."

Her lips were soft on mine, gentle with a promise that
routed any further arguments, any further thoughts . . .
leaving only room for touches, for feelings. . . .

At length I slept, dreamlessly, sinking into a vault of
sleep so deep it had seemed I lay buried beneath a
mountain that was nothing but my heavy, slumbering
body.

I dreamed not, yet even as I slept, I felt something

creeping upon me, insidious yet known, possessing me. . . .
It was like the aching of one's head after too much wine or
an injury, a dull pain that one is conscious of even as one
slumbers, yet the sleeper is too tired to rouse and experience that discomfort fully. . . .

Sunlight lay warm upon my face, rousing me to complete awareness. I lay partly off the pallet, sword in hand,
the blade half-drawn from the sheath, the time- and palm-
worn grip smooth beneath my hand. A groan I could not
suppress forced itself from my lips as I recognized the
measure of that ache within me.

Why now? *Why?* Bitterness surged, bringing an acid
dryness to my mouth. My body was sluggish, yet that
force drove it as a man may drive a floundering horse by
his strength and will. I rose, stiff, anguished, began hunting out my breeches, my mail. Joisan slept still, and I
needs must fight that force, marshal myself to touch her
shoulder, rouse her. I could not, no matter how urgent
the summons driving me, leave her behind—I would not!

She mumbled sleepily, then, as she saw me dressed, sat
up, her eyes widening with puzzlement. Then, before I
could speak, I saw understanding replace her confusion.
Understanding . . . and horror.

"Kerovan, no!" She put out a hand to me, hastily pulled
her shift back up around her shoulders. "My lord, *no,* it
cannot be—"

"Hurry, Joisan." It was difficult to stand in one place,
more difficult still to force speech between my stiff lips. "I
know not how long I can resist even by so much."

"Great Mother, help us!" Her voice broke, then she
hastily controlled herself, began searching out her traveling clothes. Her voice reached me faintly.

"When did the drawing start, Kerovan? Is it the same
as before?"

"Stronger," I gritted, my body trembling, my breath
coming rapidly as the pull clawed me sharply—this time
the demanding lure of the mountains was physical pain,

torment so great sweat started on my brow, stung my eyes as it trickled.

"Perhaps I can call up protections once more, hold it again at bay—"

"No." I could not force more than the single word but tried to put into that monosyllable all the resolution I was feeling. She touched my arm, mindsharing, and I shaped thoughts through the agony. *I will run no more, Joisan. I am done with running. One cannot run forever! I am a man, not something to be lured and tracked, as a hunter tracks prey. . . . I must face this now. No more running.*

Joisan

Fear was my only close companion as I rode. Far ahead of me I could see Kerovan, but his face, as it had been since we had awakened this morning, was set to the northeast; he did not look back.

I sighed, feeling hunger pinch my middle. Soon I must call to him, demand that we rest, eat. When circumstances concerned me alone, I might push to the point of exhaustion and beyond, but not now. My child—*our child*, I corrected myself fiercely—required that I take greater care than I might otherwise have done. The sun lay warm to my left, for noon had come and gone, yet still I shivered, thinking of the morning past. I stroked the neck of the mare I bestrode, biting my lip. I would not—would *not* weep.

The Kioga had gathered around as we walked through the heart of the camp, dressed for the trail, our packs slung upon our backs. Jonka had been the first to question me—for the closed look upon my lord's face had warned her away from any inquiries aimed at him.

"Cera Joisan, what chances? You are leaving?"

"Yes, Jonka, we must." I was faintly surprised to see
Kerovan nod. At times it seemed that ordinary speech—or
even simple understanding—lay beyond his control, so
fierce was the force gripping him. "Our thanks for all your
hospitality. We will never forget you." I paused, controlling my voice. "Gunnora's Blessing on all of you." I drew
a sign in the air, saw it take shape, faintly glowing—and
some distant part of me marked Nidu's surprise and felt a
wry pleasure that the Shaman had by so much underesti-
mated my Power.

"Our thanks lie with *you*, Cera Joisan. And with your
lord."

Kerovan turned, seeming like some stick-figure controlled by strings such as children play with, to stare at
the distant northeast horizon. Jonka's eyes narrowed. "I
see that you are in some haste, Lady. If you can bide but
a moment, I have something that will aid your journeying.
Can you tarry?"

I took my lord's arm, holding him where he was, though
I tried to make that gesture appear merely one of affection.
"Certainly, Jonka."

Jonka *was* swift. Moments later we had been given
rations of journeybread and smoked meat left over from
the feasting the previous night—how long ago that seemed
now! Under my urging Kerovan managed to eat, swallow
some fruit juice, while I forced myself to do likewise.
When I felt a gentle tug at my pack, I turned, found
Valona opening it to thrust therein a good-sized packet.
"Food for your travels, Cera Joisan. I will miss you."

I touched the little girl's fine dark hair, finding it again
difficult to swallow the sobs rising to choke me. "Thank
you, dear heart. So will I also miss *you*."

For a moment she buried her face against my jerkin,
then she was gone. I straightened to find Terlys before
me, her husband Rigon beside her. My friend held the
bridle of a beautiful chestnut mare. As I looked at her,
wondering how I would find the words to bid her farewell,

she stepped forward, thrusting the reins into my hand. "Her name is Arren, Joisan. The bravest and most sure-footed of our herd."

I stared at the horse, touched her fine-drawn head, searching for words. "Terlys . . . my thanks, but I cannot accept—"

"Yes, you can." She folded her tanned arms across her ample breasts, nodding emphatically. "The Kioga never sell their horses, as you know, but they will give them to those who are worthy. I know there has been no time for a formal Choosing, but the Great Mother will understand. You gave me my son's life . . . can I do less when you are in need?"

For a long moment I stared at her, then moved to embrace her, my words of gratitude incoherent. Her arms tightened about me protectively, and her whisper was for my ear alone:

"The Great Mother's Blessing upon you, Joisan, and upon the child you carry. If you can, return to us. . . ."

"I shall. . . ." I clutched Arren's reins as though they alone anchored me to the world.

"Cera Joisan!" I turned to see the boy, Guret, leading yet another horse—Nekia, the mount that had carried my lord during the scout. Obred and Jonka stood behind him. I tugged at Kerovan's sleeve, and slowly, reluctantly, he turned away from the mountains that drew him so. It took long moments for his eyes to focus upon the young man who stood before him, but Guret waited patiently, his own eyes dark and troubled.

My lord's voice was low and husky with effort, his words for the boy alone. "Guret . . . I must leave to answer a . . . summons. I am sorry I won't . . ." He drew a deep breath. "Nidu means you ill, I am certain—"

"M'lord—don't. I know." The boy spoke as quietly as Kerovan.

"Refuse her, Guret." Kerovan's voice was so faint I

could barely hear him. "You are strong enough . . . naysay her. Let none change your mind."

Jonka stepped forward. "Lord Kerovan, please accept Nekia as my gift. Obred tells me you and she companied well together, and if you ride into peril, you will need a good mount. Accept her, along with the Kioga's promise that always there will be a place in our tents for you and your lady."

"Thank you, Jonka." Kerovan's fingers tightened convulsively on the mare's reins. With no further word, he swung astride. Guret held Arren, as I hastened to follow him.

"Thank you, Jonka . . . thank you. . . ." My words, my thanks drifted on the spring wind behind me, answered by the summer warmth of my friends' farewells. We rode.

Recalled to the present once again, I shifted in my saddle to urge Arren onward. The chestnut mare, lacking the conditioning Nekia had received during the miles traveled on the scout, was flagging. She flicked her ears forward, lengthening her strides in a game effort to keep up with the bay.

"Kerovan!" He did not turn at my hail, frightening me. Had he gone so far already that he was beyond my reaching? I concentrated, summoning him not only with voice, but also with the mind call. *"Kerovan!"*

This time he did pause, turning to look back at me. "My lord, we must rest! Arren is tiring!" *And so am I*, I thought, watching his head swing once more toward the northeast. But, to my surprise, he did halt, dismounting from Nekia to wait for me.

Silently we shared food, a few sips from our waterskins, while the horses cropped hungrily at the thick grass. I felt myself growing sleepy . . . jerked awake, glancing somewhat fearfully at my lord. I needed rest . . . but if I allowed myself sleep, might I not wake to find him gone?

With sudden decision I fumbled in my saddlebag, bringing forth a tough rawhide thong. "Kerovan. Give me your hand."

Slowly, so slowly, his eyes broke that stare at the faint shadowing on the horizon marking those distant mountains, to regard me questioningly. Grasping his hand, I tugged until he faced me directly. Not slacking my hold, I carefully threaded my string of hide through the wristband of the Old Ones, looping it also about his flesh for a double precaution. "Give me your knife, Kerovan."

"Why?" Speech again seemed difficult for him, so great now was the pull. I watched him hesitate, frown, then shake his head as though already he had forgotten my request. With as much of my worn patience as I could summon, I moved closer until we were nearly breast to breast, my fingers seeking the hunting knife at his belt.

Grasping the blade, I jerked it out of scabbard, placing it securely within my own cloak pocket. "Now your sword, Kerovan. Throw it over there." I pointed by chance to a growth of thorny brush.

"Joisan . . ." When his fingers fumbled and shook, I lent quick aid. Then I fastened the thong's other end about my own wrist, leaving only a handspan of slack between us.

"There, my lord. If you would free yourself from me, you must gnaw through this . . . and that, I think, you will not do without rousing me. I must sleep, Kerovan." Wearily I dropped to my knees, drawing him after me by that hide bond, then stretched full length upon the ground, pillowing my head on my saddle.

His hand slid into mine, warm and strong. His voice came deeper, more assured, as if I had forced a crack in the wall of his ensorcellment. "I would not leave you, Joisan."

"I know." I made answer, but those words were a lie, for that was the fear growing steadily within me. "But I believe I shall rest better so."

Sleep I did, even while the sun westered in the sky. Yet as I slept, it was *not* afternoon. . . . No, night held me. Again I was the Other, she who had haunted my dreams so many times. . . .

Once again I walked amid the shadowed bounds of my beloved forest in the valley, feeling the night wind light on my cheek, stirring thick growth on my head that was not—or was not *quite*—hair. . . .

My senses, my *self*, were alertly attuned to life around me—and I was troubled. There had been tampering here, there was something awry within the bodies of the woodland inhabitants, both plant and animal. The ripening of fall should have begun, offering promise, through seedpod and carried young, that new life would come with the spring, but here that would not be so. Something had touched all life, a Power outside all natural laws, which disturbed the rhythms of That Which Must Be. . . .

I put out a hand (in the moonlight the downy feathering on my skin barely showed) to touch leaf, stroke bark. "What has chanced?" I murmured, putting forth all my talent to sense, to track the source of this wrongness.

Time! Time out of kilter, awry. Time had been stopped, not once but many times, just for a fleeting second or so, but such pauses were enough to disturb the internal "clock" of plant and animal. Seconds stopped, then resumed. . . . Who, I demanded of my inner knowledge, had such ability? Who had, merely, I was certain, as a demonstration of Power, caused this wrongness?

I concentrated, invoking Neave of the Fane, she who rules the continued order of life's seasons, the relationships of plant to soil, mother to young, man to maid. Thus imperiously I demanded an answer and it came.

An image sprang sharp-pictured in my mind. I staggered as if that sight was a blow as I recognized Maleron! His narrow face, pointed of chin, wide of brow, topped by black hair, a face from which blazed eyes dark and hard as onyx . . . *Maleron*, in whose dominion this forest, this

valley, and the walling mountains lay . . . *Maleron*, who
had, this year past, denied increasingly the responsibili-
ties of his rulership, preferring instead to shut himself
within the fastness of the Keep, emerging rarely and then
drained of energy, the smell of sorcery clinging heavier
than his robes of state . . . *Maleron*, whom I had once
loved as one closer to me than any other . . . *Maleron*—my
brother.

Sobs shook me as I felt the anguish of betrayal. . . .
Born of a different mother (a brief flash of a lovely, nonhu-
man face filled "my" mind), having only the faintest memories of both her and our human father, my early life had
nevertheless been full of love, of warmth, by grace of this
half brother who had ascended the throne so young, yet
still man-grown compared to me.

"Maleron . . ." My lips moved, I heard the faint croak
of my choked voice as the forest shimmered around me. I
struggled to stay—I must *know*. But it faded.

I awoke, tears stinging my eyes as I struggled to sit up.
My movement alerted Kerovan. He was watching me
closely with much of his old caring.

Hastily I averted my face, made a show of unfastening
the flap of my belt-sheath and withdrawing my knife before I severed the cord binding us together. My lord had
enough to weigh him without my "dream" evoking concern he could ill afford. I bit my lip, struggling for control,
my dream Other's anguish of discovery . . . of betrayal
. . . still vivid.

Names . . . the knowledge of a True Name was oft the
key in a spell. Now I had come from my "dream" with a
Name—Maleron. Who—or what—was he? Did he still
live? Had his careless meddling with nature caused irrepa-
rable harm to that valley I could still see if I closed my
eyes?

Questions . . . questions only, with no possible answers—
unless they came again in future sleep. I wondered again,

fruitlessly, from whence came these sendings. There must be a reason for all that was happening to me, yet—

"Are you rested, Joisan?" Kerovan extended a hand to me, drew me up seemingly without effort. His momentary concern was gone—once more his eyes were for the mountains, not for me.

"Well enough." I made the only answer I could, though fear still threatened to choke me. "Let us ride."

Ride we did, not halting even after the sun had descended. Around us the country changed, the flat plainsland now rolled and dipped, then steepened as we ascended into hilly country. Trees dotted the hillsides, their leaves that improbable fresh green of late spring. Rocks and boulders lay tumbled on the ground. I drew rein to let Arren bury her nose in a swift-running stream, the chill of the waters reaching me even as I sat astride her. The mountains were drawing ever nearer.

In the red wash of sunset, I looked to the west. Anakue lay in that direction. Longingly I thought of a hot meal, a warm bed in Zwyie's loft . . . things that, until this morning, I had learned once more to take for granted. Sighing, I urged the mare on, calling for Kerovan to wait.

We halted for the night only after I pointed out to my lord that Arren was again faltering. Nekia seemed as tireless as Kerovan, the mare picking her way unerringly among the rocks and over brush, seeming undeterred by the darkness. I remembered Obred's comment that "Nekia" meant "night-eyes" in the Kioga language.

We halted, took food, ate silently. There was no sound save the gurgle of a not-too-distant brook on its way down the hillside, and the gentle cropping noises of our mounts. Feeling chilled, I drew a woven shawl from my pack, wrapping it closely about my shoulders. Kerovan busied himself spreading our bedrolls, his only light the waxing moon, for we had deemed it safer to go fireless. I thought of the last night we had spent together on the trail, remembering the vision of that glowing horror that had flowed down the hill toward our camp.

For some reason, even as I thought of that *thing* which ran the ridges in the night, I was conscious once more of the touch of that Other. Closing my eyes, I could "see" the craggy rocks of the mountainside, the grey stone of the Keep. The Keep, which stood like a wardtower between the Waste and Arvon. . . . Maleron's Keep, it must be. What was it called? Names . . . I concentrated, blanking my mind, thus opening it to any hint forthcoming from that Other.

Long moments, then I found my lips shaping a name. *Car Re Dogan* . . . A mighty fortress, surely. The home of a ruler. But then reason and knowledge asserted themselves. I had heard no mention of any such Keep, nor of any ruler named Maleron during the three years my lord and I had wandered within the bounds of this land. My visions must thus come from the past. . . .

I sighed, stretching my weary body, too tired to worry further at the puzzle. Further enlightenment must come as part of the sendings from my Other self—nor did I doubt that she was not yet finished with her story.

After removing my boots, I once again produced a length of rawhide, without comment knotted it to my lord's wrist. He submitted quietly, before we lay down together.

Even with the moon nearing fullness again, the stars showed, and in spite of my weariness, I watched them. Slowly I raised my free hand, rested it on my middle. No movement yet—but soon, soon. Words echoed in my mind, insistently:

My lord, I carry your child. Formal words, too formal.

Kerovan, we are going to have a child. Please be glad. . . . Too pleading. He *will* be pleased, I told myself, yet doubts still surfaced. His face, when he had looked down at Ennia in my arms—twisted and withdrawn, it had been . . . why?

*Have you ever thought that we should have children,
my lord?* Stupid. There was no longer any question about
it, it was foolish to phrase my news as though there
were. . . .

A faint snore broke into my thoughts. Turning, I saw
his face, eyes closed, weariness stamped upon it like a
brand. Exhaustion had finally overcome the strength of
the pull from the mountains.

I smiled wryly. Small likelihood that I could rouse him
to hear my tidings now—and, as if in answer, a deeper
snore followed.

Sleep took me, also. The moon was nearly down
when I wakened to the clink of a shod hoof on rock. The
horses? Turning my head cautiously, I saw the dark shape
of Arren, then the white-spattered one of Nekia. Both
animals stood head-down, hipshot, plainly dozing.

Even as I watched, the sound came again, from downhill.
Someone was coming.

I tugged sharply at Kerovan's arm. "My lord! Wake!" I
spoke softly, but with such urgency that he roused
immediately.

"Joisan?"

"Someone comes."

I felt him fumble across me, then the cold touch of his
reclaimed knife on the thong. In one smooth motion, he
was on his feet, that knife in hand. Hastily I drew my own
weapon from my belt-sheath, then, thinking better of it,
laid hand to sword-hilt instead. The partly drawn blade
glimmered blue in the moonlight.

The horse stopped. I heard the sounds of someone
dismounting, the ring of an empty stirrup—then footsteps.
I swallowed, my breath catching harshly. *Is it Nidu?* I
wondered fearfully. *Does she hate me that much, then?*

The steps slowed, hesitated, then stopped. Beside me
Kerovan tensed, his body prepared to leap—

"M'lord?" Surely I had heard that voice before! I gasped,
then heard Kerovan's voice, sounding incredulous:

"Guret! What—"

Hastily I stood, my hands reaching for my pack, for the fire-striker therein. It snapped once, twice, then the wick of the candle I held caught, the feeble flame swaying with the night breeze.

It was indeed Guret who stood before us, blinking as his eyes focused on the sudden yellow flame. "Cera Joisan, I'm sorry I startled you. I've been following you since this morning. I had to come."

I glanced at my lord, searching for his reaction to the younger man's words, then realized speech was again beyond him. Even as I watched he turned, like a lodestone seeking north. I reached out, grasped his hand to keep him beside me. Sighing, I looked back to Guret. "But what of Nidu?"

His glance at Kerovan was swiftly measuring, then he phrased his response for my ears alone. "I know not, Cera. I rode from camp without seeing her, leaving my mother and father to tell Nidu and the Council that I refused selection."

"Were they angry with you?"

His face in the candlelight was shadowed, yet I could still see the emphatic shake of his dark head. "No. I told them that Kerovan had saved the scouting party—and me—at the well, then Nita told them how he had risked death to draw her from the river. I explained that I had sworn liege-debt to him, and how he had refused to accept aught from me but friendship. They agreed with me that even if I am not formally liegebound to your lord, still there is a debt between us—and the Kioga repay their debts. Your lord rides toward . . . what?"

I shook my head sadly. "I know not. I feel no taint of the Shadow, but that proves nothing."

"No matter what comes, he shall find me his shieldman. I could not do otherwise than follow, Cera."

I sighed wearily, realizing suddenly that dawn was not far off. "Thank you, Guret. It is good to have such a friend when one faces the unknown. I must sleep again, if I can. Can you watch to make sure he does not ride off?"

"Aye."

Grateful to be able to relax my vigilance even for so little, I lay down on my bedroll. I had scarcely closed my eyes when I was back again in the world of the Other.

Car Re Dogan towered before me, adding its sweeping height to the dizzying precipice fronting me. Yet "I" was swift, scorning the open road on the other side of the mountaintop, climbing the narrow trail with quick, sure strides. The rock beneath my narrow, near-taloned feet was solid, comforting, in stark contrast to the swirling muddle of my own emotions. How could Maleron have meddled so? Did he not realize that his actions in stopping the progression of Time had opened the door to sickness and the Shadow? Neither Neave nor Gunnora, the Amber Lady, looked kindly upon those who disturbed the progress of Things As They Must Be.

Sobbing, partially from the swiftness of my climb, but largely from anxiety, I scrambled my body over the lip of the sheared-off ledge marking the top of the mountain. Not allowing myself rest, I sped toward the massive door marking the postern gate to Car Re Dogan.

I scarcely saw the armsmen posted within, their shadows massive in the flickering glow of the torch-sconces as they stepped back to let me past. My eyes fastened instead on the curtained portal marking the Hall-of-State. Maleron's voice reached me:

"Send the messenger immediately. Release one of the carrier hawks, with notice to provide him a fresh mount when he reaches the Council Hall. He is to return with the Seven Lords' answer as swiftly as may be."

"It shall be as you say, Margrave."

Just as I reached the heavy velvet curtain cloaking the entrance, he spoke again. "Where is my sister?"

"I have not seen the Lady Sylvya today. She must be—"

The deep purple of the heavy velvet spilled across my wrist like wine as I thrust my arm, then my body, through the drapery. "I am here, Maleron."

He frowned at my lack of ceremony, but forebore any rebuke before the serving-man. "Be seated, sister." His deep eyes surveyed me, measuring my dishevelment. "You may go, Bern." He dismissed his man absently.

When we were alone, he gestured to the seat at his right hand. "I have granted you permission, Sylvya."

The aura of his Power was palpable, seeming to glimmer around him at every movement. That he was an Adept I had long known, but to my suddenly opened eyes that faint presence surrounding him seemed tarnished, dulled . . . darker—and, if possible, even more powerful. I found I was trembling. "Maleron, *why?* You have hurt— you may have destroyed—the valley. Why?" I held my breath, watching his face change—

"Joisan!" I was being shaken violently to and fro, so that I rolled upon the ground, the blankets of my bedroll swaddling me against movement. Guret crouched above me, his face frightened. "Wake, Cera! Wake!"

I put a hand to my head, dazed, that other reality— Sylvya's reality—still holding me in thrall. "What—" My voice seemed naught but a hoarse croak, yet Guret understood.

"You dreamed, Cera. You moaned and tossed, calling aloud strange names. Then, when I strove to wake you—I could not!"

"Kerovan?" I sat up, looking around, still half-caught by the force of that sending. It was strange, passing strange, to see around me the spring-green hillside, the rolling land, where only moments before I had stood within the bounds of that ancient Keep, stone-walled and shadowed.

"Watering the mounts. Best hurry and eat, Cera. I do not think he will wait long once they are saddled."

I made haste to pull on my riding boots, then, with swift fingers, rebraided my hair and pinned it up. Brushing off the 'broidered linen shirt I wore, I stood, belting on my knife, my sword. By the time I had splashed water on my face, Guret had packed my bedroll without any request from me. All of his actions suggested that he had been sufficiently impressed by my lord's urgency to break camp speedily as one might at the call of enemy in sight.

A clink of rock against hoof announced the return of the horses. Kerovan made haste to saddle our mounts, while Guret, after pressing upon me a slab of journeybread, tended to his own stallion.

I swung onto Arren, still gnawing at the bread, preparing for yet another day's wearying ride. Where would the night find us? Resolutely I forced such thoughts out of my mind, refusing to allow myself the energy waste of worry—either about my lord or about Sylvya—my dream Other.

As we rode, the hillocks lengthened and steepened, rising at a greater and greater angle. From the summit of each ridge the mountains ahead became clearer—changing from blue-veiled heights to tree-shrouded hills and higher, rocky peaks.

Kerovan rode mum-faced this morn, never speaking when he drew rein to allow us a brief—all too brief—halt. Even Nekia's tireless strides seemed to be diminished by such energy. Whatever drove him—be it of the Shadow or the Light—pulled him with a force as relentless as the nets the Anakue fisherfolk wove to contain each day's catch. He appeared barely aware now either of me or of Guret, though his gem-yellow eyes held a sparkle like the gleam of water in the deepest of wells.

Finally, as we mounted after our mid-morning break, Guret spoke. "Has your lord been troubled thus before now?"

"We were axe-wed when we were children," I made answer. "We have only been truly wed for three years. He told me that since our true marriage, he has always fought this drawing—though in the beginning it was much milder."

"He told me of your marriage . . . of the gryphon you

wore upon your breast that turned out to be a real creature 'prisoned within crystal."

I was surprised. To my knowledge Kerovan had never
spoken to anyone about the events that had brought us
into Arvon. *Indeed,* I found myself thinking, *he must trust
Guret greatly, for usually he never speaks of what lies
closest to his heart—the gryphon and the heritage he
bears, all unwillingly.*

Afternoon found us in the foothills, skirting great ridges
of rock thrusting up like bare bones from the softer flesh
of the earth surrounding them. We had followed Kerovan's
lead, and he continued to bear to the east as he searched
out the northern trails. There were no more rest breaks—we
must needs push our mounts, lest he, in his relentless
eagerness, would leave us behind.

Finally we rounded a huge granite scarp that sloped
upward farther than my eyes could strain, only to find it
cloven into a narrow pass. On either side of that opening
stood a pillar of the blue stone, that blessed substance that
the Shadow could not broach. Surmounting the top of
each pillar was an emblem I had seen before—the winged
globe.

The entrance the globes guarded—for such was the
impression they gave—was curtained by a swirl of grey-
blue mist, unnaturally thick, limiting sight. I blinked in
surprise. Here, where I sat Arren, was the bright sunlight
of afternoon, the rays slanting from the west, only to stop,
unable to penetrate that curtain. I could make out naught
but languid curls of the fog beyond, rolling and curdling
almost like a serpent or other living creature.

Suddenly there came a flicker of movement ahead, then
a dark shadow was silhouetted for a moment against that
faintly luminous swirling—Kerovan! I put heels to Arren,
calling his name as the mare bounded forward—too late! I
drew reign before the leftmost of the globes to wait for the
Kioga lad.

"Where did he go?" Guret swung his head wildly from

side to side, searching. "He rounded the cliff just ahead of me, but now—I can't see him!"

I pointed to that blue-grey curtain. "He went therein, and so we must follow."

He stared frantically before him, as if he could not see that entrance which lay so close now. I looked from the boy to the mist-guarded pass with a dawning surmise. That it was ensorcelled was easy to understand—but in that case, why would I see it, when Guret could not? I pointed quickly in test. "There, do you not see it? A misty wall, swirling before you?"

The young man's good-natured, open features held dawning terror. "See what, Cera? What is it you see?"

"A wall of mist. My lord rode to it, and vanished therein. What do *you* see?"

"Naught but a rock wall, Cera. I swear it, by the Sacred Horsehide of my people."

A powerful spell, indeed. How could Guret ride straight into what seemed to him a solid cliff face? The Power of illusion might well prove to those so blind to be as dangerous. And why was I able to see?

Gesturing the youth to remain where he was, I urged Arren closer, striving to penetrate that mist with eyesight or mindsend. But there was nothing beyond that my eyes could discern, and only the same blankness that had possessed Kerovan since yesterday morning met my questing thought.

Touching heel to the mare's side, I rode between the pillars. There was no physical barrier to my entrance, but I swayed, shivering, assaulted by such a sensation of giddiness that I nearly pitched from my saddle. All around me were shifting images—rocks, seeming to leer and reach, trees, bending and rippling as though before a storm wind—all in mad glimpses that blended and merged chaotically. I gasped, clinging to Arren's mane with both hands.

The mare blew gustily, turning to look around at me

with almost-human concern. It was plain she was unaffected. Closing my eyes, I fought against the glamourie that protected this place. Kerovan was somewhere ahead, and I must reach him!

After long moments of darkness, I felt a gentle peace banishing fear. Resting my hand on my abdomen, I felt it build a defense, so that I dared open my eyes. The shifting remained, but greatly diminished. Why?

My lord had plainly found the mist no barrier—had ridden in with his head up, as if the pathway for him was clear, and at the end of this trail lay all he had ever or could ever desire. Now, my hand touching my middle, I found the dizziness lessened. Could it be that the spell holding this pass had recognized Kerovan, welcomed him, allowed him free access, and that, because I carried his child, I also had the ability to see it, though some of the spell still held?

Speculations gained me nothing, and while I sat, my lord drew ever farther ahead. I longed to spur Arren after him, but there was Guret to consider. I could not abandon the youth in the face of sorceries he could not comprehend.

I turned, rode back toward the entrance to the pass. Guret sat the chestnut stallion, his dark eyes anxious. As he saw me, relief lightened his features. "Did you find him, Cera?"

"No," I answered. "And the pass is spell-guarded. Still, we must follow as best we can. I can overcome the giddiness somewhat, but I am afraid you must go blind, riding by my guidance."

"What of Vengi?" he asked, stroking his mount's neck.

"Arren felt no troubling, so I trust he will not, either. We can but try."

Grasping the reins Guret released, I pulled them over the stallion's head, so to lead him. He nipped at my mare's neck, and she backed her ears and squealed, warning him off. "This will not be easy," I said, slapping the stallion's inquiring muzzle away. Then I handed Guret a scarf I took from my saddlebag. "Tie this over your eyes. Do not loose it, on your peril, until I bid you do so."

Nodding, Guret tied the dark cloth over his eyes. Grasping Arren's reins with one hand, the stallion's with the other, I rode back to the pass. As we passed through the misty curtain, I closed my eyes, allowing Arren to pick her way for a dozen or so strides, counted for me in anxious heartbeats. Then I opened them, bracing myself for that disturbing disorientation.

It was still there, and I found I had to close my eyes again and again for long moments as I rode. Only by so doing could I overcome giddiness. Glancing back at Guret, I saw the lad sway in his saddle, his mouth white and pinched with strain. "Hold on to the saddle, Guret," I called back. My voice reverberated, echoing mockingly, making the horses roll their eyes. "Do you feel aught?"

"I feel . . . strange. As if I am riding into a dream, though I still wake. . . ." He swayed again.

"Hold on!" I begged him, the uncanny echoes making my words sound like mad laughter. If he fell, I did not know how I would get him remounted!

"The Kioga . . . need no handgrips to keep their . . . seats. I can . . . manage." He swayed again.

"Guret, don't be a fool!" I put all the snap of command I could muster into that order. "Nobody will see you but I, and I will swear by Gunnora never to tell!" With relief I saw him grasp the pommel of his saddle.

Our journey up the narrow throat of that rocky pass was a nightmare. I continued to be assaulted by the waves of giddiness but slowly learned to control them, breathing deeply, closing my eyes, and never looking too long at any one patch of barely seen ground, for the alarming sway of *change* sickened me more when I did. Still I fought for greater speed, knowing that Kerovan had several minutes' start on us.

Finally I glimpsed a dark blur ahead . . . far ahead.

Kerovan? I sent a mental call, but as before, there was no response. But, heartened at least to find that he still rode before me, and had not traversed some Gate, I urged the horses to a trot, trying to draw even with him. My left arm began to ache from the strain of leading Vengi—still, I held to those reins, sending up a silent plea to Gunnora for strength.

"My lord! Kerovan! Wait!" My call echoed hollowly, making my dizziness worse, rebounding from inside my head as well as from the rocky walls.

He—he was slowing! Turning in his saddle! I dragged harder at Vengi, dug my heels into Arren's sides, cantering toward him. "Wait, Kerovan!"

Just as we reached him the rocky walls of the pass opened out, wider, wider—

The glamourie vanished! I had clear sight again! "Guret, look!" Gaping, I reined Arren in, sitting beside my lord, gazing at what fronted us.

A valley. Beautiful rolling grasslands, bounded on my left by a towering forest. The valley might have been five and one half leagues long, perhaps half that in width. It was surrounded by mountains, vast rocky peaks with forested slopes. On my right, lit by the lowering rays of the sun, towered two high, saddle-backed peaks. And on the closer of those, near the summit—

My mind struggled for words. A Keep? Castle? A dwelling, surely, but not one constructed by humankind. Built from the sacred blue stone, it towered, seeming almost an outgrowth of the mountain itself. Curving spires, dark arched windows, narrow ramps instead of staircases—it seemed very strange, yet in no wise threatening. It clung, seeming almost without support, to the mountainside, like some improbable (and in its way, lovely) dream.

Guret's voice broke my amazed reverie. "What is it, m'lord?"

"Kar Garudwyn," Kerovan answered matter-of-factly.

"How do you know that, my lord?" I asked.

He smiled gently at me, without reply. Looking at him, I scarcely recognized this man; his face, wiped clean of fear and striving, seemed almost that of a child. My lord had always, since I had known him, appeared far older than his true age. His upbringing, his fight against the fear and hatred his "deformities" oft inspired in his own people, had given him a maturity that made him seem by far my senior—when in truth naught but two years separated us.

Now, studying him, I was struck by the remembrance that Kerovan was but one and twenty years of age. Reaching out to him, I caught his hand, held it. "Kar Garudwyn? What is that, Kerovan?"

He smiled again, still with that open, unguarded look that made him appear so young. "Home."

I gazed back up the valley at that cliff-hung stronghold, wondering what was inside. Without further speech, my lord urged Nekia forward, and the three of us rode down into that lush valley.

It was heavily populated with birds and animals—a pronghorn stood for long seconds to stare at us, wide-eyed, before trotting leisurely away. It had been long and long since humankind had ridden here.

When we reached the foot of the mountain, we sat our mounts, staring up past the trees at the steep and jutting cliff face leading to the Keep we could no longer see. There was no path, no indication of any way to reach that stronghold. I found myself wondering if those inhabiting it in ages past had been winged beings.

Suddenly conscious of my fatigue, I climbed off Arren, then removed her hackamore, letting her graze freely. "Should we unsaddle, Kerovan? Do you wish to stay here tonight?" It seemed to me that this spot, protected as it was, offered the best place we had seen for a camp.

He frowned slightly, puzzled. "Why should we stay here? Kar Garudwyn awaits us now."

I studied the sheer cliff wall facing us. "Perhaps so, my

lord, but I am no eagle, nor have I seen you sprout wings in these last moments. There is no way of our reaching it."

He laughed, still with that open, untroubled expression. "This way. I will show you."

After unsaddling the horses, leaving them to graze eagerly, we shouldered our packs. Kerovan led us east, first climbing through the fringe of trees, then treading a narrow path that wound along the naked cliff face. Guret and I, looking slightly askance at each other, followed.

The rock of the cliff continued forbidding: hard, grey granite, veined here and there with darker streaks. Nowhere did I see any means of winning up that face using less than climbing ropes and scaling irons—I began to wonder if the ensorcellment surrounding this valley had unhinged my lord's mind. Fear, which had quieted in the sight of such peaceful beauty, awakened in me once more.

We rounded a sharp outthrust scarp, to see only more of the unending cliff. Yet Kerovan had stopped, was facing the blankness of that buttressing wall serenely. As we approached, he smiled, indicating the smooth rock in front of him. "Our passage," he said.

It took all my control not to weep, tired as I was, the weight of my pack digging my shoulder, as I looked at the blank wall fronting me. My lord *must* be mad, for naught but a lizard could alight on that surface and cling there. I wet my lips, glancing sideways at Guret, saw the lad nod quick agreement, making a spinning sign with his fingers near his forehead. Kerovan turned, catching the younger man's gesture, then turned back to me, his annoyance plain. "Why do you mock me? Don't you see it?"

I remembered the times I had soothed fevered patients, and made my tone gentle. "See what, Kerovan?"

"The symbol!" Frustrated, he pointed at the blank wall. "You see it—you *must* see it!"

I shook my head. "We see naught but a stone cliff, my lord."

Kerovan turned to Guret for confirmation, then once again studied the rockface, his puzzlement growing. "But it's so *plain*."

Reaching toward the stone, he touched fingertip to its rough greyness—and I started, smothering an exclamation. Beneath his touch, light flared, violet light, and I *could* see the symbol as he traced it! A winged globe—Guret cried out from behind me, making Kerovan turn abruptly.

"It—it's gone!" Guret blinked at the stone, then looked to me appealingly, fear touching his eyes.

The symbol that had flared there so briefly, carved deep into the granite of the cliff, was indeed gone. Still—I blinked in turn, squinting, then put out my own fingers to the same spot. Warm—

Under my touch a faint blue-green glow glimmered, fading almost as quickly as it came, but for the few seconds of its life, I had been able to feel the deeply incised symbol.

"Do you mean that to you the stone is blank?" Kerovan asked, his confusion fading. "But it is so clear. . . ."

"Even as the valley entrance was to you," I pointed out. "But to Guret and me, it was shrouded in mist, filled with glamourie. Do you see a door here?"

For answer he traced again the symbol, which once more glowed faintly with a violet light. There was a groaning, a sound I heard not so much with my ears, but with that other sense I had come to associate with my use of Power, and then the rock wall swirled, darkened—

We faced a wide passage, stone-floored and walled, that curved upward out of sight.

Even with the gently angled loops of that ramp, I was hard-taxed to make the climb. Kerovan bounded ahead, as tireless as Nekia, while Guret and I lagged behind. My legs began to ache from the strain, and I was forced to pause, breathing deeply, at several points.

At one such stop Guret reached out, took my pack,

then shouldered it along with his own. "I can carry it," I protested.

"I know, Cera, but it is heavy, and you must not tire yourself to exhaustion."

I looked into his dark eyes, seeing there a gentle understanding and compassion. "How did you know?" I asked. "Did Terlys—"

The young man smiled. "I have four younger brothers and sisters, Lady. I have seen my mother's eyes grow shadowed, in just the way yours are, when she was carrying. My lord does not know?"

"No," I admitted, "and he must not, until we know what it is we face in this place. Promise me you will keep silent."

He hesitated. "Except for the weariness, are you well?"

"Completely," I made firm answer. "I am a midwife, remember. I will take no foolish risks. Have I your sworn oath?"

He nodded heavily. "Aye. I swear by the Sacred Horsehide to hold silence—unless you fall ill, Lady. Then I needs must speak."

I nodded. "That is fair."

Kerovan was striding impatiently back and forth as we toiled up the last reaches of the stone ramp.

Kar Garudwyn awaited us. In the last light of the sun the blue stone seemed shaded with a warm, welcoming glow. There were no wooden doors, such as I was accustomed to in the Keeps of High Hallack. Instead one entered through an arched portal somewhat larger than the many narrow ones admitting light and air. A short passage lay beyond, then a hall. It was large, with a circular floor, rising overhead to a domed ceiling. As we entered a crystal globe hung from the center of the dome flared into soft life, emitting a rosy light.

Tables, flanked by benches, filled the central portion, with a dais midpoint. A huge seat rose from it—seeming partially a throne, but clearly not one intended for humankind's occupancy. A ramp led up to it, not stairs, as one would find in a Keep.

I frowned, suddenly arrested by something that should have been there, filling this hall, but was not—dust. I touched the surface of a table, looking at the ungrimed pinkness of my fingertip with disbelief. After so many ages, there should be dust!

The table's surface seemed cool, smooth—not like wood, which at first sight I had thought it to be. No, this material had the color and circular veining of wood, but the slickness and glassy feel of polished stone.

"Cera!" I glanced up at Guret's whisper. "Look at the walls!"

I walked over to join him, as he stood surveying the curving walls of the feasting hall—or so I now believed this to be. What I had thought were more veinings marking the stone surfaces were instead patterns and pictures made up of many tiny gem pebbles embedded in the surface. I touched the mosaic carefully, marveling at the intricate workmanship. A dark green stone—surely that was jade. And another one with tiny fires tracing its milky surface—opal?

My searching eyes and fingers discovered a kingdom's ransom of agate, jade, opal, amber, and topaz, as well as other jewels studding the wall to form parts of the patterns. The scenes themselves were huge, swirling pictures of the sun, the mountain, plus what I realized after some study were very ancient runes—so old that I could barely recognize them for what they were. I could not read any of them, which saddened me. For I had a feeling, as I stood eyeing them, that they told the story of this place, if I could but understand their message.

"Cera!" Guret tugged at my arm. "M'lord Kerovan is not here!"

"Where did he go?" I had no wish to be separated from him in this beautiful—but passing strange—place.

"I did not see him leave. I turned, and he was gone."

Hurriedly we forsook the hall to search passages. A ramp echoed overhead with the click of passing feet— hooved feet—and we took it at a run.

Kerovan moved quickly, but without undue haste, heading for the arched portal at the end of that hallway. Open archways as we passed revealed rooms empty of furnishings, dustless and silent.

The portal before us gave way to another ramp which we ascended quickly. Beyond it, the view from the southern and western windows was dizzying, naught but a clear sweep of reddened sky and purple cloud. Fortunately the lighting globes came to life at intervals along the halls, or we would have been soon in the darkness, and eyeing the unguarded floor-to-ceiling expanse of the narrow window-arches, I did not like that thought. My palms turned sweaty and itched at the unbidden fear of falling from such a height.

As we ascended one more ramp in my lord's wake, I thought that we must be in one of the towers I had noted. A final archway met us at the top of the ramp, filled with a coruscating violet light, making me draw back instinctively. It would be death to touch that shimmering brilliance, I knew.

Kerovan put out a hand, speaking softly, words I did not know. The light grew softer, gentler, then vanished altogether. He stepped within. Taking a deep breath, I followed him.

Arched windows opened the circular room to the mountain air, making me feel a brief return of the same giddiness I had fought in the pass. Careful not to stray too close to any of those openings, I watched my lord.

The room was large, with naught but a few tables therein. Runes glowed softly on the walls, taking fire from the dying sun. A pentagram was incised on the floor; next to it, the winged globe symbol. The wind touched us here, chill with the coming of evening, making me shiver.

Kerovan stepped to the nearest table, laid hand to a

book that sat at its center. I held my breath lest the volume crumble into nothingness, as I had once seen the contents of a spell-held room do in an ancient Keep, but it remained intact. My lord moved around the room, seemingly untroubled by the giddy sweep of air outside the windows, his hands rising now and again to caress a book, a scroll . . . a rune incised on the wall—everywhere he touched came that violet glow. I could *feel* Power here, stirring like some huge animal just waking from sleep.

Guret's hand came out to clasp mine, his fingers cold.

"Kerovan"—my voice struggled to pierce that ancient silence—"who built this place? Whose things are these?"

He turned, some of the bemusement fading from his face, to see me clearly for the first time, I thought, in hours. "You do not know?"

I was growing tired of such questions, and my voice held more than a touch of asperity, I am afraid. "No, I do not. I would be happy to be enlightened, my lord!"

He came to me, putting his hands on my shoulders, his eyes intent. "All these years, this is what I have been afraid of, all unknowing. It called to me, for it holds my heritage. I was not ready to accept that part of me, until I could accept my own humanity, Joisan. Kar Garudwyr was—and *is* in a way I can hardly explain, because I just *know*—Landisl's citadel."

Kerovan

When Joisan looked at me as we stood together in that wind-touched room, high in the tower of Kar Garudwyn, I believed I saw fear in her eyes.

"Landisl's citadel . . ." she breathed, her gaze never leaving mine. "Could any Keep have stood so complete, unruined, for that long?"

"If bespelled, Joisan." I, too, was lost in wonder at this tower room, the ancient books, the scrolls undisturbed by time, the deeply incised runes not even dust-blurred. "All would have crumbled ages since, were that not so. I think"—my gaze swept on out, to the mountains ringing in this Keep—"that perhaps this citadel is barred to any chance comer—open only to he who holds the heritage of the gryphon within him."

"In other words, it waited for *you*." Her voice caught a little in her throat, her hands reached out to touch my shoulders, gingerly, as though now, in spite of all lying behind us twain, she half feared she might be repulsed. "*Power* . . . my lord, in truth that is yours. I can feel it."

I, too, could sense a growing surge within me, as of a

storm-wracked sea, tossing and ebbing. Once, as a lad, I had swallowed a draught too heady for careless drinking. Then also had my sight blurred, crossed by only half-seen visions as it did now. Knowledge came and went. I was aware—then ignorant again—until such uncertainty made me giddy. At times was I almost another—then suddenly Kerovan again.

"I know." Again arose that flow of knowledge that I could almost—*almost*—grasp, make mine. Then it was gone! I sighed, closing my eyes, only to be roused as her grip on my shoulders tightened. I was shaken—

"Kerovan! No!" Joisan's face bore tear stains, her eyes shone wide and wild. "Do not so slip away from me, not here, not now, my lord! Power—what do I care for Power, if in the gaining of it I must lose my husband? Let us get hence from this place—now!"

"Joisan . . ." I gathered her to me, forcing a steady voice, though part of me still quivered from what I felt. "No, dear heart. All the Power in the world would be too great a price to pay—if such knowledge meant losing you. No, never. . . ."

Dimly aware that Guret, with inborn courtesy, had left us alone in the chamber, I held close my lady, until the near-frantic clutch of her arms about me loosened, and I could once more put sufficient distance between us to see her clearly. I touched her pointed chin, turning her face up to mine, looking down straightly into those blue-green eyes. "Be patient with me, my lady, I ask of you. I know well all the trials I have forced unheedingly upon you—and there are doubtless many more of which I remain ignorant. However, in truth, this place surrounds me now with a rightness . . . a strength . . . that makes me sure it is our true home."

Joisan smiled, albeit a little wanly. "Patience—of all the virtues Dame Math long tried to instill in me, always she despaired of my learning patience! But the war, three years with you, have accomplished much toward her goal.

Also"—her voice softened, her fingers brushed an unruly lock back from my forehead—"when one loves truly, little is impossible, Kerovan."

I bent to kiss her, quickly, mindful of the youth waiting outside the chamber. Together we recrossed that rune-incised floor, careful to avoid stepping full on any of the patterns still glowing a dim violet.

Together, then, the three of us retraced our way to the Great Hall, where stood that dais. Carefully seating Joisan on the raised step—for my lady looked near to exhaustion—I cleared my throat. "One of us should go down the ramp before full dark, see to the horses."

Guret nodded. "I would, willingly . . . save for one thing. How would I get through that rock barrier?"

I sighed. "I know not. There is doubtless some way, but my knowledge of this place comes in spurts, then ebbs, never by my conscious willing. So it is better I see to the horses. Then we must seek out a source of water up here."

Guret hefted his waterskin. "*Is* there water? Otherwise, you should fill these when you are below."

I answered him slowly. "Yes . . . somewhere, I *know* there is water. But we must search for the source. My inconvenient memory has not enlightened me as to *where* it may be found." I grinned at him wryly. "I am no sorcerer yet, Guret, so give me not those awed, sidelong glances. I am truly but Kerovan, as always I have been."

He grinned back at me, half-abashed, half-relieved, as I slung our feed bags together and took the ramp, hurrying because I moved downward into darkness. But even as I went, the blue stone of the wall shone with a gentle glow. As I reached the valley, I whistled. Moments later, Nekia, grass tufting from both sides of her mouth, appeared. A moment later Arren and Vengi followed. I saw from the stallion's wary glances at the mares that they had repulsed his attentions. Scratching his neck, I fed him his ration of grain, well away from his female companions.

"Poor fellow . . . so they want nothing to do with you?"

He snuffed gustily, bobbing his head from the feed. I smiled. "Well, as the spring advances, you will find that changing. The maned ladies shall not be able to resist your charms for long."

Again he bobbed his head, as if in agreement, then returned to crunch greedily. I looked to Kar Garudwyn, though even in the daylight I could have barely seen its walls because of the cliff's acute angle. A faint blue glow told me that, like the ramp, the whole structure must give off light from the blue stone-metal of its building. Had it given off that faint shine every night through the countless deserted years, or did it only do so when there were those dwelling within its walls?

Weariness fell upon me like a blow as I started up the climb. The excitement of finding this long-abandoned citadel drained away, dissolving my steps into a fatigued stumble, forcing me to now and then use the wall as my support. Blue stone brightened where I set hand to it, and under my fingers it was warm rather than cold. Such touches seemed to give me a measure of energy, of well-being, pushing back my exhaustion for a few moments.

I discovered Joisan and Guret before a section of that large mosaic covering the circular wall of the Great Hall. Shouldering my lady's pack along with my own, I led the way instinctively through an archway opposite the entrance. Our feet echoed loudly on the stone floor. As before, the light globes sprang to radiant life as we approached, emitting that soft, rose-amber glow. Beyond the Great Hall, a narrow corridor stretched onward, lined on either side by those floor-to-ceiling slender arches. Joisan's voice reached me faintly, for the air here, though fresh, appeared somehow to muffle all sound.

"If we are to stay here, my lord, we must barrier these. I have no fancy to lose my footing some morn and find myself part and parcel of those rocks below."

"Aye," said Guret. "As it stands, this place is not for the clumsy . . . or the very young."

"Which, fortunately, none of us is," I said. At my words, I caught a swift glance exchanged between them, Guret's holding amusement, Joisan's a warning. I frowned, wondering what secret they shared, when Joisan spoke:

"Strange that the wind does not reach in here to touch us, in spite of these openings. Also, with walls of stone, I would expect to feel chilled with the onset of night—as I would have, if I stood within Keep walls in High Hallack. Yet I do not."

Guret looked around, again more than a little uneasy. "Witchery. . . ."

We continued to make our way down that hall (which proved shorter, somehow, to our feet than it had been to our eyes), passing through the portal at its end. We found ourselves in a large three-sided courtyard, facing the eastern heights. The jagged peaks were dimly visible through the ever-present narrow arches that framed the dark mountain night, a night which was pushed back as we entered by the glow of those strange globes. To the north and south lay arched entrances leading to other parts of the Keep. In the center of the courtyard was a fountain, its water cascading and swirling into a strange, half-familiar shape. Moving closer, I realized the flood sheeted and poured from a crystalline figure, so cunningly wrought that it was hard to divine which parts of the creature were water and which were solid.

"It is the figure of the gryphon. . . ." Joisan breathed beside me, her hand going to her breast where the tiny image of Telpher, Landisl's gryphon, had lain 'prisoned for all those years. The globe had long since been shattered; her fingers encountered only the weight of Gunnora's amulet. " 'Tis passing beautiful, Kerovan . . . making me remember so much. Has this been so all these years, or did it spring to life again just before we came?"

There was no way of answering her—as usual, my knowledge or memory remained capricious. We stood watching the flow and play of the water, until Guret broke the silence.

"Shall we bed down here, m'lord Kerovan? With the water to hand, it appears the best place."

"That seems good," I made answer, wandering over to look at a huge bowl wrought from stone which rested near the easternmost arches. Blackened traces of fire still showed within it. "Look. We will be able to cook here."

"It is perfect," Joisan agreed, before splashing water from the fountain over her face. I joined her, dipping hand into that basin, finding the water refreshingly cool. The runoff spilled into a second pool before disappearing—I wondered if its source was some mountain spring, but the liquid did not hold that bone-shrinking chill usually found in such.

We drank, then ate hungrily of the rations we had brought. Tomorrow, if we were to stay here—and, frankly, such was the peace that I felt in Kar Garudwyn, I could imagine no reason to leave—we would have to forage in the fields and forests. Also hunt, though my mind shied from the thought of so disturbing the valley below.

Joisan must have been mindsharing, for her next words echoed my thoughts. "We have food left to last us but one more day. . . ." She took another piece of journeybread, broke it, frugally stowing the remaining portion back in the pack. I must have shown my surprise as she chewed so eagerly on the tough, sustaining food, for she added, "I cannot remember when I have been so hungry. It must be the mountain air. And, of course, we did not pause at midday."

"You are right, now that I think of it. Today," I confessed, and felt some guilt at my blindness, "until we came into sight of this place, all passed in a haze for me. Though I pushed you hard, my lady, I did not know what lay at the end of our trail until I gazed upon Kar Garudwyn. Then it was as if this had always been there in my mind, waiting, its image behind my eyelids when I closed them. . . ."

We talked but little more, soon rolling into our blankets, drowsy with long riding and perhaps some strain of self-discovery. The globes on the wall shone steadily. I lay watching their reflection on the sheets of water in the fountain, wishing I knew some way to lessen their glow lest they disturb my lady. My mind wandered . . . I heard Joisan's soft breathing from the pallet next to mine, Guret's some distance away.

My eyes widened. The lights were dimming! As though my thought had reached into stone and metal, they banked to a soft red glow. Dimly, overhead, I could now make out the stars before moonrise. Somehow this small example of sorcery, more than any other that had already evidenced itself, made me aware of how attuned this place was to *my* mind . . . *my* spirit.

My old fear of Power returned to tense my body. I forced myself to relax, allowing that peace to wrap around me as a cloak against a winter wind. Power, as Joisan had shown me that night so long ago, could be used for comfort and protection, as well as by the Shadow for evil. Perhaps I would grow used to that part of me in time. *Time* . . . how long had Kar Garudwyn waited? Perhaps here, time was measured differently. . . . My thoughts jumbled, then stilled, as I sank down into sleep.

I awoke clear-headed for the first time in three days, stretching luxuriantly in the wash of sunlight from the east. Guret, I saw, was already up, his fingers busy rubbing clean the headstall of Vengi's hackamore. Joisan lay still in deep sleep, her face in shadow. Sitting up, I made to block those early rays that she might slumber a few minutes longer. Those dark marks beneath her eyes last night had troubled me. Now, at long last, perhaps we could rest, spend time simply *being*. Today we would explore the citadel further, find rooms, begin to claim this strange place, adapt it to our use.

I gazed off across the morning-revealed heights, seeing the topmost portion of the other mountain nearly at eye level—though at a considerable distance—from the arched windows on the eastern side of the courtyard. Purple mist veiled that shorn-off peak, seeming to coil snake-fashion among those faraway, tumbled boulders. I tried in vain to follow the lines of those ancient stones, hoping to ascertain whether they were naturally placed or else marked a way of the Old Ones. I could not be sure . . . there was an odd distortion when I studied any one part of the mountaintop plateau, almost like the glamourie Joisan and Guret had described yesterday when they attempted to ride past the winged globes guarding the valley entrance.

Sunlight strengthened, brightened. Rising, I sought the windows opposite the entrance that I might see more clearly.

Kar Garudwyn, the full light of the sun made clear, actually rested upon the lesser of the twin mountain peaks. Between the two lay only a torturous trail that swooped down from the rear of this citadel, then climbed jaggedly up again, so rocky a way to look as though best traveled only by those tiny, narrow-hoofed deer that forage on the lichens and mosses growing at higher altitudes.

There was a movement beside me. Joisan, her hair loosed and tumbled from its neat braids, her eyes wide as they looked out upon that twin, somewhat higher, peak, clutched my arm. " 'Tis the same . . . the very same . . ." she murmured. "But Car Re Dogan is no more. . . ."

"Car Re Dogan?" For some reason that name, though I was certain I had never heard it before, held a certain haunting familiarity. "Where—or what—is that, Joisan?"

She started, her fingers tightened on me. I guessed that she was unaware she had spoken aloud. Her eyes met mine, dropped abruptly. "I . . . have dreamed, too, Kerovan. Even as you saw the object of your dreams when we looked up at this place yesterday evening, so with the morning's light, I see mine."

"What kind of dreams?" I demanded anxiously, thinking of those strangely shifting shadows shrouding the other mountain's summit. They disturbed me. One needed no lessoning in theurgy to realize that these mountains must be as cloaked in sorcery as the rest of this haunted land— how else could they have proved such an effective barrier 'twixt east and west, High Hallack and Arvon?

"Dreams of long ago, my lord . . . a dream whose end has not yet been revealed to me. There was an Adept, once, who lived in a Keep atop that mountain over there. . . . Margrave of the Heights, he was, the watcher and guardian between the ancient land and the land from which his people had, mostly, withdrawn—High Hallack. Only there were none of the Dalesblood abiding there then, for it was long and long ago. . . ." Her voice had taken on the cadence of a songsmith's as she spoke, staring out across those twisted ways.

"Did he know Landisl?" I asked, fascinated and more than a little disturbed by and for her.

"I don't know. . . ." She hesitated, then shivered. "His place is gone, and Kar Garudwyn still stands. Oh, my lord . . . more and more I feel as though there is truly a designed purpose in our coming here. A purpose beyond finding a home, a cause we yet sense but dimly. Perhaps a reason that will be years . . . decades . . . in the revealing. I feel like a playing piece pushed hither and yon at the will of something greater—and I do not like it!"

I nodded. "In the past . . . I have felt the same. Do you recall Neevor's words to us, that day we bested Galkur? He said that *he*—Landisl—had a part in my making, and that someday I might follow a road to Power that perhaps he had walked before me. . . . Do you remember that?"

"Yes." Her voice was soft. "But I also am mindful of your answer to him . . . that you chose to follow no road which led to the holding of Power—that you wished to be only Kerovan, lord of nothing, *man* of no great talent. . . ."

I smiled at her ruefully. "You and Guret both have a

knack for summoning my own words back to haunt me. There is a time for holding to such, and a time for letting go. A time for choices of the mind, and a time for choices of the heart. And sometimes only the fullness of time can tell us if we have chosen well or ill." I drew her close as I bent to kiss her forehead solemnly. "Joisan . . . you are truly a Wise One, my brave lady."

She laughed shakily, her eyes downcast. "You give me too much credit, my lord. I can be as foolish—or as cowardly—as the next one. Just as you pointed out, sometimes we all cast away things that may be good just because we fear. Truth is a two-edged sword. Before we left Anakue, Zwyie made a foretelling for me. I awoke this morning, having dreamed of her words. 'You shall journey and you shall find a home of ancient wisdom, a place of ancient evil. What are now two shall be three . . . then six, to face that not of earth. . . .' "

"Indeed," I mumbled, my mind worrying at those cryptic words as a hunting hound might worry a lure-skin. "We have journeyed and found a place of ancient wisdom right enough. As for evil . . . could it be that well I battled?"

Joisan shrugged. "Perhaps. Foretellings are chancy matters in the best of cases."

"What means 'two shall be three . . . then six'? Three is a number of power, but not so six. Do you understand it, Joisan?"

Red stained her cheeks suddenly, she looked a little away and no longer met my gaze squarely. "I know not about the number six, Kerovan, but the two becoming three—"

"Guret!" I exclaimed. "Guret is with us, now."

"So I am," said the young man, approaching the window where we stood. "While you two looked upon the morning, I have prepared our breakfast."

After I had washed and shaved, and we had eaten, we discussed plans for the day. Guret, who had more experience as a fisherman than I, proposed to try his luck in the river running the length of the valley. Joisan wished to search the woods and fields for edible roots and growing things, while I would take Guret's bow and seek game.

When we met later in the afternoon, each of us had done well—Guret swung several fat fish from a line, I had two rabbits, as well as an unwary hedge-grouse, while Joisan's shawl bulged with intriguing lumps and bumps. As she saw us coming, she waved, beckoning us to look upon what evidently excited her. "Look!" she exclaimed, showing us several gnarled kernels. Wild grain! I shall be able to make bread, of a sort. The soil is rich. We must trade with the Kioga for seeds of all kinds—flax, grain, vegetables" —she began sorting through her booty—"wild onions, carrots, and turnips . . . this valley must have been under cultivation, long ago."

"Aye, Cera," Guret agreed.

"We will need a plow," I said, "and a harness. I wonder how Nekia will take to drawing the earth-breaking blade."

"Have you ever farmed, m'lord?" Guret looked faintly scandalized, as though he found the thought of a warrior behind a plow disturbing.

"I have turned my hand to many things since we have been in Arvon," I said, amused. "Including plowing. I can even do a fair job at smithing. Replacing horseshoes is a constant worry in the army."

"Perhaps that is one of the things you can use in trade, m'lord," Guret said. "Our smith, Jibbon, is growing old. Jerwin, the boy who died in the mountain passes last winter, was learning his trade, but—"

"Jerwin?" Joisan asked.

Quickly the boy told the story of the menace the Kioga had fled. Joisan glanced around her at the sunlit fastness of the valley, then at the mountain peaks rising above it. "Where in the mountains does this pass lie?"

Guret stood for long moment studying the position of the sun, glancing from peak to peak, in silent thought.

Finally he turned to us. "I cannot be sure," he said reluctantly, "but it must be in this very region."

Joisan looked distinctly uneasy, though I had the impression she was not much surprised, either. For me, I surveyed the peace of the valley, then the beauty of Kar Garudwyn, to learn that I could not imagine this as anything but a refuge of welcoming safety. "We were not menaced last night," I reminded them. "Naught can enter this valley that I shall not sense."

Even as I spoke, as though my words were an enlarging-glass to focus the many rays of the sun into one burning pinprick, I swung to face the southern end of the valley, whence we had come yesterday. It was as though someone had brushed a roughness across my flesh, abradingly, causing discomfort, but as yet no real hurt.

"What is it, Kerovan?" Joisan asked.

"I feel a troubling . . . southward. *Something* is trying to breach the Guardians of the pasts."

"That runner of ridges?" Guret looked frightened.

"No. *That* menace is one that gains strength when the sun is fled. I don't know what this is . . . but we must find out, and speedily."

Whistling for our mounts, we saddled and rode up the valley at a brisk canter, toward that narrow throat of rock marking its entrance. As I rode, I could feel that other presence, like a filthy cloak muffled about my spirit. Something was pushing against the valley safeguards, growing more and more angered when their protection held firm. While on my wrist—though I showed that not to my companions—my talisman took on its warning warmth and light.

As we moved toward the englobed symbols, I indeed sighted a figure without, dark, sitting silent atop a black stallion. The stranger was hooded and shrouded in a sable cloak, but as we neared, the sunlight picked out a narrow ridge of nose, and I heard Joisan's soft exclamation. "Nidu!"

Sensing my lady's strong dislike mingled with fear,

even though we were not directly mindsharing, I glanced at her reassuringly. "Such a one cannot pass the protection devices, Joisan, unless we open the way to her."

Her answer was chill. "Do not underestimate her Power, Kerovan. Even before we left the Kioga camp she was dabbling along paths better not trodden by any who value their spirits. Do you not feel that she has taken further strides along the Left-Hand Path?"

I *could* feel it. Nekia trembled beneath me, rolling her eyes and sweating as we took those last few strides to halt, facing the Shaman, just on the other side of those protecting globes. The smell of the mare's fear sweat was rank in my nostrils, and, glancing over at Guret's and Joisan's mounts, I saw they fared no better. Even the stallion, Vengi, who should have reacted to the presence of another male of his kind with open challenge, hung back, eyes rolling, not in anger, but fear.

Nidu's black mount stood quietly, wearing neither bit nor saddle, every shining line of it reflecting the afternoon sun in ebony glimmers. There was something deeply unsettling about the stallion's perfection of form, for true perfection is a thing outside of nature. As the sun caught the creature's eyes, they flashed red, deep within their depths.

"Fair meeting, Lord Kerovan—Lady Joisan." Nidu's voice held some of the low, silken hum of the spirit drum hanging by her side. "My thanks for bringing my Drummer of Shadows. You have saved me the trouble of breaching your gate and reclaiming him."

I kept my voice very level. "Guret refused your service, Nidu. I am surprised Jonka did not tell you of this."

Her dark eyes pricked at me like an ancient, keen-pointed dagger. "Jonka does not rule the Kioga, save by my will. Guret was rightfully Chosen, therefore he will serve."

"Rightfully!" My temper, usually well leashed, flared at her straight-eyed untruths. "I watched you alter the selection! Whyever you did so remains your own reason, but you called upon the Power—and a Dark one at that—to aid your will in the ceremony. Guret is thus twice free—by his own will, and by your unclean cheat during the selection!"

She regarded me narrow-eyed, as though only now seeing me as a man, not just an object to be moved aside by her will. "Do not think you can cower here behind your ancient barriers and safeguards for long, Kerovan. Give me the boy—*then* your safety, and the safety of your whey-blooded wife is assured. Otherwise—"

"Otherwise, *nothing!*" Joisan spoke for the first time. "Get you hence, Nidu, and take your insults with you. Guret goes where he chooses. He is free to stay with us until he wishes to move on, and naught you can say or threaten will alter that."

"Have you forgotten the mandrake charm?" The Shaman smiled suddenly, and for a second it seemed that her mouth bore too many teeth for one of humankind. "Best guard yourself, Lady Joisan. *Something* saved you that first time, but the next you may not be so lucky—"

I interrupted her threat with an expletive better confined to the company of one's barracks-mates, then, in cold silence, signaled the unwilling Nekia with my knees, so the mare moved to front the Shaman directly. "Get you gone, Nidu, or you will be sorry." Quickly, with my right hand, I drew the symbol of the winged globe in the air, saw it flame violet. As the symbol formed I spoke two *words*, ones that came into my head unbidden, *words* that shaped and honed Power as a smith may strike the edge to a blade.

The woman's face went ashen as those *words* struck at her like a sword-thrust. Her mount shrieked, a sound no natural horse had ever uttered, and turned, rocks and sod spurting from beneath its hooves as it raced away.

"By the Amber Lady!" I turned at Joisan's exclamation to see her arch her brows in feigned shock, then grin wryly at the Shaman's rapidly disappearing figure. "One would think she'd never heard anyone swear before."

I began to chuckle. "Your pardon, my dear. I forgot myself. It's been long and long since anyone—man or woman—rubbed my temper so sorely."

"How did you know what would chase her off?" Guret asked.

"The same way I 'knew' what would vanquish the well," I made answer. "Which is to say, I acted solely by instinct, with no forethought. Besides, Nidu might well have been able to front and vanquish what I sent against her—but her horse decided otherwise."

Guret looked at me squarely. "I know not magic, nor *words* of Power, m'lord, but I *do* horses. Whatever that . . . thing . . . was, it was *not* a horse."

"I agree that it was only that by outward seeming." I nodded. "What then, *was* it?"

"A Keplian. A Soulless One, who travels in the seeming of a stallion," Joisan replied absently, gazing through the entrance to the rolling foothills beyond, where Nidu and her unearthly mount had vanished.

"Where did you hear of such?" I asked.

"Old legends, old tales," she said. "It is said to be a harbinger of death, for one who sees or trafficks with it."

A shiver worked its way along my spine, crawling upward with icy little claws. "Do you think she will be back?" I asked.

"Oh, yes," she replied calmly—her very lack of emotion the more chilling than overt fear would have been. "Nidu is not the sort to give up what she wants."

"Which is why I am leaving," Guret said, urging Vengi forward, crowding Nekia aside in the narrow passageway. "I will ride for the camp, give my message to Jonka in person, and let *her* tell the Shaman I refuse to be Drummer of Shadows."

I made a quick motion to grab his arm, but Joisan was

even swifter as her hand closed on his chestnut's rein.
"No!" we said as one.

"Don't be a fool, Guret!" I said. "It is not just your
service she wants, but your spirit. You must not!"

"Even if you go, she will not leave us alone." Joisan's
eyes were very level, despite her pallor. "She is not one
to endure slights easily, and both Kerovan and I have
bested her, now. She will not turn aside from her revenge
just for you."

The young man's mouth was a grim line as he shaded
his eyes against the scarlet-dyed rays of sunset. "If what
you say is true, then my proper place is here, to help you
against her, and whatever she may try to unleash. Still, I
could find it in me to wish that I had done as she demanded in the first place, no matter what price it meant
for me. Not for anything would I have had this happen. . . ."

I absentmindedly smoothed Nekia's mane. "We had
best return before the last of the light is gone. We need
clear heads to plan our defenses, and none of us has
broken fast since the morning."

"Well said, my lord," Joisan agreed. "I will start back to
Kar Garudwyn, prepare food from our gleanings . . . I am
a bit tired. Perhaps you and Guret should patrol the
valley borders to make sure there are no paths down from
the heights for Nidu to discover."

I was troubled and not by any thought of the Shaman.
"Joisan, you have been tired overmuch lately. Are you
well?"

She hesitated for a second, then her small, pointed chin
came up as she smiled. "Completely, my lord."

"But—"

She interrupted me briskly. "I am the healer in this
company, Kerovan, and you may rest assured I take no
chances with anyone's well-being, least of all my own.
When we are sure that Nidu cannot enter the valley, that
we are safe, then there will be a time for talking. We are
all looking a bit worn after our journey."

What she said was true, making such good sense there was no arguing with it. Yet I found myself watching her as she cantered Arren away, back up the faint trail our horses' hooves had left, truly worried for the first time since we had found Landisl's ancient home.

When the last flick of Arren's russet-colored tail had disappeared, I turned, only to find Guret watching *me* with some of the same intensity that I had fixed on Joisan. "Guret," I said, slowly, looking directly at the young man's plain, sturdy features beneath his unruly thatch of dark hair, "does aught strike you as . . . *unusual* . . . about the Lady Joisan since we returned from the scout?"

He shrugged, turning to slap a fly that had lighted on Vengi's sweating crest. "Nothing to speak of, m'lord. Why?"

"I don't know," I said, studying him. "But I will speak of it later, to her, tonight." I caught his swift, sideways glance, and was even more certain that something was afoot, something well-known to Guret.

"For the moment," I finished, "let us divide the valley. I will take the western walls, you the eastern. Make this a quick scout, for dark is not far off. We can explore more thoroughly tomorrow."

He gave me a quick salute of acknowledgment, turning his stallion to the east. Tightening my leg muscles against Nekia's right side, I headed for the western boundary of the valley. I rode at the fastest jog I dared, my eyes on the rocky walls and forested slopes to my left, letting the mare pick her way. I sighted a few faint scars of trails, but none that I found particularly threatening—unless Nidu's "Keplian" mount had the balance and agility of a mountain crag-deer or pronghorn.

Guret was waiting for me when, after turning Nekia loose to graze with the other mounts, I reached the rampway to the stronghold above. "Look, m'lord! The way is no longer hidden to me!"

I surveyed the entrance. "It would appear that Kar

Garudwyn has accepted you and Joisan as rightful in-dwellers."

"Accepted? Are you suggesting the hold is *alive*?" His glance at the rock walls surrounding us was wary, as though he expected them to sprout hands and faces.

"No," I made answer, "but the hold and its environs are under a spell beyond anything I have ever encountered, protected by the Power. That is why Nidu could not—"

"What is it, m'lord?" Guret asked as I broke off, quick-ening my pace on the ramp.

"*I cannot sense Joisan.* It is probably nothing, but—" Without completing my sentence I began to run, my strides taking me up the ramp, then through the Great Hall in a blur, toward the courtyard with the gryphon fountain, the one fronting that twin peak Joisan had identified as the place out of her own dreams. I was gasping, hand pressed to my aching side, and it was a moment before I could summon breath enough to call out.

"Joisan!" The wind in the heights moaned outside as the sun dropped behind the mountains in a last wash of ebbing scarlet. My hooves clattered in the narrow stone passageway with its multiple slender arches. "*Joisan!*"

She was sprawled, pale as death, before the arches facing the twin peak. Arm's length from her lay the Gunnora amulet, as though she had taken it from her in response to a command, tossing it nearby.

I went to my knees beside her, raising her head, my heart stone-heavy within me. My hands shook so violently that it was many moments before I could steady them enough against her throat to feel the pulse of her lifeblood beneath my fingertips. "Joisan!"

Her breath came and went, regular, slow, deep, as though she slept. Yet her eyelids, near translucent in the glow of the globes on the walls, did not stir. "Joisan!" I called again, summoning now, reaching desperately with the mindsharing. "Wake!"

I shook her, feeling the limp heaviness of her body,

then, frantic when she did not rouse, slapped stingingly at her cheek. "Wake, my lady!"

Guret, whom I had outdistanced, came panting into the courtyard. "What happened?"

"She appears to be asleep, but I cannot wake her!"

Guret paled. "Is she hurt? Bleeding?"

"No." I looked up at him, my lady's head heavy against my arm. "There is the smell of sorcery about this."

"Nidu?"

"Perhaps. . . ." I looked over at the amulet. "Hand me that," I said, beckoning at it.

When he did so, I took it in one hand, shutting my eyes to deepen my concentration. *Gunnora,* I thought. *Amber Lady, hear me please. I know I am a male, but I ask your help for Joisan. . . .* Holding the carven sheaf of wheat in my palm, I pressed the talisman to my lady's forehead, striving to reach her, call her.

Joisan . . . wake, please. By the Amber Lady, I summon you . . . Joisan . . . you cannot leave me . . . . Joisan. . . .

I continued to shut out all else, trying to picture my call sinking *through* the amulet into my lady's mind, holding the image of her waking safe and whole. *Joisan . . . dear heart, come back!*

Suddenly her deep, regular breaths changed, sharpened into a startled gasp! I opened my eyes to see her looking up at me. "Kerovan? What chances—"

I held her close as she trembled, clutching her as though something might arise from the stone flooring beneath us to take her from me. It seemed that all the strength of my arms was not enough to shield her. "Joisan! What happened? You were lying on the floor, with your amulet flung from you as though you took it off by choice. . . ."

"I did." Her voice was muffled against my chest but I was not about to loosen my grip. "When I looked out upon the mountain peak to where Car Re Dogan stood, I knew suddenly that Sylvya was trying to reach me—and that something was stopping her. So I took off my amulet."

"Sylvya?" I questioned.

"The Other who has shared her story with me these past few months . . . she who once lived in Car Re Dogan. Oh, Kerovan, I at last discovered the end of her tale, and it was so *dreadful*—" Her words choked off in muffled sobs.

"Tell me," I commanded, believing that sharing her distress might lessen her anguish.

9

Joisan

Kerovan's voice was gentle, but his words were no request, rather a command. I knew as I gazed into his eyes, their amber darkened with concern, that it was time to part with at least one of my secrets. I sighed. "It was while you were gone that I began to dream. And in that dreaming I was no longer Joisan, but another, named Sylvya. . . ."

So I continued, telling him of the sendings that had come to me, gradually revealing the story of Sylvya and her half brother Maleron, the Adept. Finally I reached the part of the tale that had begun today, in this courtyard facing the shrouded ruins of what must be Car Re Dogan. "I carried our gleanings into here, thinking only about kindling a fire for cooking; then, while I was standing over there, near the stone bowl, facing the arches, I could *feel* her, calling me. Never had our contact been so demanding, so *real*. I put the food down, and walked over to the opening. . . ."

I turned my head to look at the arched emptiness cut into the blue stone. "I stood there, before it, knowing that

Sylvya was out there, somewhere. That she needed to tell me something. But she couldn't reach through—there was a wall between us. Then I felt a warmth on my breast, only to see my amulet glow, as though warding off the Shadow."

Kerovan shook his head, as though he already realized what my next words must be. "Yes," I admitted, "I took off the amulet, tossed it from me."

His protesting "Joisan!" rang out at the same moment as Guret's "Cera!"

"Don't you understand—I had to *know*!" I cried. "Sylvya and her fate are important to me—to us. Somehow this is so."

Kerovan made a brief, dismissive gesture. "Once done is done. What happened then?"

"I was back inside Sylvya's body, seeing with her eyes, knowing I had just confronted Maleron with that terrible accusation of being Shadowed. He tried to deny that he had taken the Left-Hand Path—I think perhaps even he was not truly aware of just how many steps he had traveled down that route. But Sylvya defied him, telling him that he was the one who had meddled with spells to stop even Time itself, and thus had brought harm to the valley she loved. . . ." I looked directly into Kerovan's eyes. "*This* valley, my lord. The one and same."

"What did Maleron do?"

"He naysaid his sister, accused *her* of being the one who was trafficking with the Shadow; then, when she would not retreat, would not take back her words, he became more and more enraged. Finally, Sylvya challenged him to prove himself untainted. Grabbing him by the wrist, she dragged him out of the room, taking him secretly down the ancient stone-chiseled road leading to the lowlands to the north, down the mountainside on the other side of that peak which is twin to this one we have claimed."

I took a deep breath, my mouth dry from talking. Guret

passed me a cup of the crystal liquid from the fountain, and he and my lord waited wordlessly while I drank. "Thank you, Guret. Ironically enough, *this* was Sylvya's challenge—" I shook the last drops of water from the drinking vessel so they spattered onto the floor. "Water, running water. Most Shadowed Ones cannot cross it. Sylvya led Maleron to a tiny stream, skipped across it, and, once on the other side, dared him to follow.

"He tried. But as soon as his foot left the bank, he staggered back, sickened. Then, when he realized that his sister had indeed proved her point, won her challenge, his anger knew no bounding. He spoke *words*—*words* the like of which Arvon has not heard for long and long— mercifully. These *words* opened a Gate, and through that Gate came hunters and hounds, like unto none our world has known before. Maleron mounted himself on a steed spawned surely in some hellish otherworld, giving the order to loose those hounds.

"Sylvya panicked. The brook could not delay them indefinitely—sooner or later there would be a crossing place for them. She ran, that ghastly hunt racing after her."

My eyes filled with tears. "Oh, Kerovan! That was long and long and *long* ago . . . and she has been running ever since."

His horror of such a fate filled his eyes. "How could such a thing happen?"

"It was Sylvya's doing. As she ran, she called out in desperation to Neave, begging the forces of Things As They Must Be to prevent the evil her brother had become from ever catching her. And those forces heard. Sylvya, Maleron—the entire hunt, quarry, hounds, and huntsmen alike—were transformed, shifted outside the bindings of Time as we know it. Sylvya could not be caught, but neither could she ever be free.

"Thus every night, at the same hour, that terrible hunt comes thundering up the ancient road, into the ruins of

Car Re Dogan. They are part and parcel of no world, rather trapped in an endless existence somewhere between. But even their half presence is deadly."

"Aye," said Guret, with a quick, indrawn breath. "Any who stands in that path then must be drawn in and destroyed. As Jerwin was."

I nodded at him.

"So that is the true nature of That Which Runs the Ridges in the night," Kerovan said. "Poor Sylvya. To be trapped ever thus is a thing beyond any horror I have yet encountered. . . ."

My hands knotted and unknotted the leathern thong holding Gunnora's amulet. "I was shown all this for some reason," I said. "There *must* be a way to free her!"

"How, when even passing contact with the thing kills?" my lord asked. "Such spells are far beyond our ken, Joisan. It would take one with the Power and learning of an Adept to undo this."

I sighed, feeling weariness flood over me, having no answer to give him. I made to rise, but even as I did so, both he and Guret put out restraining hands. "Rest, Cera," the boy said. "Our skill as cooks may not equal yours, but it shall suffice."

Thus I rested, watching them bustle back and forth, chopping roots and vegetables, skinning and preparing game, building a crude but serviceable spit, making a fire in the stone fire-bowl we had discovered earlier.

The food they served seemed to strengthen me, restoring much of the energy I had lost. We all ate in hungry silence, then, our stomachs filled, sat back for a few moments of rest, gazing out at the deepening darkness. Finally Guret arose. "I will give the horses their grain tonight, m'lord," he said, hefting the dwindling sack of feed.

"That is another thing we must trade for," Kerovan observed, "if we want to keep the horses in riding trim. How many more feedings have we?"

"If I cut down gradually, perhaps three or four," the young man said. His footsteps echoed slightly on the stone flooring as he left the courtyard.

Kerovan gestured at the eastern arches. "Can you still feel your Other?"

"Yes," I made frank answer, "but as long as I wear the amulet, she can only reach me when I dream or let down my barriers."

"I will sit up tonight and watch, lest you be plunged into another dream," he said, his mouth set in a grim line. "Even though you say this Sylvya is not of the Shadow herself, it would not be well to chance another encounter."

I hesitated, sorting through the impressions I had gained from this afternoon's contact. "She has told me what it is needful for me to know," I said at last. "The whyfor still puzzles me, but I—"

"Cera!" The shout echoed down the hallway toward us, accompanied by the beat of running feet. "Lord Kerovan!"

Together we rose as Guret plunged headlong into the courtyard, nearly toppling into the fountain in his rush. "The Great Hall!" he gasped. "There's something there! Something . . ." He tried to steady his breathing. "Something that cannot be seen, or heard, or felt—but it is there, nonetheless! I swear it, by the Sacred Horsehide!"

My lord started for the entrance, his words reaching us faintly as we hurried after him. "I sense it, too, now. A questing, an opening . . ."

"As I started to walk past the throne, it was *there*—just there." Guret's words came quickly. "I could almost see something. . . ."

I hastened my steps to a near run to catch up to Kerovan. "A questing? Nidu?"

"No." He sounded positive. "I know not what it is, but there is no taint surrounding it, such as accompanied that one." He frowned, the faint click of his hooves on the stone coming ever more rapidly. "But the boy has the right, there is *something*. . . ."

"What?"

"Something *familiar*. I cannot recall—" He broke off as we burst into the Great Hall with its circular dais holding that huge, oddly shaped throne. As soon as I entered the room I, too, could feel the troubling.

Hesitantly, we began to walk around the chamber, toward the spot facing the throne—and as we took each step, that troubling grew stronger. There was Power alive here, ancient, growing evermore potent in the ages since it had last been tapped. It seemed to mist against our faces as my lord and I approached its center (Guret, perhaps wisely, having chosen to watch from the shelter of the archway). I sniffed, detecting a sharp odor I could not put name to in the air.

Kerovan paused by the ramp leading up the dais to the throne, then, his face set, put out one hoof, beginning that ascent.

"Kerovan!" I made as if to grasp his arm.

"No," he said, his voice ringing hollowly, overlaid with another, alien tone. "This is what I must do."

I felt the resistance against my bone and flesh increase as I made to follow him, and stepped back, defeated. No spell I had ever enjoined could break down barriers of this kind. This, then, was for my lord to face alone.

Reaching that massive block of the quan-iron from which the seat had been carved, he hesitated for a long second, then, in one smooth motion, sat down. His hooves dangled by nearly a handspan, and he needs must squirm to find a comfortable perch thereon. Clearly, none of humankind had been the original occupant of the throne.

As if his presence in the seat were a signal, the mist before my eyes began to take on visible form, curdling in the center. Two widely separated blocks of the blue stone underfoot began to glow, azure light growing upward from between them, shimmering in the air. The Power centered between them, suspended like a web between pillars. It flickered, becoming visible as I backed away, suddenly frightened, thinking of the child. The forces uncoiling here in this room were vast—I had no wish to be trapped in some arcane backlash.

Violet trails uncoiled and crawled within that web of Power, coalescing, then stretching upward, moving into the form of a living creature—a gryphon!

Telpher! I thought, the image of the beast that had protected me during the battle with Galkur filling my mind. "Telpher?" I called, stretching out my hand toward that shape.

It turned eyes the color of gentle flames in my direction, opening its mouth as though to speak.

Joisan! Kerovan's mindsharing reached through my concentration, bringing a warning. *Touch it not—what you see is but an image of the Unlocker of Gates.*

I turned to see him raise his hand, his fingers forming a sign I did not recognize; then, quickly, he sketched the winged globe that seemed to have been Landisl's Power symbol. His mouth moved, twisting into an utterly alien shape as he spoke a *word*—one that I could not hear with my ears, except perhaps as a distant pain, but perceived with the inner sense.

I turned to see the gryphon image ripple in its center, then split and tear apart in lines of searing violet light. I put up a hand to shield my sight, and then Kerovan, with a sudden leap down, was beside me, his hand raised as if in greeting. "Come," he called, using the ancient word from the Old Tongue.

He extended his hand toward the light—

There came a sudden clap of sound so high-pitched as to be only a sharp pain, and a wave of brilliance engulfed us both as a twig is swept by the spring floods.

Staggering back, I tripped over the edge of the dais, sitting down with a jar. My eyes watered and ran, my nose filled with the odor one can sometimes scent after a lightning strike. I struggled up, only to see not one, but *two* forms sprawled on the stones before me!

"Guret? Kerovan?"

There was the sound of running feet, then hands on my shoulders, helping me to rise. "Cera? What happened? Who is *he*?"

I swayed dizzily as I stood, looking up at the youth's concerned face. If it was Guret who stood with me now, then *who* was the other man sprawled beside my lord? My heart seemed near to fighting its way out of my breast as I stumbled forward with the Kioga lad's aid.

"Kerovan?"

My lord was sitting up, one hand to his head, dazed. The man beyond him groaned, rolling over, his sword and mail scraping against the stone flooring. He went helmed, and his equipment could have been forged at the same fires as my own sword and mail, or Kerovan's. . . .

A man of the Dales? Here, in Arvon? Brought to Kar Garudwyn by some sorcerous Gate, the like of which we had traversed?

Questions flooded my mind, but for the moment it was plain the man was in no condition to speak. I hastened to his side, touched fingers to his throat. His war helm made a half screen across his features, but my questing fingers found that our "guest" had a pulse, and a strong one.

"Who is he?" I asked as Kerovan made an unsteady way over to join us.

"I know not," my lord answered. "The old Knowledge awakened and seemed to act through me—I knew what must be done to assist the one trapped within the Gate, but as to whom our guest may be . . ." He shrugged.

"Help me with his helm," I directed. "Guret, bring some water and a cloth."

Carefully we removed the man's helm. Beneath it was truly a Dalesman's face, hair a shade or two lighter than my own, the weathered skin of a rover, well-cut, even handsome features. The man looked to be some years older than my lord—

I gasped as my mind suddenly rearranged those features into familiar lines—this man I knew! *"Jervon!"* I stammered, hardly believing my own sight. "How—what—"

Three years ago, when I had first followed my lord into the Waste, just before our entry into Arvon, I had met this man. At the time he had companied with a woman of the Old Race, Elys. The three of us had traveled the Waste for many days, searching after Kerovan, for, in their kindness, Jervon and his lady had been moved to aid me. Without their help I could never have made that perilous journey that had ended so abruptly as I was dragged down into a trap dug by the Thas, those repulsive Dwellers-In-Darkness. The last sight I had seen as the earth caved away beneath me had been this man's anguished face as he strove vainly to reach me. And now he was here, in Arvon.

"Jervon?" I saw Kerovan frown, as if trying to remember, then his eyes widened. "It cannot be! Where is Elys?"

After I had been captured by the Thas, Jervon and Elys had aided my lord in *his* subsequent search for *me*. He had told me that at one point in their journey together, his two companions had been warned back by the Power— for Elys was a Witch, and one of no small talent. The time was not right, she had said, for the two of them to walk the road leading to Arvon. Sadly, he had bade them farewell and ridden on alone. Kerovan had told me of Elys's wistfully expressed hope that someday the way into the ancient land might be opened to them. . . .

Carefully steadying Jervon's head on my knee, I wet the edge of the cloth Guret brought me and wiped his face. He seemed to rouse slightly, and when I gave him to drink, his eyes opened, blinking in the light. "You are safe, Jervon," I said quietly. "Do you remember me? I am Joisan."

"Joisan . . ." His eyes widened, and I could see memory rush in.

"Where is Elys, Jervon?" my lord said, bending over so the Dalesman could see him. "I am Kerovan, remember?"

"Kerovan? Here?" His eyes wandered around the circular chamber, plainly disbelieving. "Where—"

"You are in a place of the Old Ones," my lord said. "You came through a very ancient Gate. Do you not remember? And where is the Lady Elys?"

"Elys . . ." For the first time he looked to both sides, then sat up with a jerk, though I strove to hold him still. "She isn't here?" Panic awoke. "She *must be*— Elys! *Elys!*"

The Great Hall rang with his shouts, and it took the combined strength of the three of us to hold him down, lest he run wildly through Kar Garudwyn, risking a terrible fall if he suffered a misstep too near one of the open arches.

"Jervon!" I clutched at his shoulders. "Jervon, *listen*. If you would find Elys, you must *listen* to me!"

His eyes were frantic, and for a moment I feared he might plunge into madness, so terrible was the grief I sensed. Then he sagged. "Elys did not come through the Gate with you," I said as clearly as I could. "Where did you come from? It may be that Elys was left behind, and you must return for her."

"In the Waste," Jervon said dully. "We were in the Waste, in a portion we had never traveled before, and we came upon a road. A strange road. My lady said there were visions there, of the ones who had withdrawn out of High Hallack so long ago." I heard a swift indrawn breath from Kerovan. "On either side were great faces of stone carved, and then something Elys called the Great Star—"

"The road!" my lord exclaimed. "That is the road where Riwal and I first found the crystal gryphon! What happened to you there?"

"We reached the end, where the road simply ran into a solid facing of cliff, and thus ended. But Elys said that it was no true end, rather a stepping-off place for one who possessed the Power to summon and open."

"Did she try the Gate?" I asked.

"Yes," he made slow answer. "And I believe it opened

for both of us. We were hand in hand, before that cliff, then . . ." He shook his head. "We were . . . *not*. In a place between, a place where we possessed no bodies, rather only our spirits had meaning. I saw, but my eyes did not comprehend. But Elys was with me! I *know* she was! That was the one thing I could still feel—her handclasp!"

"What happened?"

"Time was strange." He fumbled with words, as though he could not make them serve his meaning. "It stretched forever, it seemed, and yet no time passed at all. We were being drawn toward a violet light, and I saw what seemed to be a creature. One out of legend, with the wings and foreparts of an eagle, but the hindparts and ears of a lion. A gryphon."

"That was the Gate," Kerovan said. "Was Elys with you still?"

"She was—but then something seemed to pass between us, and I felt her hand torn away."

"What was this 'something' like?" I asked, my throat tight. If Elys had been trapped between the Gate and its portal, how could we hope to find her?

"It was . . ." He frowned, as though the shock had partially erased his memory. "Of the Shadow," he decided, horror settling in his eyes as if it had always been there. "I could not see it, but it seemed to make a droning noise, and its stench . . ." He shook his head. "It gave off a yellowish light. Its touch was . . . loathsome."

"Oh, no," I mumbled, feeling my heart dropping within my breast, till it lay like an anchor-stone.

My lord nodded soberly at me. "I am afraid so, my lady. Can you discover aught from Sylvya?"

I hesitated, remembering well that sleep that had claimed me almost past my waking again. Then I nodded. I owed Elys a debt that I had never paid, and the people of the Dales are raised to acknowledge and repay such, even as are the Kioga. "I will try," I said. "But you must mindlink with me this time, Kerovan, so you can aid me if I go in too deeply."

He nodded. "Agreed."

As Jervon watched anxiously, Guret behind him, I sat down on the dais, with my lord sitting behind me, so that I could lean back against him. His arms came up to steady me. I tried to keep my face from betraying any inner fear or disquiet as I carefully removed the Amber Lady's amulet. Guret moved forward to take it.

Even as it left my fingers, I could feel Sylvya's presence quest inward, seeking, and knew that she again had something she must convey. Closing my eyes, I surrendered myself to the will of that Other, but this time I went conscious of Kerovan's presence like the support of an arm around weary shoulders.

For long moments it was dark, then the otherness swept over me, whirling me away from the here and now to . . . where? I was noplace I had ever seen or experienced, either in my life or hers. Though I was once more within Sylvya, this time she was *not* reliving moments out of the far past. Instead, I knew the turmoil and utter horror of what it meant to be caught outside the bounds of Time itself, of having no physical world to surround me.

I was running—but I had no feet, no legs, and my surroundings never changed. Still, within my mind, my body was running, my blood coursing through my veins, my breath catching in lungs that burned with each breath— but I had no blood, no chest with which to draw breath!

Struggling to calm myself, I faced these conflicting messages from a body that did not exist—and all the while, I fled from that ghastly hunt dogging my footsteps (except that I had no feet, of course). Behind me, there was a massive wave of Power, an anger that knew no bounds nor leashing, and that anger flickered yellowish, lighting this uncanny not-place with a fetid, diseased glow. That wave of powerful anger was Maleron's manifestation here between time and worlds.

But I knew—or Sylvya told me, it amounted to the same thing—that there was now come a change in the hunt. There was a force trapped here with us, a force of Power. That presence was like a clean light shining through the dank mists of a fen, and I knew that light was Elys. She was ensnared.

Could I free her? Take her back with me? Even as the question flickered within my mind, there came a fresh wave of knowledge from Sylvya—and experiencing that knowing, I was nearly lost in fear.

The spell holding this dreadful hunt between worlds and times had become faded with age, its arcane bindings stretched and pulled thin, as one may draw out the strands of linen from a spindle—but even the strongest thread has a breaking tension. Even as I focused the sight of my not-eyes on the bindings of that spell, they stretched, tore, then rippled away. I caught a faint backlash of Power from the world where my body still rested, then glimpsed a narrow, knifelike face, skull-thin, with long dark hair waving wildly in the night breeze.

Nidu! As I watched the Shaman, the roll of her drum reached my ears, and I saw the blood and fat-smeared rock upon which she had sacrificed to work her spell—her spell to loose the bindings holding That Which Runs the Ridges in thrall, releasing it onto an unsuspecting land.

She might never have accomplished such a feat of sorcery, had she not somehow used Elys to direct her summoning. The Wisewoman's Power had served the Shaman as a focusing point in this deadly liberation.

I felt the Power that was Maleron waxing, swelling into a force so deadly, so inimical to all that I had ever known, that I panicked, struggling to free myself from such proximity. *Kerovan!* I shouted with part of my mind, using the name as my own focusing point. *Kerovan! Reach me—*

It was as though I was one trapped in a raging fire or a roaring flood, struggling helpless, until something akin to a lifeline began to tighten, drawing me back to safety. The grip of that malevolent Power swung in my direction, clutching at me, seemingly grinding the flesh from my bones—

Kerovan! Along that insubstantial but nevertheless real binding I felt strength flow, so that I was able to claw my way out, free myself—

With a rush that left me too dizzy to even move, I was back in the Great Hall of Kar Garudwyn, held tight in my lord's embrace, with Guret clinging to one hand, Jervon to the other. My relief was so great I nearly sobbed aloud, to breathe again, smell clean air, feel my blood move in a warm, living body.

"Joisan!" Kerovan laid his cheek against my hair, clutching at me as though I was indeed one rescued from a physical death. "What happened?"

I was so wearied I could barely whisper, but managed to direct Guret to bring my collection of simples. There was a cordial within, distilled of a mixture of carnation and dragon's blood, that, when two drops were mixed with a cup of water, would help me regain a measure of my strength for a while—and would not harm the child. Under my direction, the boy prepared the cup, then Kerovan held it for me while I sipped.

Gradually, steadiness gathered again in my limbs, my hands stopped their trembling, and I was able to sit without support, my head clear. Finally I faced my lord and Jervon, trying to summon the courage to deliver such devastating news. I was too tired to choose the easiest of words, so I expressed myself as bluntly as possible.

"I was within Sylvya's body, as she was trapped inside that hunt. There was another force of the Light also trapped, and I recognized that presence as Elys. Nidu has drawn Power from her, using her as the focusing point of her spell-breaking. And she has succeeded in her attempt!"

I looked up at Kerovan, trying to control the shivers still threatening to wrack me. "She is mad, my lord. The anger she felt at us today has overcome any lingering traces of sanity. When she could not break the forces shielding this valley, she turned wholly to the Shadow for the worst fate she could find to unleash upon us! Tonight when that hunt wends its way up the mountainside, when it reaches the end of its set run in the ruins of Car Re Dogan, the bonds holding it out of time will be released by her drumming. It will be *free* to continue on as a flesh-and-blood threat—no longer a phantom manifestation—tonight, it will become *real*. All that stands within its path will be swept away, so great is the force the Shaman has unthinkingly released."

Kerovan looked around blankly at the walls of the Great Hall, and I knew, even though his expression did not change, the depth of his feeling for this place—a place that had claimed him as lord, where he finally felt at home. "And we and Kar Garudwyn lie in a direct path from that other peak," he said. "It will sweep over this place, then continue on through the valley, toward Anakue and, eventually, the Kioga grazing grounds."

"It will be free to rove wherever it wishes—or Maleron chooses to take it," I made swift agreement.

"And Nidu was the cause of this?" Guret asked.

"Aye," Kerovan said. "But I doubt greatly that the woman has even the faintest idea of what she has so thoughtlessly unleashed. She can no more control such a Power of the Dark then she could stem a flood with her naked hands."

"Who is Nidu?" Jervon wanted to know. "And how came you and your lady here, Kerovan?"

As my lord swiftly recounted the barest bones of our story to the Dalesman, I quietly arose and set about gathering up the herbs, candles, and other materials that might prove necessary in a contest of spelling, carefully placing them in my bag of simples. My hands shook as I did so, for I hated to even imagine myself pitted against Nidu's sorcerous powers—not to mention the aroused wrath of one of the true Adepts, freed now after centuries of bondage.

"What are you doing, Cera?" Guret asked, coming over to watch me.

"Gathering together my materials," I said, carefully locating my wand and placing it in the top of the bag.

"But Cera"—Guret was pale—"you cannot hope to stand against such a foe!"

Swift as a blade in battle, Kerovan was by my side, though there had been no true mindsharing between us— rather simple knowledge of a common threat to all we had gained at such hardship. "My lady has courage for two, but she will not stand alone. Kar Garudwyn is my home— *our* home—and I will not lose it after the finding of it has taken years of wandering and fear! We *must* stop that thing"—he looked down at me earnestly—"and stop it we will."

10

Kerovan

"No, my lord!" The Kioga youth shook his head violently, then his eyes traveled from me to Joisan. "We have no chance against such an enemy, Cera!"

I put a hand on his shoulder, feeling tremors I could not see. "Rest easy, Guret. Joisan and I travel alone in this attempt. I have another duty for you this night, and that is to ride southward to warn the people in the fisher-village of Anakue, and then your own people, of what may come their way in the event we are overrun."

"M'lord, you are mad!" Guret's voice broke slightly in his vehemence, but his gaze was level as it held mine. "You did not see Jerwin after he stood in the path of that . . . *thing* . . . and I did. My lord, there was naught remaining for us to even bury! Lumps of flesh . . ." He swallowed. "Shards of bone no bigger than the tooth of a yearling. You also did not see my blood-friend, Tremon, wither like a sapling uprooted, shrinking into himself with each dawn until we all waited for him to die with *hope*, rather than fear!"

"Guret . . ." Joisan reached forward from beside me to lay hand on the boy's arm. "Kerovan and I—"

"No!" He faced us. "You don't understand what I'm trying to *tell* you! It's death to cross the Shaman, and doubly so to stand in the path of that thing! It is folly to throw your lives away in such a fashion!"

Joisan glanced up at me, and I caught her wry unspoken words. *He may very well have the right of it, my husband. . . .*

Probably, I agreed with her mindsharing, but aloud I said, "Guret, this will not be the first time we twain have faced the might of an Adept from the Left-Hand Path." I did not add that three years ago we had had allies like Neevor and Landisl, creatures whose command of Powers dwarfed that possessed by any of humankind.

The youth might have mindshared, so quickly did he seize on my unspoken thoughts. "But this time there is no crystal gryphon . . . no talisman or ally out of the past to aid you. You have said over and over to me that you are not one who commands Powers, m'lord. True, I have seen you do things here in Kar Garudwyn that I know *I* could not do—but are you equal to this? I think not. Two of humankind cannot face—"

"Three," said Jervon from across the circular chamber, his tone as flat as one who comments on the weather. "I company with you, Kerovan."

"No, Jervon," my lady protested, "if Kerovan and I have little Power with which to defend ourselves, you have—"

"Even less," he agreed tonelessly. His hand sought the pommel of his sword, resting there as if he grasped the hand of an old friend. "However, I can wield cold iron, which many of those of the Shadow cannot endure. And I am not one to be easily amazed or bemused, after these many years roving the Waste with my lady Witch. You are going to try and rescue Elys, as well as save this land. I can do no less than stand with you."

I pulled my mail shirt over my head to give myself a heartbeat's duration to think, then my eyes sought and measured his expression from across the chamber as I settled the cold metallic weight around me. His gaze challenged and captured my own for a long moment, and I could see therein the pain that he had kept so well masked. Realizing how I would feel in like circumstances, if Joisan were the one trapped within the bowels of a Shadowed One, I nodded. "Very well. You share our path tonight, Jervon."

"And that is another thing!" Guret broke in. "The path! You cannot even reach the other peak now that the sun has set. You must needs ride back down the valley and around the mountain to come in from the north—you will be too late! The thing travels its run before midnight, that I remember clearly!"

Drawing my sword, I checked its edge, making sure its sweep out of my scabbard was smooth, swift. When I was satisfied, I made short answer. "Not if we take the old trail running between the two peaks." Picking up the saddles, I nodded to Joisan to carry the hackamores. I noticed that she also had donned her sword and mail. Briefly, I wished I could induce her to travel southward with Guret but knew better than to broach the subject. I knew the look in her eyes when her mind was made up.

"The trail between the peaks?" Guret sounded even more aghast, if that were possible. "In *daylight* that path looked treacherous—by night, you'll kill yourselves and the horses, too!"

"The moon is waxing near full again," Joisan said. "We'll manage."

"Nekia has good night-sight," I added. "She will find the trail. We will be cautious."

The Kioga youth threw his hands into the air, emitting a hiss of exasperation. "By the Mother of Mares! I can see there's no turning you, m'lord. But in that event, I ride with you tonight—not southward."

"No," I said flatly. When he began to protest, Joisan moved toward him, drawing him aside.

Guret, you must do as Kerovan says. . . . I caught part of her thought, then her mind slipped away from me.

The Kioga youth shook his head, then whispered something to her. My lady's lips thinned and she flushed, her eyes sparkling with anger. The lad smiled faintly as he confronted her. With a movement that whipped her chestnut braid like a horse's tail before battle, she turned and addressed me, her words very fast and clipped.

"Kerovan, Guret has just pointed out to me that to reach Car Re Dogan in time, we must ride, all three of us. Vengi will not suffer a stranger, but he *will* carry double. And you alone must ride Nekia—she trusts you. I have never ridden the stallion, and neither has Jervon. I think we must perforce take Guret with us."

· Suspicion flared strongly as I eyed her—what had the boy threatened her with to sway her to his way of thinking? But there was no time for argument . . . I nodded brusquely. "So be it. Now we must go, and swiftly."

The four of us descended the ramp from Kar Garudwyn hurriedly, with no more speech. I saw that indeed the moon was very bright, light enough to make out large runes by, thus bringing the chances of our journeying safely along that perilous trail up from naught to slim . . . but, as I had pointed out earlier, we had no choice.

Wary snufflings were the only greetings our mounts gave us as we called and whistled for them among the eerie blue-touched shadows. "Nekia," I murmured as reassuringly as possible, "come here, girl, to me . . . come on."

The slightest delay was maddening, but I curbed myself to stand patiently, speak coaxingly. If the horses took fright and stampeded, we were all lost.

"Come on." I heard Guret's voice. "That's a lad, Vengi."

Finally the stallion pawed, snorted, then footed a hesitant path over to the Kioga lad. The mares followed. As swiftly as we could, we saddled them, then, still on foot, turned back toward the ramp.

The animals blew in alarm at the strange entrance before them but, after more coaxing, were persuaded to set hoof to that sloping stone way. I led the group with Nekia, my own hooves clicking against the rock path. The trail was almost—*almost*—too tightly curving for the horses to take, but we managed. Within moments, my heart labored under the effort of guiding the mare up the incline swiftly enough so that the others would not run up on our heels, while insuring that Joisan and Guret would not be left behind.

After the first moments I began trailing my left hand along the ramp wall, for when I did so, the stone emitted a weak blue glow to partly offset the gloom of the passageway. Finally, with a last scramble and heave, we were out on the plateau, facing Kar Garudwyn. I struggled to catch my breath, spittle flooding my mouth in a bitter rush. We had barely begun our race.

Last up the rampway was Jervon, mumbling a breathless epithet before he spat over the cliffside. "What a scramble!"

"I didn't realize getting the horses up would be so hard," I agreed. We paused only a second, gasping, then, mounting, I led the group toward the back of the citadel, skirting to the left along a narrow path that wound along the mountaintop.

Looking down from the towers, it had been difficult to make out the exact beginning of the trail between the peaks. Now I was forced to bend low in the saddle as I searched, scanning the ground to my left where the plateau dropped away into a rush of black air and wind. Moonglow silvered the rocks below, softening their outlines, but did little to lessen my wariness. A fall from this height could be nothing but fatal.

I squinted, blinking, until my sight began to blur from sheer strain, trying to discern the trail I *knew* must branch off to my left somewhere in this area. *Light . . . if only I had light,* I thought, and even as the word crossed my mind, one of those odd bits and pieces of ancient knowledge surfaced. Holding my wristband before me, I spoke aloud the word in the Old Tongue for light—"Ghithé!"

My wristband began to glow, sending out a wavering pattern of blue-gold, almost as though my flesh had sprouted flames. Nekia snorted, skittering sideways, and I heard Joisan's gasp behind me. "Kerovan! My ring, the one that came from the Old Ones!"

Cautiously I twisted in the saddle to see that her finger was also lit by the cat's-head ring. These artifacts, it seemed, still responded to the proper command.

When I turned back, my eyes fastened on a break in the rocky escarpment surrounding the plateau—peering at it closely, I realized the gap marked our path.

"Hold!" I cried, raising my wrist in signal. Climbing off the mare, I bent over, studied the now-revealed way before us by the moonglow and the light from the Old Ones' gift. It was narrow—scarcely wider than our mounts at some points—plunging downward in a dizzy sweep before leveling out for a space, only to climb at a gentler angle toward the other peak. Nekia stretched out her neck, peering down at the trail, then shook her head, snorting, her eyes rolling white-ringed.

"I don't like it much, either," I told her, "but we must take it. Can you see it, Nekia? Well enough to give the others something to follow?" After a second the mare tossed her head, almost as if she understood my words and was agreeing to attempt the descent.

"Should we ride or lead them, Kerovan?" Joisan asked, and I did not miss the tremor in her voice.

"Ride," I made answer, working to keep my own tones steady. "If we try to lead them, we could slip and pull them after us. Besides, their night vision is better than ours." I paced downward a step, testing the footing. "The path is dust over rock—slick, but they can dig a footing, I hope. Try and ride as still in the saddle as possible, keeping your weight forward over the shoulders so they can balance. *Don't* lean back. They need their hindquarters free."

I glanced over at Jervon. "Vengi cannot carry double down this way." I jerked my rope free from my saddle, tossing it to him, as did Joisan. "Knot these together, then anchor the line to one of these rocks, then around yourself in case of a slip. I will go first, then each of you, in turn. Ready?"

All three nodded. I mounted Nekia with a quick motion, turning her to face that downward trail which bore such a disturbing resemblance to a child's sliding path. "Come on, Nekia," I said, shaking my reins, squeezing her sides with my legs. She snorted, putting a tentative foot over the side of the plateau, then jerking it back in the next instant. "Come on," I said again, gentling her with a hand on her shoulder.

She put out one forefoot again, the other following it, then her hindquarters humped beneath me as she was over the side. For several strides she managed a mincing walk, legs bunched together for balance, swaying like a dancer—then, as the slope steepened even further, she was sliding downward, nearly sitting on her tail, with me poised over her withers, trying not to move.

In a last rush of dust, we were down, and safe.

"Joisan next!" I shouted, looking up, moving off the trail to give her room. Arren was plainly balky, but finally, after my lady gave her an audible boot, she, too, came. Guret followed, then the three of us watched as Jervon inched his way downward, finally losing his balance and sliding down on his rear, fetching up beside us ghost pale from dust. Had the situation not been so desperate, he would have aroused our amusement.

"Are you hurt?" Joisan asked as he climbed stiffly to his feet, brushing at his breeches.

"No," he said as Guret extended his arm and freed his

stirrup that he might mount double behind him. "But in the unlikely event we *return* to your citadel, *I* shall take the long way 'round."

"May the Amber Lady grant we *all* may do so," Joisan agreed dryly. "The crag-deer are welcome to this their range, with no envy from me."

We moved along this comparatively level portion of the trail, the light from my wristband still helping to pick out the sharpest, most jagged rocks. The world appeared tenuous, insubstantial, as though the moonlight leaching its color had also stolen some of its reality. There was no sound save for the scurries of small night-dwellers and, overhead, the muted winging of an owl.

The trail sloped upward again, ascending in a long curving angle to the top of the peak where Joisan said Car Re Dogan had once stood. Nekia's muscles strained as she began the climb. I leaned forward to give her free rein, digging my fingers into her mane, wishing Kioga saddles were equipped with breast-collars. If the saddle slipped . . .

But it did not, and eventually we were able to halt on a ledge to breathe our mounts, staring upward at the last short section of trail. I could see what appeared to be ruins farther up, the same ruins we had noticed this morning. By moonlight their shifting was even more pronounced and disconcerting. "This is akin to the glamourie protecting our valley," Joisan said thoughtfully as she sat beside me.

I glanced over at her, seeing in the wash of pallid light the heavy braid of her hair falling down her back, the shine of her eyes. Below the half sleeves of her mail, her Kioga blouse was dark with embroidery against the white linen. Swept by the sudden knowledge that this might well be the last time in life I looked so upon my lady, my awareness of her caught in my throat like something tangible.

I love you, Joisan, I thought, making no effort to link

my mind with hers. Even at this moment some vestiges of the old reserve still held, and I feared that if I gave way even by so little to my feelings, I would be unable to ride on that last small distance. I wanted to tell her—how I wanted to!—but the words stayed within me, mine alone.

"We may be forced to ride blind, my lord," she continued quietly, not guessing, of course, the nature of my thoughts. "The horses, if they react the same as they did yesterday, will remain unaffected."

"Do you know—has your vision shown you—what now lies at the top of the peak?" I asked.

"No."

"Guret," I called, and the Kioga youth urged his sweating stallion over beside me. Vengi was the strongest of the three mounts, but it was fortunate that neither the boy nor Jervon was heavily built. The Dalesman had scrambled the steepest parts of the trail afoot, clinging to the horse's tail for an anchor. "When we reach our destination, we will leave the horses with you. The sight of that . . . *thing* would surely panic them. I want you to guard them."

I made my words as positive and inarguable as I could, and to my relief, Guret nodded. "Very well, m'lord."

"Let us go," I said, turning Nekia to that last stretch of trail.

We moved upward in single file, and with every stride the disorientation surrounding the ruins grew stronger— for, I was now sure, we rode into the remains of a once-mighty stronghold or Keep. Crumbled walls thrust raggedly upward, the moonlight doing little to illuminate them— instead, they seemed to absorb any and all light, so that they hulked as ebon shadows in the night.

And they *changed*. I would stare determinedly at what appeared to be an almost-recognizable wall, or courtyard, or balustrade, only to have it ripple, crawl, then melt before my eyes, sometimes changing into another form, sometimes disappearing entirely. My stomach lurched as we approached a tumbled high barrier to our path, only to have Nekia, ears forward, walk calmly up to and *through* its seemingly solid surface. I shut my eyes as we reached the top of the peak and continued on, for the distortion grew stronger, my vision blurring until at times I saw double—or even triple—images of the roiling landscape.

At last I opened my eyes upon a trail—one that stayed in place, making me believe it truly there—leading in from the right. Looking back along it, I saw that it wound a curving path to the east, back through this forest of pillars and ruins—both real and hallucinatory. That trail, I thought, came from the direction of the Waste and, beyond that, the land of my birth, High Hallack. Was this a trail of the Old Ones? Had the place called Car Re Dogan been some kind of watch-keep set on the mountain border between the ancient land of Arvon and the newer one of humankind?

There were no answers for my questions as I turned to ride on, letting Nekia pick a cautious path along the ancient trail, keeping my eyes narrowed to barest slits. "Is all well?" I called.

Murmurs of assent greeted my hail. We left the summit, began a downward path, only to find walls of rock rising up on either side, higher and higher, until we rode in a near tunnel, except where the moonlight washed down from the open roof. Without knowing how I knew, I became aware that we were nearing our goal.

Ahead of me the path curved, which turning I followed, only to emerge into a great space, mostly open, but containing some of the ruins near the mouth of the half tunnel. Again they swirled and dissolved, only to reappear in other, almost-identifiable shapes. Ahead stood a great walled area, not roofed, oval in shape. The road led up to an archway, then disappeared therein. Colorless mist coiled, snaking along the ground, though the night had been clear.

Halting Nekia with a tightening of my knees, I swung

her to face the others. "Ahead lies our battleground.
Guret, the horses stay here."

I dismounted a trifle stiffly, feeling the ground sway
beneath my hooves for a second. Joisan swung off Arren,
and I moved quickly to steady her. In the glow of the
moon and the faint phosphorescence of the fog, her face
looked spectral, hollowed, her eyes bright sparks. "It is
approaching, Kerovan. I can feel Sylvya."

"Then we have no time to lose," I said. "Is that place
ahead its lair, do you think?"

"No," she answered, her brows drawing together as
though she struggled with an elusive memory. "Sylvya
knew this place. It was not of the Shadow . . . it has been
here for longer than any can tell. . . ."

Leaving Guret at the mouth of the passageway, Jervon,
Joisan, and I walked cautiously up to the archway to look
within. The road ran straight down the middle of the oval
enclosure, but on either side of it there were niches in the
walls. These were spaced at regular intervals, and each
was walled three-quarters of the way up—as though each
of those niches had once enclosed an inhabitant, placed
standing up so that he or she might look out upon whom-
ever passed. On the front of each niche was a rune, the
ones at the far end barely more than a tracing, so ancient
were those symbols.

As I stood poised to look within, I realized with sudden
shock that, empty as those hollowed-out spaces appeared—
and there were some twoscore of them—they were *not*
untenanted. I gasped, swayed, feeling the *attention* of
those within that enclosure turn to me!

"Kerovan!" Joisan whispered, her nails digging into my
arm above my wristband. "They are still *alive* in there!
They want to know who I am, and why I have come
here!"

I wet my lips. "Not alive, no." I chose my words, for
"memories" were stirring within me, odd sortings of that
inconvenient and inconstant knowledge that erratically

flickered and guttered within me, obedient in no way to my own will. "They are the Guardians, ensorcelled into a kind of life, mostly a repository of memories and wisdoms of their kind—which is *not* the humankind we know. It is their duty to question and challenge all comers, but I think we have little to fear."

We looked out upon that silent expanse of openings, so awed we nearly forgot the dire reason for our coming. I was conscious still of that measuring appraisal and wondered whether these Guardians existed only to examine, or if they still had the Power to determine who was allowed to walk their road. If That Which Runs the Ridges came here each night, perhaps all they could do was watch, for, alien as they were, I sensed from them no taint of the Shadow.

I noticed that at this end, close to the archway where we crouched, there was one niche not walled—it stood open, unmarked. Had the last of the Guardians been lost? I wondered.

"Do we dare go within?" Jervon whispered. "We should search out the best place to make our stand—"

He stopped abruptly as I shushed him, then, hearing it, too, he tensed. I swung around, sword out, as a low throbbing resonated through the air. "Joisan? Is it—"

"*No*," she said. "Don't you hear? It is a drum!"

The sound rippled and rose, making a kind of strange, sick music. "Nidu! She's here!" I looked to the others. "We must find her—she's drumming to guide it here, so it will be released!"

"Yes," Joisan agreed.

I scanned the ruins behind us, seeing that the mist was thickening, gleaming in the moonlight as it curdled and sank, seeping along the rocky ground like blood from a death-wound. That throbbing thickened in my veins, and I realized to my horror that the mist was responding to the Shaman's drum. "The mist! She's out there, somewhere, in the mist! We have to find her!"

Sword out, I dodged into the ruins but was baffled by their rippling, now made even more unnerving by the strange vapor. Several times I thought I saw the crouching figure of a sable-clad woman, only to have the shape dissolve into a rock or chunk of broken pavement at the last second. Once I narrowly missed shattering my sword.

Finally, realizing that my eyes would avail me naught in such a search, I began prowling through the ruins with my wristband held out, reasoning that its runes would warn me of the Shaman's presence. And still that thrum-thrum-thrumming rose and fell through the shadowed expanses, threatening to turn my mind from its purpose, ensnare it in the quavering rhythms of the Shaman's song.

"Kerovan!" Joisan's voice reached me faintly, for the encroaching mist seemed to swallow certain sounds as it amplified others. Had it not been for the glow from her cat's-head ring, I might not have found her as she crouched beside the archway into the place of the Guardians, Jervon beside her.

"Did you find her?" I asked, glancing from one to the other.

"There is no more time to search, Kerovan."

Even as she spoke, I heard the droning sound, felt the thudding vibration of That Which Runs the Ridges as it approached from downmountain.

To see it in a vision was one thing, I speedily discovered, to confront it in the flesh very much another. It swirled up the road into the oval court of the Guardians as a sickly yellow-toned cloud clotted with streaks of scarlet. Its whining drone was enough to drive one keening away in madness—I found myself unable to force my eyes to watch it for more than a second or two before I must needs look down or away—

And the stench! Foulness like all the Shadow poured into a distilling flask and bubbled over an alchemist's flame, the noxious smell of the thing swept out to engulf me. I gagged, holding one hand over my mouth and nose, pinching viciously at my nostrils so the pain would help me keep control. Beside me Jervon retched uncontrollably.

Worst of all was the wrenching *alienness* of it. There was an overwhelming sense of a force totally outside nature, completely skewed, perverted from Things As They Must Be. I thought wildly that I must run, run away from such horror. I climbed to my feet, clinging to a boulder for support, then half turned back toward the horses—

It was then that I saw Nidu. The Shaman crouched on the other side of the oval, close to one of the niches, cowering, though her fingers continued to beat out the wild summoning rhythm. Then the tempo changed, from the thrumming to a sharper, more staccato tattoo. As if in answer, the thing within the Guardians' space began to spin, widdershins, pulsing larger with each revolution.

My sword was again in my hand, though I had no memory of drawing it. I concentrated on my anger, trying so to drown the fear that was still urging me back toward Nekia. *I will not run*, I thought. *I took oath that I was done with running, and I will not let myself be forsworn. . . .*

Gazing at Nidu, I remembered her harassment of Guret, her mockery of me, her cruelty to Elys—but the memory that gave me the strength to take that first step toward the Shaman was that of her sneering voice calling Joisan "whey-blooded."

I had moved three steps toward the Shaman, toward That Which Runs the Ridges, when Jervon and Joisan both moved to front me. "No!" Jervon shouted over the sound of the drumming—no longer a tapping, it had become a thunderous booming rivaling that of the worst storms I had faced. "You cannot!"

I brought my sword up, motioning him to step out of my path. "I have no taste for killing in cold blood, either, Jervon, but it must be done before she looses that thing!"

Joisan shook her head. "*No*, Kerovan. We must let her finish!"

"Why?" I stared at both of them, wondering if the sight of the thing had unhinged their wits.

"Because otherwise we will never see Elys again!" Jervon shouted. The drumming resounded through our bodies now, shaking the rock beneath our feet. *Rum*-dum-*dah*-dum . . . It seemed to fill the world.

I lowered my sword, realizing he was right, then crouched with them behind the archway. In spite of my resolve, it was torture to watch the whirling of that thing, knowing that whatever form it took when released from the spell completely would be even deadlier.

With a final turn, it exploded outward until it nearly filled the open area—then, in complete silence, the yellow miasma vanished, and the Shadowed hunt stood in its place.

There were perhaps a score of beings in the center of the Guardians' oval. Many were beautiful. All of them, I knew instinctively, were deadly. As they milled, confused, I scanned them from the concealment of the archway, seeking Elys.

Four mounted forms looked to be as nearly of human-kind as I, though their skins shone golden beneath their helms. Their armor glimmered blue in the moonlight, seeming to shed a faint phosphorescence. These were the huntsmen, armed with long-lashed whips that trailed sparks. Their white hounds bore some resemblance to those from which the warriors of Alizon take their name, but these creatures were much the larger, moving with a sinuous, reptilian grace, red-fanged jaws lolling open, while their eyes seemed to drink in all light, reflecting back nothing but pitted darkness.

Several insubstantial, wavering forms appeared to be those of humankind, men and women alike, their eyes holding both pain and a terrible purpose. One of these in the forefront, a youth, wore the distinctive embroidered linen of the Kioga. Looking upon him, I remembered Obred's words about young Jerwin: ". . . I am haunted by the thought that he met a death that is not yet finished . . . an unclean death . . ." So the Kioga leader had the right of it—all those who had been killed by That Which Runs the Ridges during the centuries had gone to be part of it. Sickened, I tore my gaze from those pitiful wraiths—

It was then that I saw their leader. Maleron sat atop a tall white steed, like unto the ones the huntsmen bestrode. The animal (for it resembled a horse in the same way the "hounds" resembled dogs) arched a scaled, sinuous neck, pawing at the ground with a clawed forefoot. Its master gazed around him almost casually, but even from the many spans separating us I could *feel* the Power emanating from him. A scarlet cloak billowed off his shoulders, his features were regular, even handsome—a typical man of the Old Ones. We could have been brothers.

With a final drumroll, the Shaman stepped from her spot of concealment. "Adept! I am she who released you from your long confinement!"

Jervon moved suddenly beside me, his breath hot against my cheek as he whispered, "Kerovan! Can you see aught of Elys?"

"No," I made answer.

"I do not see Sylvya, either," Joisan said worriedly. "I can feel her, though—she is somewhere among those who front us. Elys must be using illusion to conceal them."

For long moments Maleron sat unmoving, then his unhelmed dark head turned to regard Nidu as if she were the lowliest of servants. Finally he inclined his head in the briefest of nods. "My thanks, Shaman."

"You can best tender your gratitude"—the black-robed woman straightened, her fingers resting on her drum as though she drew strength from it—"by ridding me of my enemies. They are your enemies, also, Adept."

Maleron lifted his brows skeptically. "I have been free for less than a hundred heartbeats," he said. "I find it difficult to believe I could have made enemies in this time and place with so little effort."

The Shaman's voice shook. "They are cowards, hiding behind the Light! They have gathered to destroy you here and now, before you can even taste of your new-won freedom! Kill them!" She waved a sticklike arm in our direction, as though she could see us in spite of the concealment of the archway.

Maleron shook his head, frowning. "Judge me not so summarily, Shaman. *You* may tread the Left-Hand Path, but I do not. I am but a seeker after knowledge and Power."

Nidu began to laugh wildly. "If you truly believe that, then you are a greater fool than you are a sorcerer! Within your menie are all those who were killed by even the most passing of brushes with you and your hunt—fell death results from your most casual touch. Is that the mark of the Light?"

The Adept's features hardened as he raised a hand toward her. But before he could move or speak, something rippled before my vision and there came a shrill scream!

"Elys!" Jervon lunged forward. I had only a second to see the two women huddled together and, confronting them, two shadows of such dire black that they seemed naught but holes ripped in the fabric of the night. Reddish sparks awakened and died within those twisted Shadow-creatures, and even looking at them made my stomach knot painfully.

The Dalesman was out and running toward the two women, who, unseen by all before this moment, must have been crawling toward us until the Shadow-creatures had sniffed them out. I heard Maleron's shout over all— "*Sylvya!*" Hate trembled through the air in palpable waves. In response to his signal, the huntsmen urged their mounts toward the Dales warrior.

My sword was in my hand and I, too, was running. I reached Sylvya and Elys, who was standing with steel drawn, only a few strides behind Jervon, Joisan at my side.

We had only time to back each other, forming a rough circle of drawn steel, before the four riders were upon us.

Their only weapons were those hunting lashes, but those, I speedily discovered, sparked and flamed as they were wielded. I took a glancing sear across my thigh before I was able to parry. As my steel crossed his weapon, sliding down until we were wrist to wrist, I saw his teeth flash as if the touch of iron pained him. Remembering the evil well on the plain, I raised my wristband. His white mount screamed and reared as the runes on the talisman flamed. The rider reined it back toward me, still in such deadly silence that I wondered if his race were mutes.

Once more the lash curled fire toward me, but this time I was able to duck beneath it and, daring greatly, stepped forward, under his guard. It was a chance, breaking the circle, but if I could—

There! The point of the sword slipped inward, grazed his breast.

A thin shriek broke from him as violet flame licked outward from even so small a point of contact. As I stepped backward, closing the circle, he wavered, then fell, wreathed now in lines of light, to lie jerking. As I watched, his flesh—if flesh it was—began to shrivel, as though it were being consumed from within. I turned away just in time to see Joisan use the glow from her cat's-head ring to bewilder and panic the mount on my left.

Within another second, her sword had found the rider's throat. I shouted a wordless encouragement as I gave her a warrior's salute. We both turned toward the next golden-skinned foe, only to find Jervon's steel transfixing his middle. With a heave, the Dalesman stepped back, pulling his weapon free. The remaining huntsman backed away, then as the four of us, swords ready, advanced on him, he turned and ran.

Before his mount could gain the archway, though, the Adept shouted a harsh phrase and, with a shriek, the creature tumbled flaming from the saddle of his white steed. I stared at the writhing, burning thing on the ground, feeling my throat tighten with horror. This was truly *Power*. If Maleron could slay with a word, how could we ever hope to prevail against him?

I backed a half step to close the circle again, seeing Jervon do the same. My shoulder brushed Joisan's on my right, Elys's on my left. And beside the Witch stood the creature my lady had named as Sylvya . . . Maleron's half sister. My quick glimpse of her had shown me that she was not completely of humankind—a glimmering white down crested on her head, extending along her arms, which were bared by the short tunic she wore. In the moon-misted darkness, I had only a vague impression of a pointed-chinned face with overlarge eyes—beautiful in its way. Certainly a far cry from Nidu's description to the Kioga of the hunt's quarry as a rapacious, foul harpy.

I turned my head back toward the Adept at Nidu's shriek. "See, Powerful One! They are your enemies and will strive to kill you! Loose your hounds!"

The sorcerer looked over at us, his eyes glinting cat green in the eerie glow of the mist. "I know you not, you four, but if you ally with *her*—this traitress—then you are indeed my foes. Step aside from her, and you may depart freely."

I found my voice, worked to keep it steady in spite of my fear. "Leaving you free to ravage and destroy as you will?" I shook my head. "Nay, Maleron."

He started as he heard me speak his name aloud, and I knew a brief satisfaction that I had been able to threaten him by even so little. Names can have great Power in spelling—if only I had the knowledge of how to use such a potent weapon! But my mind remained untouched—no such intuition surfaced.

"Loose the hounds!" Nidu shrilled again. "I will guide them, Maleron!"

He nodded at us grimly. "So be it." Gesturing, he reined his white mount away from the creatures milling at its feet. Their narrow-snouted heads pointed up at him, then began to swing back and forth as though they possessed no sight in those pitted caverns serving them as eyes. The Shaman's drum began to throb again and I felt a warmth suffusing my body as it responded to those beats. A light that was also heat began to pulse forth from each of my heartbeats. I heard Joisan cry out, turned my head to see waves of heat and light lapping out from her, also.

"They hunt by blood-warmth!" Elys cried urgently. "We must stop the drumming! Lend me your will, sisters!"

I struggled to step forward, bring my sword up, and felt sweat burst from me as though I stood mailed in the summer's sun. But I could not stir.

Throb . . . throb . . . throb . . . *throb* . . . *throb* . . .

Scarlet waves burst across my vision as I strained to keep my eyes focused on the hounds. I could no longer discern the difference between my own heart and the beats of the drum. Behind me, I could hear Elys chanting, but the sound was as far away as fallen Ulmskeep. Pacing slowly, their jaws hanging open enough to show narrow, dripping tongues, the hounds advanced on us. They were only a few lengths away from me—

Throb . . . throb . . . THROB . . . THROB . . .

Gasping for air through the wash of heat, I strained to raise sword, move my feet—

THROB! **THROB!!! THROB—**

With blurring swiftness something gleaming flew through the air toward the Shaman, knocking the drum from her hands. I could see again! I could *move!* The drum quivered, impaled on Guret's short spear. From the archway I saw the Kioga youth straighten from a throwing stance. I shouted a quick word of thanks, then flexed my knees as I dropped into a swordsman's guard-position. At least the youth had given us the chance to go down fighting—

Behind me, Elys's chant rang out loudly, and, mindsharing, I sensed that Joisan, at least, was doing as the Witch had demanded and was aiding her in whatever spell or protection she strove to raise. The hounds, barely a sword's length before me, hesitated, their slender heads weaving as if they were puzzled. Then, slowly, those heads swung toward Nidu as she crouched at the foot of one of the niches.

The woman gave a gasping cry of horror as gradually the outline of her body began to shimmer. It was as though the entire light of the moon were suddenly concentrated upon her, and I could feel warmth streaming from the Shaman even from where I stood. Elys's voice rose higher, higher, became more commanding—

The pack leader turned, those pitted eyes naught but wells of shadow. Nidu screamed thinly, scrabbling for her ruined drum, but the heat radiated from her as though she were filled with a score of suns—

The hounds leaped, but their target was the Shaman. The black-clad woman went down under their writhing, sinuous forms with a shriek that was hideously stillborn.

I found I could not watch and turned my eyes back to the Adept. Maleron turned away from Nidu's body with a half shrug. "That one should not have meddled with what she could not understand," he said. "Perhaps her fate has lessoned you, half-man?"

I felt heat flood my cheeks at the casual gibe but forced myself to face him squarely. "You are so inured to death that naught can reach you, Maleron. Can you not see that your time is past? We stand ready to stop you before you can Shadow this land as you have Shadowed this lonely mountain for these many ages."

"Stop me?" He chuckled, and the sound was enough to make the hounds, still tearing at the ravaged thing that had been the Shaman, stiffen and whine. "There are none left who can stop me, half-man . . . beast-man. . . ." He swung off his white mount with a quick, sure motion, facing me nearly eye to eye across the moonlit oval of the ancient Guardians. "Any who might have been my peers have vanished. They are less than memory . . . less than dust."

I hesitated for a long second, watching him summon his Power as a soldier will gather his weapons. A faint, dark light began to flicker around him, and suddenly he seemed even taller, his eyes radiating palest ash-silver. I took a breath, lifting my wristband, ready to stand against him with all the Power that was in me—

All the Power that was in me . . .

It flooded into me, filling me, and yet this time I remained myself, not some other. I knew that the knowledge had bided its time, and that this time I was to be no unthinking, unknowing instrument of an ancient wisdom— but truly myself, more myself than ever before. Landisl had so waited until I had accepted my heritage, found my home, was ready.

"Not so," I said, and my voice rang forth as though I had sounded the charge for a full company, filling this ensorcelled burial ground. I heard Joisan gasp, but I could not look away from the Adept now. My eyes bore into his as I strengthened my Will, and after a second he had to brace himself to meet my gaze. "It is time for you to realize just what you have done, Maleron, and in that knowing will lie your fate."

His eyes narrowed and the darkness around him blazed like a wind-fed fire. "Who *are* you?" He faced me squarely. "I know you not, yet—"

"You know me," I corrected him. "We were neighbors long ago, Margrave of the Heights. Your sister was far kin to me, though you were not, since your father's first lady was of humankind. Do you remember my Name?"

He backed half a step, shaken. "Landisl? But you are not—"

"I am," I said. "I am of the heritage of the Gryphon, if not the blood. Kar Garudwyn is my home, just as Car Re Dogan was yours. But you, with your meddling and dabbling along that Shadowed Path, have dishonored what your ancestors built. Look around you!" My shout rang like the clang of a sword upon shield. "Your home is dust and illusion, fallen into ruin because of you and your evil. Look, and look well!"

Slowly his head turned until he could see through the archway behind him to the ruins holding those shifting hallucinations that had once been walls, and courts, and rooms for living. "No," he whispered. "No . . ."

"Sylvya was right, Maleron. You trifled with that which should not even be thought of, and as a consequence, your entire Keep, your line, and all that you call yours fell after you departed. There is naught here for you, except to resume the evil you have wreaked for these ages— slaying and stealing spirits. Is that what you want?"

He did not answer, only stood staring wide-eyed. I could see shudders wracking his body. Pity stirred within me for a brief second, but I quenched it sternly. Ten heartbeats' worth of remorse could never make up for ten centuries of destruction. . . .

The Adept turned back to me, his eyes dull and hopeless. "I see," he said softly. "What must I do? How can I mend . . . ?"

"You cannot," I said inexorably, again quashing those brief stirrings of sympathy. Landisl's wisdom was mine for the moment, greater and fuller than my own, and the truth was inescapable. "If the Light has surfaced within you at last, it cannot be for long. The Shadow has held you in thrall for time out of mind, and you must act quickly, while you can think with your wits undarkened."

"I must undo—"

"No," I said, shaking my head. "It is too late for that, Margrave. It is a hard thing to know, but it is the truth. The most good you can do now for the world is to ensure that you will never again have the opportunity to work evil."

I pointed to that empty niche waiting by the archway,

and violet light flared up from my hand to outline it. The coursing of the ancient Power through me was beginning to make me tremble, but grimly I held that channel to the other open, focusing all my Will upon Maleron.

"Your rest, Adept. For all these ages you have wished for rest from that mad chase. There it lies."

He turned back to me for a long second, then his shoulders came forward in defeat and he nodded. His eyes, no longer greenish-silver, but leaden, went past me to Sylvya, who had moved up beside me. "Your forgiveness, sister," he said, reaching a hand toward her in supplication.

"It is yours, my brother," she said, and I heard her voice for the first time. It was a high, musical trilling, as though she sang rather than spoke.

Maleron turned back to the niche, still blazing with that coruscating light, his shoulders straightening again. Head high, he walked deliberately to that opening, stepped within, then turned to face us. Crossing his hands on his breast, he closed his eyes. The Power flickered through my open fingers again, almost without my willing it, and as I slowly raised my hand, a wall of the blue stone Landisl named quan-iron grew to cover the niche, not stopping three-quarters of the way up, as for the other Guardians, but enclosing the opening completely.

As the wall reached his chin, I saw the Adept's face for the last time—and watched an expression of peace flow across it just before the quan-iron encased him.

"Walled in," Sylvya whispered beside me. "Forever. . . ."

"No," I said heavily, feeling a strange, life-ebbing sensation as the Power began to leave me. "He is gone. If we were to open the niche, we would find naught but dust within."

That trickle of waning strength widened, to become a wash of exhaustion. I staggered under such an onslaught of weariness as I had never experienced—even after Nita's rescue. Jervon grabbed my arm, slinging it across his shoulders, steadying me. I tried to stand, brace my knees, but it was too much effort to even hold my head up. And yet, within me was the knowledge that the next time I used the ancient Power, it would be easier . . . though the exercise of such Will would always exact a toll in physical energy and strength.

"Kerovan!" Joisan was at my side, Guret with her.

I am unhurt. I used the mindsharing, for even my tongue was too heavy to move. *Must . . . rest . . .*

"Joisan!" Sylvya's trill held alarm. "The captured ones . . . and those Shadow-creatures . . ."

I looked up to see the hollow, *needing* eyes of the boy Jerwin fixed on us. With the other men and women once of humankind, he was moving toward us, past the spot where the hounds had pulled Nidu down. I looked for the Adept's white beasts, but they were gone. As they drifted silently closer, the sad wraiths were somehow infinitely more threatening. Lowering me to sit on the rocky floor of the Guardians' enclosure, Jervon stepped toward them, sword held out, then fell back in the face of those pitiful stares. "I cannot cut them down!" he gasped. "I am a warrior, not a butcher! What do they want?"

"They are not-dead," Sylvya whispered, fear making her voice even more alien. "They seek death, or life—it matters not which. They will steal our lives in their blind search to reclaim what was taken from them."

I tried to climb to my feet, summon strength to meet this new threat, but even if I had been ringed by fire I could not have crawled a sword's-length to avoid the burning. Sickly, I watched those hollow-eyed ones draw closer, wondering if I could manage to kill what should have died long ago. . . .

Then a shimmer of red-flecked blackness moved off to my right. The Shadow-creatures were also closing in.

11

Joisan

As I knelt beside my lord in this place that Sylvya's memory named as The Setting Up of the Kings, he turned his head to look up at me. His face was naught but a misty blur now that the light from his wristband had died out, and his eyes no longer glowed the brilliant amber that had faced down even an Adept of Maleron's ability. I knew that the Will he had expended to sway the Margrave, convince him to withdraw from Arvon, had sapped his strength as no physical battle could. Even as I tried to support his head, his hands slid along the rocky ground and he lay still.

For a terrible second I feared the worst, but, mind-sharing, I knew that this was simple unconsciousness—not the blankness that is death. At Sylvya's urgent "Joisan! Guard yourself!" I scrambled to my feet, sword in hand, watching the wraiths and those two Shadow-creatures draw closer to our little band. Maleron and Nidu were gone, but with them went all semblance of an enemy we could speak to, possibly reason with—the hilt of my weapon slid in my sweaty grasp as I tried to think of some way to fight these new threats. Somehow, eyeing them, I did not think steel would avail us this time. And Kerovan was so far spent that he could not even protect himself.

Beside me, Guret shuddered. "Jerwin . . . Cera, it is Jerwin! But I saw him die!"

"He *is* dead," I said absently. The insubstantial form of a woman stepped toward me, her hand held out pleadingly. She had the black hair of a woman of Elys's race. I wondered how long ago she had been swept up into such a hideous fate. "They are all dead, Guret. They want only to rest—" I stopped as my own words made me think about the nature of death . . . how it was part of life, if things followed a natural path. Nature . . .

A thought niggled within me, tantalizing me with a possible solution, then it was gone as the wraith before me reached out a transparent hand and, even though I told myself to stand firm, my flesh shrank away from any contact with it. Cold . . . wrenching, numbing cold radiated from the woman, and I knew if I suffered her touch, she would crawl within me, seeking to rest in my warmth—

The thought was so repellent that I needs must force myself not to step over Kerovan and retreat. Jervon cried out, backing away from the blackness seeping along the ground toward him—one of the Shadow-creatures. I knew that they were even more dangerous, that they sought to drain our Power, our spirits, as the wraiths hungered for our life and warmth. They would seek out the one holding the greatest Power—

The two Shadow-creatures flowed by Jervon, heading directly for me. "No! Joisan, you must get away!" Sylvya stepped before me, her trill sharpening in her anxiety. "Your daughter, Lady! They seek your child!"

I shrank back, my heart hammering as I realized she was speaking the truth. My bootheels were against Kerovan's side now—the wraith-lady reached for me again and I took yet another step, so that I balanced with one foot on either side of his body. If I retreated any farther, I

would be abandoning my lord in order to protect my
child—

No! I could not—*would not*—choose one over the other!

My hand went instinctively to my breast, seeking the
crystal gryphon—but of course that was gone. My groping
fingers brushed only the Amber Lady's talisman, the rip-
ened wheat and grape-bound amulet of Gunnora—*Gunnora*.
I looked again to the moon, that orb that is also Her
symbol. "Gunnora," I said clearly. "Amber Lady, hear
me, please! Give these poor creatures the rest they crave,
I beg of you! You who protects the young and we who
carry them—help me!"

As before, the amulet began to glow, sending amber
ripples of light out to envelop the wraiths. Like frost in
the morning sun, they began to fade . . . fade . . . and
then, with a final glimmer, they were gone!

Leaving only the two Shadow-creatures. I walked quickly
up to Sylvya, who motioned me yet again to retreat.
"No," I said firmly. "Give me your hand, my sister. I will
not escape at the price of leaving my comrades here to
face them—living with that knowledge would be worse
than succumbing to them here and now."

I forced myself to stare at the two Shadow-creatures,
ignoring the stomach-twisting *wrongness* they exuded, that
of beings completely outside their rightful time and place.
Like tiny rips in the fabric of reality, they seemed, as they
slowly flowed to front the two of us—

Not just two of us, I realized suddenly, *three*. Within
me was a child holding greater Power than any of us here
could claim. But an embryonic Power all the same, unable
to think or reason. *Little one*, I thought, reaching out for
Sylvya, *lend me your strength, also.* . . .

Sylvya's hand grasped mine, and I realized with this
first touch that it was only through the child that she had
been able to reach me for these many days. It was as
though she were the holding link in the chain between me

and my daughter (for daughter it was, Sylvya was right—the spirit that touched me now was clearly feminine).

Shutting my eyes, I let my awareness travel inward, seeking the strength that the child possessed but could not shape or direct. There! It was as though I had discovered another Will, one that inhabited my body but did not belong to me.

Touching that other strength, that Power, I channeled it, directed it outward. . . .

Those Shadow-creatures were not properly of this world. Therefore they could not be allowed to stay. Using the child's Power as I would use a tool to cut, I *opened*—

I heard Elys cry out, raised my eyes to see a flash of violet light over our heads and, beyond it, a glimpse of stars—*black stars on a paper-white sky*.

The world reeled past me as I glimpsed that strange otherness, that place beyond the Gate I had opened. Steadying my Will, still clinging to Sylvya's hand, I gestured at the Shadow-creatures. "Your home lies there! Go!" And with all the Power that lay within me, I *pushed*.

There was a hideous moment of touching, of resistance; then it broke, and, with the sound of a mountain falling, my world turned inside out.

12

Kerovan

The night was gentle against my face, yielding like fist-fuls of wool, filled with the quiet sounds of talking. I lay on a hard, rocky surface, but my head was pillowed on something yielding and warm. For a moment I lay content *not* to remember, simply to rest, to know that I lived. I did not want to open my eyes. That gesture would tie me again to the real world, to striving, and pain, and discovery. . . .

Idly, I identified the voices I could hear.

"Pass me the waterskin again, please, Jervon. I have never been so thirsty, it seems!" That was Elys. Somehow, without seeing them, I knew she was sitting beside her lord, their sides touching.

I heard the gurgle of the liquid. My own mouth was dry . . . I resisted the urge to lick my lips. Waking would bring demands, and for the moment I wanted none, save only to know I was alive, and so was my lady . . . for Joisan sat beside me. The softness pillowing my head was her lap.

"Here, Lady Sylvya." There came the sound of footsteps.

"I have some selka juice here. Perhaps you would like it."
Guret's voice.

"My thanks." That was Sylvya's trill.

So . . . we had all survived. I wondered idly how the
Shadow-creatures and the wraiths had been bested. I had
drifted in and out of consciousness for several minutes
during that battle, hearing but not seeing, and now I
remembered a jumble of words. Sylvya had spoken of a—
Hastily my mind skittered away from memory when it
pressed too close. I could not have heard correctly. . . .

"How is he, Joisan?" That was Guret, sitting down
beside my lady.

"He has been asleep," she said, and I felt her touch,
lighter than the night air, on my hair, smoothing it back
from my forehead. I could tell from her voice she was
smiling. "But now he begins to wake, though he has not
yet consented to open his eyes."

Found out, I lifted my eyelids hastily, then strove to
get up. The reality of the task proved far harder than the
idea—but finally I sat, looking around me. We were in
the ruins, outside the Guardians' place. The horses were
tethered nearby, and a small blaze threw back the last
shadows of the night with brave yellow flames. Jervon,
Elys, Sylvya, Guret, and Joisan were gathered around it.
There was no sign of any of our enemies.

"The Shadows . . . the wraiths—" I began, only to have
my voice crack from dryness. Joisan handed me the
waterskin and I drank thirstily as she explained that they
were gone, defeated.

"How?" I asked, around a mouthful of the journeybread
Guret produced from his saddlebag.

"The Lady Joisan," Elys said, her voice holding a faint
current of amusement. "First she persuaded Gunnora to
grant the wraiths the peace of true death, then she opened
a Gate to send the Shadows back whence they had come.
And to think three years ago I told her that some small

share of the Craft might be awakened in her if she strove hard and was patient!"

My lady smiled. "And so I owe my success to you, Elys, for telling me I might be able to learn. And for giving me those first few hints as to how to seek wisdom within myself."

"It seems you have been an excellent student," Elys agreed wryly. "I feel fortunate that we are comrades, not opponents!"

"But to open a Gate . . ." I shook my head. "Only with Landisl's Power to draw on was I able to do such, even in a fortress steeped in sorcery, where the reserves had been strengthened through ages of waiting. How could you . . ."

Joisan looked away, and it seemed to me I saw a faint flush redden her face even more than the firelight. "I had Sylvya to help."

"The Shadows . . ." I frowned, trying now to remember. "And Sylvya was speaking. She said—" I stopped as the full memory rushed back in. I looked at Joisan and knew the truth. *Why didn't you tell me?* I demanded silently. *I never guessed—it is true? You are going to have a child?*

Her chin came up as she met my gaze unflinchingly, but her mouth trembled. *We are,* she admitted. *I tried to tell you, but there was no time. . . .* For a long second she watched me, as though she had never seen my face before. *Tell me, Kerovan . . . are you—please say you are—glad?*

I heard a rustle and glanced over to see Guret and the others gathering up the provisions and moving away to saddle the horses. I stood abruptly. "Let us walk for a moment."

Joisan followed me into the place of the Guardians, until we could no longer see the fire. I needs must still move slowly, but the better part of my strength was returning. As we stepped through the archway, I glanced over to see the once-empty niche—it was almost impossible to believe that we were still in the same night as the battle. I paced on a few more steps, thinking.

"Kerovan!" Joisan grasped my arm, swinging me to face her, her eyes pleading now. "Tell me what you are thinking!"

For answer I touched her hand, feeling the roughness left by hard work, yet the fine bones beneath the skin. "I am thinking that I love you very much, my lady," I said simply. "And that I cannot wait to see our daughter. I cannot believe Gunnora has smiled upon us after so long." Drawing her to me, I held her tightly, feeling a quiet joy rise up between us and overflow, spilling outward until I was sure even the ancient Kings could feel it.

When I finally released her, reluctantly, she touched my cheek. "It was the child, you know, that held the Power to open the Gate. We are going to be very busy, Kerovan. Raising an ordinary babe is taxing enough, but this one . . ." She shrugged, smiling. "Ah, well, we have never been overfond of boredom, either of us."

I shook my head in wry agreement. "Still, I could wish for a few less alarums and excursions," I said. "When will it—she—"

"Around the time of Midwinter Feast," she told me. "We will have to gather plenty of firewood."

"Guret and I will have to block up the arches," I said, then a memory struck me. "He knows, doesn't he? He guessed?"

Joisan nodded.

I shook my head. "I should feel a fool, since I was so blind," I told her. "But I thought I was so different that I never let myself hope—"

"I know," she said. "So you want to ask the lad to stay with us?"

"The Kioga need a home," I said. "Now they can rove their mountains again without fear. The grazing in the valley is rich. . . ."

She nodded thoughtfully. "Perhaps . . . there was a purpose to all this," she whispered. "Remember that Obred said that when the Twins came to walk the earth, the Kioga would find a new land?"

"I remember," I said. "And in a few days, when we have rested, we'll ride south, the three of us, to tell them they can return to the mountains in safety."

"And what of Sylvya?" she asked. "The valley is very precious to her also."

"As Landisl's only remaining blood-kin," I said, "Kar Garudwyn may be more rightfully hers than it is mine."

"Not so," Sylvya trilled, and we turned to see her step through the archway. "The heritage of the Gryphon belongs to you, Kerovan, for it chooses its master or mistress. I would ask of you only the chance to work with you and your lady to restore the citadel, and my valley."

"We shall all work together," I said. "Joisan and I, you, Elys and Jervon, if they desire. There is room—Arvon is wide."

13

Joisan

We rode together from The Setting Up of the Kings, Sylvya behind me on Arren, Elys on Nekia with Kerovan, and Jervon and Guret astride Vengi. As we picked our way north, down the ancient mountain road, I looked to the east, whence we had come so long ago, to see the first flush of early dawn. So many dawns since our journey had begun . . . so many, and yet at this moment, all the world felt fresh and new, as though this were the first of them.

I looked longingly at a brooklet that ran beside the road for a space, thinking that the first thing I would do upon my return to Kar Garudwyn would be to find an isolated spot in the valley stream and bathe—or, perhaps we would find something to serve as a tub in one of the unexplored rooms of the citadel. . . .

I heard a soft, sad breath from behind me and turned, to see Sylvya's wide eyes fixed on the tiny rivulet of water. "What is it, sister?" I asked, concerned.

"The brook . . ." Pain overwhelmed her for a moment. "Only yesterday, or so it seems to me, I challenged my brother to step across that running water and he failed."

I reached back to clasp her hand. "He is safe now, and at peace," I told her. "Try to think of him thus . . . and remember that you saved the valley."

She nodded, and I turned back to guide Arren, seeing the first touch of scarlet and orange lap over the mountain peaks, spilling down their granite bones in washes of glorious color. It would be a beautiful day—

I sat up suddenly, feeling a tiny stirring within me. It was the strangest sensation, one that I had heard described many times before but had never understood until I felt it for myself . . . a small quiver, as something within me wriggled and stretched and *lived*.

Our child . . . I looked ahead to my lord, seeing him talking with Elys as he expertly reined Nekia along the ancient roadway. For a moment I considered making the effort to mindshare this new happening, then I decided to wait until we were alone. There would be time, after all. Time for all tellings, and for many, many dawns. . . .

The road ahead warmed and brightened, as the sun rose.